TALES OF SILVER DOWNS

DRUID

BOOK 3

KYLIE QUILLINAN

First published in Australia in 2016.

ABN 34 112 708 734

kyliequillinan.com

Copyright © 2016 Kylie Quillinan

All rights reserved.

Apart from any use as permitted under the *Copyright Act 1968*, no part may be reproduced, copied, scanned, stored in a retrieval system, recorded, or transmitted, in any form or by any means, without the prior written permission of the publisher. Enquiries should be addressed to Kylie Quillinan at PO Box 5365, Kenmore East, Qld, 4069, Australia.

A catalogue record for this book is available from the National Library of Australia.

Ebook ISBN: 9780994331557

Paperback ISBN: 9780994331540

Large print ISBN: 9780994331571

Hardback ISBN: 9780648903932

This is a work of fiction. Any similarity between the characters and situations within its pages and places or persons, living or dead, is unintentional and coincidental.

Cover art by Deranged Doctor Design.

Proudly independent. Please support indie authors by legally purchasing their work.

This work uses Australian spelling and grammar.

LP08072022

*For my dear friend, Claudia,
Who doesn't read fantasy
and will probably never see this.*

1

ARLEN

I sat cross-legged in front of a pond. Its depths were clear and calm, with just the slightest ripple. The woods around me rang with birdcalls and the rustle of leaves from various forest creatures. I stared into the pool and concentrated on letting go of all thought.

As my mind became as calm as the water, my body also relaxed. The mossy ground was cool and slightly damp beneath my linen trousers. A beetle crawled over my bare foot. I inhaled, filling my lungs with the scent of moist earth, cool water and rotting leaves. I watched the water and tried not to let anxiety crowd into my mind. Eventually, I would master control of the Sight. If I waited long enough and kept my mind still enough, the waters would show me something. A voice from behind me disrupted the stillness I concentrated so hard on.

"Arlen, Oistin asks that you go to him."

I sighed and pushed my irritation aside. It was not the boy's fault I had managed to achieve the calmness I sought only moments before he spoke.

"Did he want me urgently, Pilib?" My gaze never left the water, hoping I might yet See something.

"He asked that you go immediately. He's in his bedchamber."

I nodded and heard just the faintest rustle of leaves as the boy retreated. I shouldn't have been able to hear him at all, but he was an apprentice just newly arrived. He had much to learn yet. With one last wistful glance into the pond, I climbed to my feet and brushed the dirt from the seat of my trousers.

As I set off through the woods, I wondered what Oistin wanted. Perhaps he intended to ask me to take a new boy under my wing. Perhaps he merely planned to ask after my studies. I pushed the thoughts from my mind. There was no point in speculating. I would find out soon enough.

The stone lodge stood in the middle of a large clearing deep within the woods. The remoteness of the location suited us, for those training to be druids spend much time alone. Surrounded by woods as we were, there were plenty of quiet places for a druid to wander off by himself. Many a day had I spent perched in the branches of a tree, or sitting on a flat rock, or roaming the woods, reciting the lore we learned, practising calling the elements, or trying to master the Sight.

The heavy wooden door of the lodge stood open. It was rarely closed. Inside was cold and dark, for evening approached and the lamps had not yet been lit. The aroma of vegetable soup and fresh bread made my mouth water and reminded me I hadn't eaten yet today. I made my way through the corridors to Oistin's quarters.

As the master druid, Oistin had a bedchamber that although modest, was far larger than the one I shared with three others. I rapped softly on the open door, waiting until he bade me enter. The room contained a bed, which was neatly made, some shelves, a cupboard, and a large desk. Its window looked out at an elegant rowan tree. Oistin sat behind the desk, examining a piece of parchment which he held close to his face.

"Arlen." He placed the parchment on the desk and waved me in.

"You wished to see me?"

"Yes, yes." For a moment, Oistin looked puzzled, as if he couldn't recall why he had summoned me, then he nodded. I suspected he wasn't as forgetful as he sometimes pretended. He ran our community with tight reins and rarely let an important detail slip. "I have a task for you."

I waited.

"I am sending you to Braen Keep to be an advisor to Hearn. You will leave as soon as you pack your belongings."

"Master?" My carefully cultivated calmness evaporated.

"It's a new stage of your journey, boy. A grand adventure. Great responsibility."

"You're sending me to the king?"

"He needs a trustworthy advisor. Someone honourable. Someone who will guide him with the country's best interests in mind."

Oistin looked at his desk, at the window, at the rug-covered floor. Anywhere other than at me.

"Master, I don't understand."

How could he have forgotten? Oistin knew my greatest failing as a druid. He knew why I was the person least suitable to undertake such a task.

"I know it might seem intimidating. You'll be surrounded by more people than you're accustomed to. It'll be noisier. You'll need to find a quiet place of your own where you can continue to practise your craft."

"How will I advise the king?" I asked. "You know I have no ability with the Sight."

Oistin sighed and finally looked at me.

"You will do what you must do, Arlen. Now, go gather your belongings so we can send you on your way. Tonight you will dine in the king's hall."

"Does this mean my training is concluded?"

He studied me before he responded. He knew there was a personal task I planned to complete as soon as I finished my training. A task I had never kept secret from him and that I had no intention of postponing. I would repay my training and serve as druid wherever he wanted to send me — once my task was complete.

"Your training is suspended," Oistin said. "You must continue to learn what you can in the meantime. When Hearn no longer requires you, you will return here to finish your training."

I left Oistin's bedchamber with my head held high and my shoulders straight. I breathed deeply — in, out, in — as I strode along the corridors to my own bedchamber. A sigh of relief when I arrived to find it empty of my fellow druids. Our accommodations were sparse: four narrow cots, each draped with a grey blanket, one cot against each wall. A well-worn rug covered the wooden floor. Our belongings, such as they were, were stored in boxes beneath our cots. We were permitted two boxes each. Our bedchamber was in the middle of the lodge, so there were no windows. The stone walls were bare with the exception of a small shelf holding a lamp, which I lit with trembling hands.

I sank onto my cot and dropped my head into my hands. I had grievously offended Oistin. Why else would he punish me in such a way? To send me away, my training incomplete, was a clear indication I had failed.

I had always expected to leave the community eventually. Other than those few druids who remained here to teach, most stayed only for the ten years of our training. They departed to perform the roles for which we had studied: advisor, confidante, teacher. They interpreted visions and signs, performed ceremonies, led festivities. All except for me.

Twelve summers had passed since the druids came to take me from Silver Downs. Twelve summers during which I studied hard and learned all I could, yet I showed little sign of ability. Small charms that my fellows performed easily required many long hours of practice for me. I could not call on the elements until several years after all my fellows had mastered the practice, and even now the air elementals still eluded me. I found it difficult to interpret the signs, for it seemed they could be read in several ways, depending on one's motive. But the area in which I had most soundly failed was the Sight. No matter how many hours I practised, I never Saw even the briefest vision in the waters. But despite that, the druids believed I was intended for them.

I had a secret reason for pursuing my training, despite my lack of ability, and it pained me that Oistin had seemingly chosen to disregard this now. I had confided in him many years ago about my sister, who had been stolen at birth by the fey queen, Titania. He knew I planned to search for her as soon as my training was complete. Once she was located and safely returned home, I would again be at the druids' disposal — for the rest of my life. It seemed to me to be a fair exchange.

Given my lack of ability, there must be another reason the druids had selected me all those years ago. If Oistin had Seen the path that lay ahead of me, he had never hinted at it. So this assignment was completely unexpected. How would I advise the king with no Sight?

2

ARLEN

There was no point sitting here feeling sorry for myself. Oistin had made his decision and I would not shame myself by arguing with him. From under my bed, I retrieved the boxes that held all my worldly belongings. Two spare pairs of linen trousers, three tunics. A pair of socks, long overdue for darning. A well-worn pair of boots. A thick cloak. A sack in which to pack my belongings if I travelled from the community.

The other box contained a comb and a few small mementoes of Silver Downs, for as a boy I had been permitted to take from home only what fit in my pockets. A black raven feather, gathered on some long-forgotten expedition. A stone plucked from one of the twin rivers that crossed our estate, worn perfectly smooth and round from the waters. A small wooden dagger one of my soldier cousins made for me. I remembered him wrapping my fingers around the dagger as he taught me to use it. And the final item: two small, flat blocks of wood bound together with a faded yellow ribbon. It contained a single day's eye bloom, taken from a bush on the very edge of Silver Downs, swiftly plucked as I walked away for the last time. This was everything in the world that belonged to me.

I pulled on my socks and boots, then quickly packed the rest of my belongings in the sack. I pushed the boxes back under my cot, which would likely belong to someone else by sundown tomorrow. Cots did not stay empty around here for long. Clutching the sack, I left my bedchamber without another glance.

When I returned to Oistin, he still sat at his desk, although whether he stared at the parchment lying there or at his hands in his lap, I couldn't tell.

"Aah, Arlen. Are you ready?"

"I am at your command, Master."

"Then we shall send you immediately." He went to the door. "Come."

"May I ask something before I leave?"

Oistin's step faltered and he paused before turning to face me.

"Of course, and I will answer if I can."

"Will you tell me what I have done?"

"Whatever do you mean? This is a great honour. Some druids spend their whole lives angling for a position at court."

"But not me. You know this is the last thing I desire. So I would know what it is I have done to cause you to punish me in this way."

Oistin sighed and for the first time I noticed how old he looked. His face was lined and his eyes shadowed.

"Arlen, this is not a punishment."

"Then why do you send me? Why not Niall or Donat? They would be better suited to such a position than I."

"Give yourself time to settle in. It won't be that bad. You've been here a long time and I suppose you think of this as your home. There is always a sense of grief at leaving one's home behind."

"You know I despise politics. I have little patience for it. I am entirely unsuited to advise the king."

"I think Hearn will find you refreshing. He has enough sycophants surrounding him. An impartial advisor will be welcome."

"You know the other reason I am unsuitable. That hasn't changed. I will be useless to him."

"I haven't forgotten. The visions will come with time. Patience. Practice."

"I've had patience. I've spent hundreds of hours practising. And still I See nothing. How can I advise the king if I cannot See?"

"He doesn't need to know that you See nothing. You have common sense and wisdom and enough knowledge of politics, history and geography. Your Sight will come eventually, but in the meantime, you can still guide Hearn to make the right decisions."

"You want me to lie to the king?"

"I'm not suggesting you lie to him. Merely that you don't tell him what he doesn't need to know."

"Master, is there no one else who can do this?"

Oistin's mouth twisted and he laid his hand on my shoulder.

"Arlen, I regret that I have to ask this of you. But it must be you who goes. I have Seen it."

"Tell me. Please."

"There is little to tell. I Saw you at the king's side with a shadowy woman behind you. That is all."

"That doesn't mean I am intended as his advisor, only that for some reason, at some time, I might meet the king."

"I feel this deep in my bones, Arlen. A sure certainty. You are meant to be at Hearn's side. You will be instrumental in something he must achieve. It has to be you."

"And what of my sister? When will I be able to search for her?"

Oistin looked at me steadily and at first I thought he would not reply. When eventually he spoke, I felt like I had been punched in the stomach.

"Your sister will be important to the kingdom's peace," he said. "It is crucial that you find her, but not yet. Certain events must occur first. If you search for her too soon, everything will be ruined."

"You have Seen her?" I whispered. "She is alive?"

He nodded. "But I must caution you, Arlen. Do not search for her until I tell you. Peace is fragile and tenuous. Your sister will either make peace or irrevocably destroy it."

I sucked in a deep breath and bowed my head.

"I understand. If you wish me to go, I will go."

"I will send someone to visit occasionally, so you can return any news. Ronan, perhaps. He itches to be out in the world and away from here. Don't send a messenger unless the matter is dire. Wait until I send someone we can trust."

I nodded.

"Let's send you on your way, then."

As I followed Oistin out to the stone circle that stood not far from our lodge, druid after druid came to pay their respects, for already word had gone around that I was leaving. About two dozen druids lived in our community and I knew them all. Most were youngsters, arrived only in the last couple of years. A few were master druids who stayed to guide the younger ones. And then there was me. I stayed because I had not managed to complete my training. Yet I was about to step into one of the most highly coveted positions.

I said my farewells quickly. There were none here I was close to. There had been good friends over the years — boys who came to the community around the same time as I had — but they all moved on eventually. They mastered their studies and left for whatever role Oistin chose for them after their ten years were concluded.

By the time we reached the stones, only Oistin remained. The stone circle was ancient and we had no knowledge of those who set it in place, or why they would select such a site deep in the woods. I rested my palm against one of the stones, seeking a connection with it, and received a faint sensation of peacefulness and endurance.

"Farewell, Arlen," Oistin said. "You have studied long and hard and your journey is not over. Keep up your practice. Find a place where you can study and meditate in quiet. That which you seek will come when the time is right."

"Of course, Master. Thank you for everything."

"Step into the centre of the stones, then. Keep your eyes closed until you stop moving. Someone should be there to meet you. Hearn is expecting you."

Dead leaves crunched under my boots as I followed his instructions. I closed my eyes and waited. There was nothing left to say.

Oistin murmured an invocation to the air elementals, asking them to take me to my destination. I had never before travelled in this manner, although I knew what to expect and, in theory, I knew how to summon the elementals to send me through the stones. I resisted the urge to open my eyes and check what happened.

Soon enough a gentle breeze flowed around me. It circled my legs and moved up my body, bringing with it the fragrant scent of honeysuckle. I clutched my sack of belongings as the breeze grew stronger, whipping around me, faster and faster. There was no other sensation of movement, only of wind swirling around me, as if I was in the eye of a storm.

Eventually the wind died down. It became once more a gentle breeze that wafted around my legs. Then that, too, withdrew and I was alone.

3

ARLEN

When I opened my eyes, I stood in the centre of a much larger circle, the stones of which were taller and wider than any man. Despite Oistin's promise that someone would meet me, I was alone. Grassy fields and a few ash trees surrounded the stone circle, but nothing that might be a commoner's lodge, let alone a king's. The sky held no trace of smoke that might signal a home, only a few clouds and the golden blush of sunset. Not the most auspicious of beginnings.

I dropped my pack in the middle of the circle and sat on the grass. I had no idea which direction Braen Keep lay in. As the sun sank, the air grew cool. I shivered in my linen trousers and my stomach growled. I had not thought to bring any supplies. I could probably make enough of a meal if I left the stones. There would be mushrooms or nuts or any number of things I might eat, but I might miss whoever was meant to meet me. So I waited. I would not let Oistin down by disobeying him on my first assignment.

Darkness fell and stars appeared. I should have used this time to meditate, perhaps on my failure with the Sight, but instead I leaned back on my hands and stared up at the sky. It had always fascinated me. The sun. The moon. The stars. The beauty of it all. Had anyone ever persuaded the air elementals to let them travel the skies? Could I touch the sun if they were willing? Stand on a star?

My thoughts wandered to my lost sister. I had heard the tale of our birth more times than I could count. How Eithne struggled in labour for almost a day before the first babe was born. It was a girl child, as she had known it would be, and she had already determined the babe would be named Agata for her own mother. No sooner was the child born than Titania revealed herself.

Nobody knew how long the queen of the fey had watched. Perhaps she had only just arrived, in which case the timing was fortuitous for her. Or maybe she had looked on all through that long day. Before anyone could move, Titania snatched up the babe, still coated with birth fluids and not yet even wrapped in a blanket.

"The child is born of a fey," Titania said. "She should be with her own kind. If you want her to live, you will not follow."

Then she disappeared and the child with her. Before Eithne could make sense of what had happened, her womb contracted and it was only then she realised there was a second babe. I was born and Eithne named me Arlen.

"The child has been unSeen this far," said Brigit, who was wife to Eithne's brother and midwife for the births. "Even my own Sight didn't show him. If you acknowledge him as your son, she will steal him, too."

Eithne was distraught at the loss of one child and unwilling to give up another, but she knew the wisdom of Brigit's words. So I was given to Cryda, a servant who had recently borne a child, and she nursed me with her own babe. But I grew up knowing that Eithne had given birth to me, although Cryda was the one I called Mother. We had neither seen nor heard of Agata since then. I was a young boy when I first vowed to search for my sister and bring her home if she still lived. I reasoned that since I had been unSeen, Titania's instruction not to follow Agata did not apply to me, only to those who had been present for our births.

As night deepened and moonlight shone on the ancient circle surrounding me, I took my woollen cloak from the sack and wrapped it tightly around my shoulders. It kept out the night breeze, but still the chill crept underneath and I began to shiver. I knew techniques that would keep me warm, if I could attain the right level of focus. Settling into a meditation pose, with my legs crossed and my back straight, I closed my eyes and tried to let go of my thoughts.

It was difficult at first, for I was distracted by my bodily need for warmth, but eventually I stopped feeling the cold. I passed the night in the peacefulness of deep meditation, not even noticing when the sun rose, and only opening my eyes when someone spoke.

"Are you going to sit there all day?"

Standing over me was a man perhaps a couple of summers younger than I. He wore dark blue trousers and a shirt of the same colour. He gave me a friendly grin and reached out to help me up.

"Bram," he offered. "You the druid? From Oistin?"

"That would be me," I said. "My name is Arlen."

"Come on, then. I'll take you to the keep."

We bore west, walking through ankle-deep grass that still held the lushness of late summer, although that season was past. The ground sloped upward gently. We walked in silence for several minutes.

"Did you not expect me yesterday?" I asked eventually, thinking I should try to make conversation.

Bram shrugged and his ears turned pink.

"We was busy yesterday. Hearn couldn't spare anyone to come get you until this morning."

Perhaps Hearn wasn't enamoured of Oistin's belief that he needed a druid advisor. We walked in silence and eventually we came to the top of a long slope. In the distance, still a couple of hours' walk away, stood a town.

"You walked all this way to fetch me?" I asked.

"Set out at first light," Bram said.

I wondered why he didn't ride a horse or perhaps bring a cart, but I didn't ask. It seemed politics were at play even before I arrived. I would need to learn fast. The sun was past its zenith before we reached Braen Town. I had never been to a town before, so I had no sense of its size compared to others. The streets were dusty and poorly paved, and the air stank of rotting refuse. Skinny children crouched in the dirt, watching forlornly as people rushed past. The adults looked downtrodden and surly. I made eye contact with a woman and she raised her lip in a snarl. I was careful not to look directly at anyone else after that.

It took at least another hour to wind our way through the streets. Eventually we reached a tall stone wall set with heavy wooden gates which stood open. Bram greeted the two guards stationed there as we passed through. Inside were fewer people, although this side of the wall seemed no better maintained than the other. I saw bare earth, stunted trees, and paths in need of repair. My spirits sank. I was used to greenery and solitude and the peacefulness of the woods. Here was all dirt and dust and people rushing. Surely Oistin didn't expect me to stay here for long.

Braen Keep was far larger than the druids' lodge. My memories of Silver Downs were faded, but I had always thought it to be a large lodge. However, even it paled in comparison to the king's keep. Like the town around it, though, Braen Keep was poorly maintained. Weather and mould darkened the grey stones, window shutters hung crookedly, and the roughness of the thatching suggested it leaked. A raven perched on the roof cawed and I had the uncanny sense that he warned me away. We entered through a small side door, guarded only by a single man who nodded at Bram.

Inside, the keep was dim and dusty. There were no lamps or candles lit, despite how little sunlight reached through the shuttered windows. Bram led me up several flights of stairs and along twisting passages before we reached a small bedchamber with an ill-fitting door.

"This is where you'll sleep," he muttered as he put his shoulder to the door to force it open.

The bedchamber was no larger than the one I had shared at the druid community, but it contained only one bed rather than four. The rest of the furniture consisted of a wooden chair, a small chest of drawers, and a single shelf. Wooden shutters covered the window, but there were no curtains. There was no rug on the floor or blanket on the bed. Nevertheless, it was reasonably clean, although it needed a good airing, and would be quiet.

"This will be ample," I said.

Despite its plainness, a bedchamber of my own was a luxury. I had never slept alone, even during my boyhood days at Silver Downs.

"You'll need a blanket." Bram's ears were pink again. "I'll get someone to send one up. And a candle."

"Thank you." I should try to make an ally of the young man. After all, he was the only person I knew here. "You've been very kind to walk all that way to fetch me."

Bram stared at the ground. "Just doing my job."

"What exactly is that?"

"I fetch things. Run messages. Things like that."

"Then you will be a useful man to know should I need to send an urgent message." I tried to give the impression he might someday be privy to secret information, but Bram looked unimpressed. I swallowed a sigh. I knew nothing about politics.

"Would you show me to the kitchen?" I asked. "I've not eaten since the evening before last. Or do you think Hearn would want to see me immediately?"

"He'll call for you when he wants you."

"Wise advice," I said, feeling like a fool.

I left my sack on the bed and followed Bram along the twisty hallways and down three flights of stone steps. I paid careful attention to our path, for fear I would not find my bedchamber again.

The kitchen seemed to have no order and nobody in charge, which was a far cry from the community's kitchen. The heat from the wood stoves and two hearths was stifling, and the aroma of beef stew filled the air.

Bram showed me where I could obtain some bread and a mug of ale, and a spot where I could eat without being in anyone's way. I sat beside two guards who looked up at me blearily, then returned their attention to their meals. They had probably just come off a night shift and I thought better than to try to make conversation with them. I would not win any allies by pestering people.

Bram had disappeared, so I ate my meal, then managed to find my bedchamber with only one wrong turn. A neatly folded blanket and two candles sat next to my sack of belongings on the cot. I placed my spare clothes and my cloak in the dresser. They barely took up one of the three drawers. What else was I supposed to put in there? Surely nobody expected me to have enough clothes to fill three drawers.

I managed to force the window shutters open. The wood was swollen and they probably wouldn't close properly again, but at least I could air out the room. Winter nights would be cold with shutters that didn't close, though. I pulled off my boots and stretched out on the cot. Might as well sleep while I could. Who knew what sort of schedule Hearn might expect me to keep once I commenced in my new role as his advisor?

Hearn kept me waiting for four days. The time spent alone didn't bother me, for I was used to solitary days. When I was hungry, I made my way down to the kitchen and helped myself to bread and ale. Nobody ever commented on my regular presence, although one of the guards who was often there for a meal at the same time soon began to offer a friendly nod.

I secured the loan of a small bronze bowl, which I filled with water and carried carefully back to my bedchamber. I spent hours peering into the bowl's shallow depths, hoping to catch a glimpse of something. Past. Present. Future. Maybe. But the Sight remained as intangible as ever, and all I saw was the smooth interior of the bowl and the reflection of candlelight on the water's surface. This was what I was doing when Bram finally came to say Hearn had sent for me.

I followed Bram along the keep's twisty hallways. He paused outside a thick wooden door flanked by two guards on each side.

"In there." Bram indicated the doors with his thumb.

"Thank you," I said.

"Don't thank me till you know what he wants."

Bram left. I hesitated, wondering whether the guards were supposed to open the door, but they kept their gaze fixed straight ahead. It seemed their duties extended only to keeping people out, not helping them go in. I pushed open the door and entered the king's audience hall.

There were only five people in the room, and although I had never seen Hearn before, the stout man lounging on a massive chair padded with rich purple cushions had to be him. He appeared to be deep in conversation with a man standing in front of him. Behind Hearn stood two guards and to his left was a much smaller chair on which a woman sat.

I wondered how it had taken me so long to see her. Even seated as she was, I could tell she was tall and skinny to the point of ungainliness. She held her arms awkwardly, as if she didn't know whether to fold them in her lap or across her chest or rest them on the arms of the chair. Her face was long and horsey, with a large nose and protruding ears. She wore a deep purple gown that looked like it was intended for a woman with a much larger frame.

As I met her eyes, a jolt passed through my body and it seemed that somebody said *pay attention for she will be important*. Was this a glimpse of the Sight or merely my own brain being overly dramatic? The woman broke our eye contact to look down at her hands and the moment passed. Trying to cover my discomfort, I strode forward. I stopped a few paces away from Hearn and bowed.

Hearn paused his conversation to look me up and down. He was a large man in his middle years, with a physique that was turning to fat. His hair hung almost to his shoulders and his eyes were unintelligent.

"So Oistin has sent his plaything to me." Hearn's voice boomed, far too loud for the distance at which I stood.

"Your Majesty, I understand that I am to advise you," I said.

"Have you not sufficient advisors, my lord?" asked the man he had been conversing with, eyeing me with clear displeasure. He wore a frilly shirt which he kept straightening and a moustache which he probably thought was more impressive than it really was.

"I have more advisors than any man should have to suffer," Hearn said. "But it seems the druid master thinks I need one more. Well, let's see what kind of advice you give, druid. You'll stay for as long as your advice pleases me, despite what Oistin says. Go now. I'll call for you when I want you."

I hesitated. Was he not going to introduce me to the others? I desperately wanted to know who the woman was.

"Are you deaf, druid?" asked the other man.

I bowed and left. The heavy door closed behind me with a thud.

4

AGATA

"Agata, my dear, you look like you have been rolling around on the ground. Whatever were you doing?" Titania reached over and plucked a leaf from my hair. She waved it in front of my face, her eyebrows raised. "Hmmm?"

I held her gaze and willed myself not to blush.

"Looking for birds' nests."

Titania's face said clearly that she didn't believe me, but she wouldn't question me further. That wasn't her way. As long as I looked suitably meek, she would let it go.

"Well, straighten your clothes and sit down. And Agata," she said as I moved to take my place at her feet. "Do fasten your gown properly."

She looked pointedly at my chest and I realised my gown was only partially laced up. This time I couldn't hold back my blush. I had taken it off earlier in order to climb a tree more swiftly and hadn't realised I had failed to tie my laces again. I could only guess what she thought I had been doing. I fixed my gown and sat on the edge of the dais, where I could see Titania from the corner of my eye, and ensured my gown covered my legs.

The dais stood at the edge of a circular clearing in the woods. This was fey territory — Titania's realm — and we were deep in the heart of it. The fey realm sat side by side with the mortal realm, not that I had ever visited that fey-forsaken place. I had no interest in mortals and no reason to visit their realm.

Oak and elm shaded the clearing, but lush grass covered the ground despite the thick canopy. Titania's magic gave her realm whatever appearance she wished, and the seasons changed only at her desire. Guards stood behind the dais, a full dozen of them. Not that she needed their protection. This was her place and her people. Nobody would dare attack her here and even if they did, Titania could protect herself with her magic. More guards ringed the clearing and in the centre stood a group of fey. Men and women and a few children. They waited silently and without moving, even the children. Appearing impatient was a certain way to bring Titania's wrath down on oneself.

Titania sat on her throne. Her gown pooled around her feet, shimmering like blood, and her dark hair was artfully arranged to flow over her shoulders in a cascade of curls. Her fingernails — half as long as her fingers themselves and the shade of congealed blood — tapped against the arm of her throne.

"Where is he?" she hissed, barely moving her mouth. This was why she liked me to sit so close, so she could speak to me without anybody else hearing. I was the only one she could confide in.

"I haven't seen him all day," I answered quietly.

She waited for Oberon, king of the fey and her husband, although not my father. She had never told me who my father was and I had never asked. He obviously meant nothing to her, so there was no reason for me to care either. He was probably just some fey she had a brief affair with.

"He knows I hate waiting for him." Her fingernails drummed against the curved arm of her throne.

"He'll be here soon."

It was a lie and we both knew it. Oberon did his own thing. He might turn up, but then again he might not.

"I'm not waiting any longer," she said, then raised her voice for the guards. "I will hear the first petitioner."

The guards communicated silently with hand signals, and within moments a fey woman crossed the grassy court and sank to her knees. She bowed her head and waited for Titania to address her. I shifted slightly to get more comfortable and prepared for a tedious day. I had long ago perfected the art of looking attentive while retreating into my own mind.

My legs had gone numb and I had long since stopped listening when a soft whistle caught my attention. I turned my head slowly, trying to seem as if I just happened to look in a different direction. If Titania thought I was restless, I'd earn a sharp kick in the ribs. That was another reason she liked me to sit so close.

Sumerled waited in the shadowy depths of the woods. He tipped his head as my gaze met his, beckoning me to come to him. Irritation flared within me. He knew I couldn't leave until Titania allowed it. I gave him the tiniest shake of my head, although even that was more than he deserved.

"Are we boring you, my dear?" Titania's voice was dry and I knew even without turning that her words were directed at me.

"Of course not, my lady," I said. "But he is little more than a child and doesn't understand restraint. I don't control him."

"You should learn to," she said.

I swallowed the retort that came to mind, about how she was unable to control Oberon, who hadn't yet showed his face today.

"Yes, my lady."

She sighed and with a wave of her hand silenced the current petitioner. He stopped as suddenly as if she had slit his throat.

"Enough," she said. "Leave."

The clearing emptied, the fey departing swiftly and silently, even the one whose petition had been cut off. I didn't move. The instruction to leave was unlikely to apply to me, and Titania would only be crosser if I presumed to depart.

"Agata, come to me," Titania said.

I stood, my movements graceful, just as she had taught me. I would never move with the sinuousness that Titania did, however much I tried, but I could be graceful and elegant when I remembered. My skirts drifted down over my legs and I gave them a tiny shake to ensure they lay properly. Of course Titania noticed with a frown and I mentally admonished myself. Had I moved correctly, there would be no need to adjust my skirts. She didn't comment, though, and her usually observant gaze was somewhat distant. Perhaps she still wondered about Oberon's absence. Eventually, Titania looked me in the eyes. She had a way of staring that made me feel as if she peered inside my brain.

"What is our role?" she asked.

"To rule the fey," I said automatically.

"And how do we do that?"

"By being regal and authoritative at all times."

"Were you regal and authoritative today?"

I hesitated and her gaze sharpened.

"No, my lady," I said quickly before she could admonish me. "I was distracted."

"And it showed."

"It won't happen again."

"Make sure it doesn't. Now go. See what that boy wants. I've had enough of listening to whining fey for today anyway."

I turned to leave but stopped as she said my name.

"Don't ever turn up for court looking like that again."

My fingers twitched, but I held them at my sides and didn't let them stray to check my gown was fastened properly or that no more leaves were caught in my hair.

"Yes, my lady."

I fled before she could change her mind.

5

AGATA

Sumerled had at least enough sense not to stand right on the edge of the clearing, where he would have been visible to everyone. He waited further back amongst the trees. Oak and ash and beech grew thickly here, leaving little space for the sunlight to penetrate.

"What took you so long?" His voice held a whiny tone that made my fingers itch to slap him.

"Shut up," I hissed. "Just move. Before she changes her mind."

I held my gown up to my knees and ran through the woods with Sumerled at my heels. We fey know how to move swiftly and silently, although it had taken me somewhat longer to master than is usual for a fey child. Titania had often bemoaned my slowness to learn.

I inhaled deeply as we ran, savouring the aroma of moss and trees and damp leaves. The fey woods were home. I couldn't imagine ever living anywhere else. Some fey did, of course. Some chose to live in the mortal realm. Titania's opinion of such fey was scathing.

Although I had no desire to venture into the mortal realm, I was just the tiniest bit curious about it. Could it really be as bad as folk said? I pictured it as a wasteland, all brown and grey and dead. How did mortals survive in such a place. Where did they live? What did they eat? Did they wear clothes like ours? Did they live alone or in groups? What kinds of creatures inhabited their world? A sprite flew past my nose, near enough to brush my skin with its wings.

"Shoo," I muttered, adding a small burst of speed to get away from it.

The sprite laughed and flew away. Or at least I thought it laughed. I heard the sprites only as the faintest tittering. Sumerled claimed he could hear them clearly. I was never quite sure whether he lied, although it was true my senses didn't seem quite as sharp as those of most fey.

"Where shall we go?" I called over my shoulder once we were far enough away from court.

"Anywhere you like," he called back.

If it was my choice, I knew exactly where I wanted to go. My favourite place in all the fey realm was a pretty pond shrouded by elegant weeping willows. Their branches draped right down to the ground, forming a green curtain all the way around the pond. The water was warm and came from somewhere deep underground. In the morning, soft white mist hung over the water. Emerald-green moss surrounded the pond and a nearby patch of bluebells scented the air perfectly.

It would take us some time to get there, even running as fast as we were. I had never seen another living being there — not even a sprite, and they tended to be anywhere one didn't want them. There, I could pretend I was far away from the politics of court and from Titania, whose expectations I never quite managed to live up to. Somewhere where nobody watched to see when I would disgrace myself next and where nobody tried to befriend me just to get closer to Titania.

There was no point wishing for what I didn't have. Things could be much worse. If I lived in the mortal realm, I'd be far enough away from court, but I would be surrounded by stupid, uninspired, insipid mortals. The worst day amongst the fey was surely a hundred times better than any day in the mortal realm. I stopped thinking and pushed my legs faster as I hurtled over rocks and ducked under branches. If I ran fast enough, maybe I could outrun my morose thoughts.

"Slow down," Sumerled called from behind me. He might be able to move more quietly than me, but I had always been swifter.

I ignored him and ran even faster. He would know where to find me. This place was where I always went when I truly wanted to get away from fey intrigue. My legs were tired by the time I reached the pond. I had long left Sumerled behind, although he ran so silently that I never knew exactly where he was. I should have a few minutes to myself before he arrived, though.

I was hot and sweating from the run as I stripped off my gown and dived into the pond wearing just my underthings. The water was clear and blissfully warm. I took a deep breath and ducked under until my hair floated out around me.

The pond was so deep that if I held my breath and dived down, I couldn't touch the bottom. I had always wondered whether anything lived down there. Maybe some of the Old Ones who inhabited this land before the fey arrived had retreated to lonely places like the depths of a pond. The thought that there might be something down there, watching as my toes dangled above it, made me uneasy. I surfaced and splashed back to the edge. I was hauling myself out of the water as Sumerled arrived. He looked at me for a long moment and I felt almost naked in my dripping underthings.

"Now that's a nice sight to arrive to," he said, with a smirk.

"Too bad you're so late," I said easily. I wrung the water out of my hair and sat on the mossy ground, leaning back on my elbows and enjoying the cool shade. Sumerled sat beside me, a little too close. He leaned in, his breath hot on my neck.

"What do you want to do now?"

His breath tickled my neck and I shoved him away.

"Don't be disgusting."

He shrugged, but didn't seem offended. "I didn't do anything."

"I know exactly what you were thinking."

He leered. "I doubt you know *exactly* what."

I glared and his smile wavered a little. Nothing untoward had ever happened between us, but I was never entirely sure whether he joked when he said things like that. Resolving to ignore him, I lay down in the moss and fanned my hair out around me to let it dry, then closed my eyes.

The air was just warm enough that I didn't feel chilled, and I was pleasantly drowsy. The chirps of water bugs drifted past. Something made a small splash in the pond. Again the thoughts of hidden Old Ones rose, but I didn't let myself open my eyes to check that we were still alone. They were probably more myth than truth anyway. Even if they had existed long ago, it wasn't possible for them still to be here somewhere, waiting. The fey were the longest-lived of all species.

I must have drifted off into sleep, because when I next noticed my surroundings, my mind was fuzzy. Fighting my way out of sleep was like swimming back up from the bottom of the pond. Eventually I managed to open my eyes. The light hadn't changed, but I could tell the day was late. The fey woods had a certain tone to them as night approached, even though the light and temperature remained constant. I rarely ever slept so soundly, but there was something about this place that made me deeply relaxed. I reached over to poke Sumerled in the ribs.

"Sumerled," I said. "Wake up. I need to go back."

He grunted but didn't move. I poked him harder.

"If you don't wake up, I'm going to leave you here."

He opened his eyes and squinted at me. "Just a little longer."

"I'm leaving now."

I twisted my still-damp hair up into a knot as I climbed to my feet. It was only then I noticed the rock right next to where I had been lying. It was about the size of my head. I stared at it for a long moment. My thoughts were jumbled and my ears rang. Surely I would have noticed that I lay down next to a rock that large?

"Sumerled, did you put that there?" I poked my fingers in my ears, trying to relieve the pressure that made the air sound like it vibrated.

He had closed his eyes again and seemed to have sunk back into sleep. I toed his ribs.

"Sumerled!"

"I'm awake," he grumbled, sitting up. "What's the hurry?"

"You mean apart from the fact that we've been here all afternoon and Titania will be wondering where I am?"

"It's not like she'll send someone looking for you. She always knows where you are. It's peculiar."

"Don't say things like that," I said. "You never know who might be listening. Did you put this rock here?"

He gave me a bewildered look as I pointed.

"What do you mean? Why would I put it there?"

"Is it some sort of game? Leaving a rock right next to my head for me to find when I wake up?"

"Of course not. I didn't do it. I never even saw it before."

"Then how did it get there?"

He shrugged. "It must have already been there."

"It wasn't. I would have noticed."

"Then you explain. How did it get there if I didn't do it and it wasn't already there?"

I stared down at the rock and an uneasy feeling crept over me. My skin began to pimple. Someone else had been here while I was sound asleep in my underthings.

"Somebody must have snuck up and put it there while we were sleeping," I said.

Sumerled started to laugh, but stopped when he realised I was serious.

"Who? And why?"

"I don't know," I snapped. "I just know it wasn't there before. So either this is one of your stupid games or somebody snuck up on us."

"I would have noticed if anyone came here," he said scornfully.

"Apparently not."

We glared at each other for a minute.

"I have to get back." I pulled on my gown and slid my feet back into my slippers. I didn't wait to see whether he followed.

6

IDA

It is a long time since he first trapped me in here. I was sure he wasn't strong enough to contain me. But somehow he was, and he has. His druid brother shows him how to trap me in the box inside his head. How to envision the box, how to make sure it is solid and real. How to hold the lid closed, even when he sleeps.

I try many times during his long life to escape. Sometimes I almost do. When the pain starts in his stomach, he knows his end is near, and hope rises in me once again. I watch those last long months as the disease eats his insides. I feel the fatigue and bone-crushing pain with him. At times it is hard to remember whose pain it is. We have shared his mind for so long that sometimes I think my thoughts might have really been his to start with. The box he keeps me in dims my view of the world. I can see what he sees, hear what he thinks, but only if I concentrate. Most of the time it seems like too much effort. Instead I sink down into the darkness and wait.

He prepares well for his death. He spends time with his druid brother, who coaches him in how to keep me trapped inside his mind. They think that if he can keep me confined as he dies, I will die with him. I am not so sure and I am not ready to die.

When the moment comes, I am ready. As his mind drifts into

silence and his heart stutters to a halt, I push hard against the lid of the box. As prepared as he thinks he is, he finally loses control in those last moments. I burst out of the box and finally I am once again free in his mind. I immediately think, *Out*, and suddenly I stand beside him.

I look down at his corpse. He lies on a bed, soft pillows under his head and a fine blanket drawn up to his shoulders. He is much older than when I last saw him. Then he was a boy of only nineteen summers. Now he is an old man, withered and wrinkled and yellowed. How many years has it been? I have felt the strength leaving his body as time passed. The aches in his knees and hips and the throb in his lower back. The way his hands shook and didn't quite do what he wanted them to. I felt his frustration with these things and then, later, his acceptance.

I finally notice the woman who sits on the opposite side of his bed. When he looked at her, he must have been seeing a memory, for she looks little like that now. She has aged just like him, although her eyes are still sharp and her hands steady. She glares at me.

I ignore her and glance around the bedchamber. The coals in the hearth spit sparks and the air is fragrant with healing herbs. Heavy curtains drawn over the windows prevent me from seeing whether it is day or night. The room is well furnished with solid wooden furniture and expensive bedclothes.

"It's been more than sixty years," the woman says. "And yet you look exactly the same."

I stretch my arms, feeling my skin tighten and my joints move. Muscles flex and contract. Blood races through my veins. My heart pumps. I inhale and air rushes into my lungs. I hold it there a moment, then exhale. It is intoxicating, being alive again after so long.

"He spent his life trying to atone for what you did," the woman hisses. "You should have died with him."

"As you can see, I did not." I arch my eyebrow at her. Oh, the flexibility of muscles and movement.

"The lodge is well warded. You won't be able to leave this place."

"That would be a shame for you, wouldn't it?" I say. "For I don't think you and I could live here together."

She glares at me but says nothing further. I notice the way she holds his hand in her own, the way her grip tightens as she swallows whatever it is she burns to say. She helped him confine me all those years ago. I should probably kill her, but I turn my back and leave the bedchamber.

The lodge feels quiet and solemn as I stride along the hallway. The air is heavy with grief. There are people here who mourn his death and not just his wife. The boy experienced much sadness in his life as he watched first his parents, then his brothers grow old and die. There were other lesser griefs which were not as personal for him. The loss of wives in childbirth for two of the brothers. Children born still and quiet; others who fall ill and die before their second birthday. He rejoiced in the sounds of running feet and the laughter of children, even as he sorrowed that none of them were his.

As I reach the bottom of the stairs, folk appear in the doorways of various rooms. Their solemn faces turn to surprise as they see me. Nobody steps forward to challenge me as I stride through the lodge. Until I reach the front door.

A young man steps out in front of me. He is probably about the same age as the boy was when he created me. We stare at each other and understanding crosses his face. He squares his shoulders and clears his throat and I recognise the boy in his actions. Not a son, for he never had one, but trained by him perhaps. I haven't been paying enough attention recently to recognise his face. His voice is amusingly earnest.

"When the great bard died, the creature he had imprisoned in his mind broke free."

I feel his power immediately. He is not as strong as the boy, but he understands his ability. I will not be trapped again. Before he can speak another word, I wave my hand towards him. He goes tumbling back into the room he came from, gone before his expression can change.

I open the door and step out of the lodge. Drizzling rain kisses my skin and for a moment I close my eyes and lift my face to greet it. Too long have I been bereft of feeling, locked inside the boy's mind.

When I open my eyes, someone else stands in front of me. Like the boy's wife, he too has aged, although he still holds his back straight and his head high. The dark hair is silver now, but it still hangs in braids to his shoulders. His face is not as wrinkled as the boy's and he stands without aid of a cane, which is something the boy has not been able to do for some years. It is his druid brother. Without him, the boy might have been able to return me to his mind all that time ago, but he wouldn't have known how to keep me there.

We stare in silence, each waiting for the other to make the first move. Rain runs down his face, but he doesn't try to wipe it away.

"Keeping you confined was his dearest wish," the druid says, at last.

"I cannot be confined," I say. "Not any longer. I will live my own life."

"You live only because he created you. He knew he was wrong to do so. It was done in a moment of rashness without any understanding of his ability."

"But I live now."

"Brigit has warded the lodge." He gestures towards my feet. "You are standing right in front of the line she has drawn. Take another step and the wards will kill you."

I extend my senses, feeling, tasting. I sense something, a lingering power of a type I am unfamiliar with. I hesitate. What if his words are true?

"Step back into the lodge," the druid says. "We will allow you to stay here, provided you cause no harm. You can still live."

"That is no life," I say. "Confined to the lodge just as I have been confined to his mind for so long. I will not live like that."

"Then cross the wards and die," he says. "Those are your options."

I hesitate on the doorstep, looking past him to green fields and grey sky. Heavy clouds. Fog shrouding distant mountains. There is a whole world out there. A world I have yet to experience, for the boy never travelled again after his journey to capture me. He was content to pass the rest of his life on these grounds. I cannot be content with that. Not now.

The cold rain against my skin raises goose bumps and with each passing moment, I remember more and more of what it is to be alive. I can't go back. I can't stay. I can only move forward. Even if this is my death. I raise my foot and take a step.

White sparks blind me. Pain shoots through my body. My vision fails and I taste blood. All I can think is, I don't want to die. I gather my power and push the pain away. It is difficult and I strain, already panting. She is strong, the boy's wife, and her wards are powerful. They wrap around me, writhing up and down my limbs. They cling, suppressing my power. The pain is like nothing I have ever imagined. I am weakening. Dying. But no. I *will* live. I will not die now, not when the boy is dead and I am finally free.

I fight back, *pushing* at the wards. I fear I am not strong enough, but first one weakens, then another. One by one, the wards fizzle and fade away. I am left trembling, vastly weakened. My heart pumps once, then more strongly, and blood starts to flow in my veins again. I take a deep breath, filling my lungs with cool air. My head begins to clear, although the pain is still strong. I ignore the discomfort and take a shaky step forward. The druid backs away. His face is pale as he raises his hand towards me.

"Enough," I say, and my voice is stronger than I expect. "You have already seen that her wards cannot control me. You can do no more than she. Move out of my way."

"The people out there are innocent," he says. "They had no part in what happened to you. Do no harm to others and we will not have reason to come after you."

I force out a laugh, although it nearly chokes me.

"Come after me? You would dare? You have seen my power. And I will only grow stronger now that I am free. There is nothing you can do to me."

"Perhaps not I alone," he says. "But my brethren will aid me. And there are others like Brigit. Together, we can stop you."

"No," I say. "No mortal can stop me. Not now. Not this time."

He opens his mouth as if to argue, but closes it without another word. He steps aside, leaving the path clear for me. I walk on unsteady legs. The sensation of having a form is already familiar from the last time, although my legs never trembled like this back then. I force myself to take one step after another, away from the lodge.

"Ida," he says from behind me.

I had forgotten I ever had a name. Ida. This is what the boy named me all that time ago when he first created me. Ida. It means thirst. He thirsted for me.

"Ida, please."

Without looking back, I raise one hand and flick my fingers. I hear a thud as his body slams against the stone wall of the lodge. He doesn't speak again.

I walk on. Away from the lodge. Away from those who confined me.

I am free. And this time I will not be stopped.

7

IDA

I stride down the road that leads away from the boy's home. I have no plan, no idea of where I am going. Just the notion that I need to be away from here. I dealt with his apprentice easily enough, and even the druid posed little problem. My power grew while I languished inside the boy's mind and it will continue to grow. I have not forgotten how to feed it.

I look up at the grey sky as I walk. I am tempted, briefly, to halt the rain, but it is pleasant to feel its chill dampness on my skin. Cool rivulets run down my face and neck and limbs. They drip beneath the bodice of my white dress and trickle into my shoes. It has been so long since I have felt anything and I savour it.

I walk until the rain finally ceases of its own accord and then I walk some more. In the distance across some fields, I see a lodge. Sturdy grey stone, smoke rising from a chimney. Should I make that my home? But no, it is too close to the boy's lodge, where his wife and the druid are.

I continue to walk. Eventually my stomach starts to feel hollow and a growl emits from it. I recognise the feeling from before: this is hunger. It means I need to eat. Far off in the distance, smoke rises.

Where there is smoke, there are usually mortals. And mortals will have food. I keep walking.

The day is drawing to a close as I reach a small stone lodge. It is weather-beaten and the thatch roof is poorly made. The front door creaks loudly as I tug it open. A screaming baby immediately assaults my ears. I try not to listen, but the shrill noise reverberates through the lodge and worms into my head. I cover my ears as I walk down the hallway. How can they stand such noise? Why does nobody stop it?

The kitchen is devoid of inhabitants. I inspect the pantry, but it is almost bare. Just a few soggy turnips and an almost empty sack of barley. My hunger has grown so great that it almost eclipses the continuous screams of the child. Something gnaws at my insides. If I go long enough without food, will my stomach start to eat itself? I cast my gaze around the room, desperate for something to eat.

A half loaf of bread rests on the workbench. I rush towards it, ready to devour it. But it is dry and hard. Stale. I hesitate, but there seems to be no other food in this sorry place. I lift the bread to my mouth and bite into it. It is dry and I almost choke trying to swallow it, but I force it down.

My stomach still growls after the bread is gone. I return to the cupboard and inspect the turnips. They are soft and spongy to touch. I think I recall they should be cooked before eating, but perhaps that isn't always necessary. I take a bite from one, but it tastes nasty and I spit it out. No, these cannot be eaten without cooking. In fact, I think they will not be edible even if cooked. I let the turnip drop to the floor. The baby continues to scream.

I search the room again, but there is no other food. I consider checking the other rooms, but memory tells me that mortals usually only store food in the kitchen. I leave and continue walking. I feel drawn in a particular direction. There is one of the boy's blood out there somewhere. It is as good a destination as any.

Night has long fallen before I reach another lodge. This one, too, is poorly made, but the contents of its kitchen are more substantial. A cooking pot hangs over banked coals with the remnants of the inhabitants' dinner. A savoury scent arises from the pot. A vegetable stew of some sort. I take a bowl from a shelf and spoon the stew into it. There is even an end of bread which tastes like it was baked only yesterday. Together they make a satisfying meal and my stomach finally stops trying to eat itself. I leave the bowl and spoon on the workbench and leave.

I walk through the night, still following the invisible trail that leads to the one who shares the boy's blood. It is a fine evening, clear with a waning moon. The air is crisp, but not too cold, and walking keeps me warm enough. I had forgotten how fragile mortal bodies are, that they cannot withstand cold or heat or lack of food.

The sun rises over distant mountains, casting the sky a fiery shade of orange. I continue to walk as the sun creeps up through the sky. Twice more I stop to eat. On both occasions I encounter mortal women in the kitchen. One raises a knife at me, threatening. I merely wave my hand towards her and she drops the knife to clasp her throat, wondering why she can no longer breathe. She falls to the floor and is still long before I finish eating the porridge she was cooking. The other has the sense not to threaten me. She merely backs into a corner and waits. I ignore her and when I leave, the quiet sounds of her sobs follow me out the door.

As the sun sets and my legs become too tired to continue, I encounter a small village. It is nothing much — merely a dozen or so tiny lodges clumped together. I select the finest, although even that is poor. The inhabitants flee when I announce that I require their lodge, and I sleep soundly.

At dawn, I rise and break my fast with bread and honey from the kitchen. I had forgotten honey. Sticky and fragrant, sweet almost to the point of sickliness. After I have eaten, I continue walking. The sky is patchy with clouds, but no rain falls. The crisp wind holds a hint of winter's approach.

Towards the end of the day, I come upon another village. Although it is far larger than the last, it is no grander. Skinny, dirty children flee ahead of me. Weeds struggle through the cracks in the roads and every lodge looks ready to fall down in the next strong wind. I follow the widest road and trust it will lead to something more habitable. Eventually it does.

There is a stone wall, far taller than me. Soldiers guard a wide wooden gate which, like everything else in this village, looks to be in need of repairs. I merely look at the guards and they swiftly open the gate. None meet my gaze as I walk through, drawing ever closer to the one I seek. He is near.

Ahead is a lodge much larger than the others I have seen, larger even than the boy's home. Someone important must live here. I walk past dusty garden beds and empty fountains. People scatter ahead of me, hiding behind stunted trees or barns in sore need of maintenance. I approach the front doors. They look sturdier than those at the gate, although it would cost me little effort to blast them away.

I look at the two soldiers who guard the doors. The men tremble and one immediately moves to open the doors for me. The other hesitates, one hand lingering on the sword at his waist. I am tired after my long walk and have no patience for silly mortal bravery. I point my finger towards him and he pales as his chest tightens. His heart pumps one final time and bursts. He falls to the ground, already dead. One arm flops out across my path, and I frown as I step over it. Mortal bodies are so messy. I wish they would have the decency to fall away from me as they die.

Inside the lodge is dark and the air smells musty. The wooden floor needs polishing and a thick layer of grime covers every surface. I stride along the hallways, wondering whether I should seek food first or a place to sleep. Food, I decide, as my stomach growls again. It seems to need feeding at unreasonably common intervals. The scent of roasting hares reaches my nostrils.

I follow the aroma to the kitchen, where a skinny woman removes two hares from a spit over a fire. My mouth waters at the meaty scent, and it is all I can do not to rip them from her hands, but I know they will be hot and will burn my tender skin. The woman's eyes meet mine and like most of the mortals I have encountered, there is no fight in her. She merely places the hares on a platter and waits to see what I want.

"Where do you serve these?" I ask her.

The woman points towards a door at the other end of the room. It leads down another dark hallway. I glance through open doors as I pass. None hold anything of interest until I reach the room at the very end. To say it is sumptuous would be a lie, but it is a large room and appears well used.

A wooden table at one end is positioned on a raised platform. The chairs at this table are finer than the others with elaborate swirls carved along their backs. The rest of the room contains two more long tables, these with plain wooden chairs. Only two tables — the one on the platform and one of the others — are set ready for dining. Dark tapestries cover the stone walls and the lamp lighting is inadequate. The air smells of long-eaten meals and spilled ale.

I go to the table on the platform. Up five shallow steps and I am looking out over the rest of the room. I seat myself in the finest of the chairs and wait. Only minutes pass before a man enters the room. His form is overly substantial and his beard needs cleaning. He stops at the steps leading up the platform and glowers at me. Perhaps he thinks it is his place in which I sit. Other men crowd behind him. They exchange mutters as they watch.

"Are you the one who was in charge here?" My voice is pleasant and even, for he has not yet offended me.

Discontent radiates from him and I know immediately that he can feed my power. He is not the one who drew me here, the one with the boy's blood. That is the one I need most, but the man who stands glaring at me can nourish me in the meantime. He seems to take a very long time to decide what to say and I begin to wonder if perhaps he is simple. At length, he clears his throat.

"My name is Hearn," he says, "and I am king."

"Well met, Hearn. Come and sit beside me."

I arch my eyebrows at him. My voice is musical and enticing. He will either respond or he will be dead. Either way, if dinner is not served shortly, somebody will die.

He hesitates a moment longer, then walks towards me. I wait to see whether he will bluster or try to threaten me, but he merely pulls out the chair beside me and squeezes his substantial form into it. My chair is wider, perhaps built for his girth. He reaches for a mug, and swiftly a serving woman is at his side, pouring ale into it. I have only to glance at her and she quickly fills my mug too. I raise it in Hearn's direction.

"My name is Ida. And this is now my lodge."

In response, Hearn drains his mug. The servant refills it and he drinks again. Only then does he look at me.

"Well met, Ida," he says.

It seems I will find no opposition here.

8

ARLEN

I was meditating on the floor in my bedchamber when someone knocked on the door. It took me a moment to find my way back into the world outside my mind. I had to push the door hard to open it, for it stuck against the floor. The woman who waited there was the one I had seen when I met Hearn. The one who was all limbs and angles with a horsey face. She smiled timidly at me.

"Druid, I realise we have not yet met, but Hearn bade me show you around the keep. I am Derwa." She paused for a moment. "I am handfasted to Hearn."

"You are the queen?" I was so surprised that she had come all the way to my bedchamber that I spoke without thinking.

She smiled a little sadly.

"I suppose you could say so."

"Forgive my rudeness, my lady." I bowed. "My name is Arlen."

She acknowledged me with a slight nod and looked away, fiddling with some stitching on her sleeve.

"Well met, Arlen," she said, after a moment. "I understand you have been sent here by Oistin."

"I have, my lady. This is the first time I have lived anywhere other than with the druids since I left my home as a boy of ten summers old."

"You were not permitted to return home?"

"We remain with the community for the duration of our training. After that, we depart for whatever role Oistin allots us."

"And what position did you last hold?"

"My lady?" I probably had a strange look on my face, but I hadn't been prepared for such a question.

"Your previous posting. What was it?"

"This is my first."

"But you must be more than twenty summers old."

"I am indeed, my lady. But my studies were incomplete and I stayed to remedy that."

"In what manner were they incomplete?"

I studied my bare feet. I couldn't afford for Hearn to find out.

"My lady, with all respect, I would prefer not to say."

"Of course." Her tone was brisk. "You are under no obligation to tell me anything. Your role here is to advise the king, not to entertain my simple curiosities. Hearn has asked that I show you around. Would you like to see the gardens?"

"I would, my lady, for I have seen little other than my bedchamber and the kitchen since I arrived."

I followed Derwa through the hallways and outside. The gardens she led me to were meagre things and not deserving of the name. Those bushes that still lived were overgrown and yellowing. The grass was worn down to the soil in some places and too long in others. It seemed even the birds found this place unattractive, for the gardens were devoid of their chirps and chitters. Likewise, there was no buzzing of bees or fluttering of butterflies. The wind was sharp with a hint of frost, reminding me that winter fast approached.

Derwa said little as she led me around the pitiful gardens. I hadn't even known Hearn had a wife, so I knew nothing of her and could think of no conversation we might share. If she minded my silence, she didn't comment on it. After we had walked through the gardens in their entirety, I thanked her and retired to my bedchamber. Why would the queen seek me out? Given Hearn's cold welcome, it made no sense that he would direct her to show me around. Yet I kept remembering the thought that crossed my mind the first time I saw her, that she would be important.

My peaceful life had been turned on its head. Only days ago, I had held no expectation of leaving the community until I mastered the Sight. As a boy, I knew I would go to live with the druids, for a child who is to be torn from his family and taken to live with strangers must of course be prepared for such a fate. Normally the druids know when a child is intended for them and they arrive on the day of birth to say small charms over the babe. But not me. My mother believed she carried only one babe, not two, and it seemed nobody else foresaw my birth either.

But when Fiachra, my mother's brother and a druid himself, first saw me, he sent word to Oistin. A few days later, two druids arrived to say the charms I had missed out on. And on my tenth birthday, two of their community came to fetch me. Whether they were the same two or not, I never knew.

As a young boy, I used to go up to the grassy knoll that was the highest point on the estate. From there, everything I could see, all the way to the distant woods, was Silver Downs. I used to sit there and pretend I was already a druid, that I had mastery over the elements and could call up a storm or ask the earth to divide, demand that the rivers rise up and cover the lower pastures or summon a fire to sweep over the lands. That was what I knew of druids as a child.

I did not know of the many hours of learning the lore and the history of the lands around us. I did not understand I would spend most of my days in silent contemplation. I thought it was all about charms and magics. I had some understanding that we studied the fey, and even as a boy I knew this would be useful for when I went to find my sister, but I did not know I might be sent to advise a king who did not want me.

Four more days passed before Hearn summoned me again. This time he sat in a smaller room which was sumptuously appointed with tapestries on the walls and knotted rugs on the floors. Two boys who appeared to be barely into their teens sat on stools in front of him.

"Druid," Hearn said. "Sit."

He pointed to a stool which stood slightly apart from the others.

"Boys, tell the druid what you know of battle." Hearn leaned back in his chair, hands folded over his girth.

"We have been learning about strategy," one of the boys said. He was broad-shouldered and already I saw shades of the man he would grow into. His dark hair was too long, like Hearn's, and his eyes were cunning. "We must know our enemy. If he has few soldiers, we can beat him if we have more. If he has many soldiers, we can beat him if we divide his army. We must choose the location for the battle and make it one that is favourable to us. We must arrive first, so our soldiers can be rested. That way we can engage the enemy as soon as they arrive, while their soldiers are still tired from the march."

"Well done, Brennus," Hearn said. "Girec, do you have anything to add?"

The other boy, younger by perhaps two or three summers and small for his age, shook his head. He stared down at his scuffed boots and didn't speak.

"Of course you don't," Hearn said. "I despair of your ever learning anything." He turned to me. "Well then, druid, what do you think of my foster sons?"

I took a moment to look each boy in the eye. Brennus stared back boldly, while Girec barely glanced at me before returning his gaze to his boots.

"Who is your enemy?" I directed my words at the boys.

From the corner of my eye, I noticed Hearn start. He hadn't expected me to speak to them. Perhaps he had intended that I would observe only. Was he trying to impress me — or intimidate me?

"The enemy is anyone who opposes the king," Brennus said. Although his voice was confident almost to the point of insolence, he glanced at Hearn, as if gauging his approval. He was not as self-assured as he pretended to be.

"Girec?" I asked.

Girec started to shake his head, but stopped at Hearn's exasperated sigh.

"The enemy are those who oppose our freedom." His voice was barely more than a whisper. "Those who take our land, or steal our people away to be slaves. Those who burn our fields and steal our cattle and leave us to starve."

I nodded my approval at him.

"So, druid, which one is best suited to be my heir?" Hearn cocked his eyebrow at me and waited.

I hesitated. How could I make such a determination after only moments speaking with them? If this was a test, the wrong answer might jeopardise my chances of Hearn ever trusting me. From his obvious favour towards Brennus, it was clear the older boy was the chosen one. But it seemed clear to me that Girec was the better choice, if these two boys were the only options.

"There is much more to kingship than being able to identify one's enemies, my lord," I said. "I know nothing of their strategy or cunning, their fairness or compassion, their wisdom or sense of justice. I would not presume to identify the one you have chosen based on such a brief interview."

Hearn seemed satisfied enough with my response and continued instructing the boys. Brennus and Girec focussed all their attention on the king. Hearn hadn't forgotten me, though. The occasional sideways flick of his gaze, checking whether I still paid attention, told me this was all for my benefit.

I tuned out Hearn's words and focussed on the boys' body language. The way they both faced Hearn directly, with straightened shoulders and heads held high, told me they wanted to please him. Brennus often followed his answers with a sneaky sidelong glance towards Girec, suggesting he thought the younger boy should be impressed with him. When Girec paid him no attention after a response Brennus clearly thought was particularly witty, Brennus turned his back slightly towards him. If Girec noticed the snub, he didn't react. He seemed entirely focussed on Hearn, although nothing he said seemed to satisfy the man.

At length, the lesson was over and Hearn dismissed his foster sons. They left the room at a run, Brennus elbowing Girec out of the way in order to pass through the doorway first. Hearn turned to me.

"Druid, there is a feast tomorrow night. You will attend."

He left without another word.

9

ARLEN

A boy pounded on my door the next morning with a message asking me to meet Derwa in the afternoon. Once again, we walked around the pitiful gardens and I found myself enjoying her company. She spoke more easily this time, and her observations displayed a sharp and intelligent mind. After that, it became a habit for us to spend time together each afternoon and a tentative friendship of sorts blossomed between us.

Hearn had told her to keep me busy — she admitted it with obvious embarrassment — but I also sensed she was lonely. She didn't have ladies-in-waiting trailing after her, or even a maid. It was a curiously lonely existence for someone who should have been surrounded by fawners and flatterers.

"I supposed nobody briefed you on court etiquette before you came here?" she observed as we made our way around the dusty courtyard.

"I never expected to have a position at court," I said. "And there was no time for anything else the day Oistin told me. He sent me as soon as I had packed my belongings."

"Curious. I wonder why it was so urgent that you come? Hearn had already made it clear he didn't want one of Oistin's druids here and two days later he received a message that you would arrive that evening."

"I can't imagine he was pleased with that."

No wonder Hearn seemed to dislike me as soon as he saw me. Derwa grinned and for a moment I forgot how strange she looked with her long face and her awkward limbs. She was almost pretty when she smiled.

"He was extremely displeased. But something you need to understand is that when Hearn summons you, you should wait outside the audience hall. He will call you in when he is ready. It will go easier for you if you accede to at least some of his expectations."

And I had walked straight in that first day.

"I had no idea," I said.

"Of course you didn't."

I shot a glance at her, wondering whether she mocked me, but her face was unreadable. Since she was in a talkative mood, I gathered my courage to ask what I knew I probably shouldn't.

"Why are you always alone? You have no flock of maids trailing after you, no herd of women who want to be able to say they are intimates of the queen."

"They fear me." Her voice was emotionless. "Even as a child of five summers, I knew I didn't look like everyone else. I certainly don't look as one expects a queen to. They fear my ugliness will tarnish their reputations if they are seen associating with me."

I wanted to protest she wasn't ugly, but it would be a lie. Instead, I waited to see if she would offer more. Clouds shrouded the sky today and the wind made lingering outside unpleasant. Derwa shivered and wrapped her cloak more tightly around herself. My mouth tasted gritty from the dust kicked up by the wind.

"You didn't look away when you first saw me," she said, finally. "You looked me right in the eyes as if you saw into my soul."

"I felt it, too," I admitted. "Something inside me said you would be important."

She glanced at me, startled. "To what?"

"To my duties here. To the kingdom. To everything."

To me, I added silently.

Derwa was quiet for a while and I knew her well enough to understand this was no easy silence where she simply didn't feel the need to speak, but rather that she didn't know what to say. The air seemed to grow colder by the minute and I wrapped my cloak more tightly around me.

"I've never been important to anything," she said, long after I had decided she would say nothing further on the subject.

"You are the queen. How could you not be important?"

"I always expected to handfast well, despite my looks. But I never thought, or desired, to be queen. My father owns a massive estate that borders near half of Hearn's land. Joining their two estates together in an alliance of marriage provided significant benefits to both parties. With my father's land and not inconsiderable army, and Hearn's wealth and power, both men gained greatly. And I acquired a husband who was not as intelligent or prudent as I might have hoped for."

Derwa's voice suggested she saw some irony in the situation, although I couldn't imagine how. Hers was not an unfamiliar tale. Many women handfasted with men chosen by their fathers for political or strategic reasons. Some eventually grew to love their husbands. Others at least came to respect them. Derwa, it seemed, had neither.

"Are you very unhappy?" I asked.

She sighed a little as she considered my question.

"Unhappy, no. I have the kind of security that few women gain, even if my husband is petty and stupid. Lonely and unfulfilled? Yes. I could do so much *more* if Hearn wasn't so afraid someone might realise I can actually think. He wanted a pretty, vapid wife. He was reluctant to handfast with me, even to gain such substantial holdings as my father settled on me. I suspect there were other inducements I wasn't told about. Do you know he wasn't supposed to be king?"

"I knew Hearn had an older brother who disappeared some years ago," I said.

"There were two older brothers. One was an excellent horseman, yet he died in a fall from his horse. The other disappeared one night and has never been seen since. Folk said he took off with a travelling girl. A musician or a bard."

"You think…"

Her lips were pursed. "Hearn was supposed to be the soldier son. He was meant to go off to war. But with both brothers dead, and his father following them to the grave shortly afterwards, the role of king fell to him."

"And you became queen."

"And I became queen."

"Why does he dislike me so much? You said he didn't want me here, but is there more to it? He is barely civil to me."

"He fears you will report back to Oistin on everything you hear. That's partly why I am supposed to keep you occupied. So you have little chance to hear what he doesn't want you to."

"And the rest of the reason?"

"To keep myself occupied, I presume. But he tries to offend you in the hope you will choose to leave. He will look weak if he sends you away."

"He hasn't offended me," I said. "I've hardly spoken to him."

"You should have received chambers suitable for an honoured guest, not a servant. That was your first test. To see if you would complain about your lodgings."

"I don't need fine accommodations. The bedchamber I have is perfectly adequate for my needs."

I didn't mention the door that only opened if I put my shoulder to it or the shutters that didn't quite close.

"I suppose druids are accustomed to having little." She sighed. "I might have been a druid myself, had I not been the oldest daughter. That life would have suited me well."

I could picture her walking gently through the woods. Meditating. Memorising the lore.

"I've always had an affinity with nature and the elements, especially that of water." Derwa reached out to caress the naked branch of a young ash tree. "I remember as a child playing with the water elementals, creating fountains in a pond. But the oldest daughter of a powerful landowner would never be permitted the indulgence of being a druid."

I hardly needed to ask whether she would have preferred such a life. The longing in her voice was unmistakable.

"Had you ever met Hearn before you were handfasted?"

"Oh, yes. We met on a number of occasions, although I had never spoken more than a few words to him. But I knew who he was and what he looked like, which is more than many young women can say about their intended husbands. He has changed of late, Arlen," she said suddenly, the words coming out in a rush. "He has never been a clever man, but he used to be petty rather than cruel. Recently though…"

"What?" I asked. "What has he done to you?"

She waved away my question.

"Nothing I can't handle. But there's a meanness about him now that wasn't there before. Or perhaps he just never let it show. I don't know. I'm tired, Arlen. I think I will retire to my bedchamber."

We walked back to the keep in silence and stopped just inside the main entrance. I wanted to offer some comforting words, something she might hold close in difficult moments, but my mind was blank. Instead I touched her lightly on the arm, barely letting my fingertips graze her sleeve.

"Farewell, my lady."

She gave me a sad smile. "Farewell, Arlen."

10

ARLEN

I passed the rest of the day in silent contemplation of my borrowed bronze bowl. I was still getting used to sitting on the hard floorboards, which left my backside numb. I was more accustomed to a seat of moss or fallen leaves or even bare earth to better enhance my connection with the natural world. But there were no woods here, just a few scraggly trees, and I didn't desire to make a spectacle of myself by practising where folk could observe.

I had never before felt self-conscious about my studies. In the community, it was not unusual to come across some druid or other meditating or practising the Sight. Druids walk silently — one of the first things we learn is mastery over our bodies — and we can glide through the woods without disturbing our brethren. Here though, folk might be more inclined to stop and stare, perhaps even interrupt with questions. And they made so much noise when they walked that I wouldn't be able to concentrate. Perhaps nobody would be interested anyway but I preferred to work behind a closed door.

I concentrated on clearing my mind. For hours, I stared into the bowl. Occasionally I thought I glimpsed something in its depths, but even as I stared it melted away. It might have been nothing more than a ripple in the water's surface, caused by my own breath, or a glimmer from the sunlight through the gaps around the shutters. I pushed down my frustration. This was a skill even the youngest apprentice could learn. If I could master the Sight, I might actually be of some use to Hearn.

The light began to soften and the air became colder, signalling the approach of dusk. I pushed the bowl away. Another fruitless session. Oistin had always said my ability would come eventually, that sometimes those who struggled the greatest became the most proficient. But even so, he admitted I was well past the age of any druid he had known to be unable to See.

I had tried every technique for opening myself to the Sight. Hours of quiet contemplation. Silent walks through the forest. Lying back to observe the sky, letting my thoughts float as high as the clouds. I had even once tried inhaling the smoke made by burning a particular leaf which was supposed to open one's mind. Nothing. No matter what I did, the result was the same: the water at which I stared so intently, be it in bowl or pond, was always empty.

The fact that none of a druid's skills had ever come easy to me was a constant source of frustration. I studied harder and practised longer than anyone else to achieve a modicum of proficiency. Even a task as basic as summoning the elementals was a struggle. If they responded, a druid could do almost anything: summon rains or fire, make mountains rise up out of the ground, or travel to the furthest edges of the earth in no more than a few hours. There was nothing magical about any of this, just a working relationship with the elementals. With great difficulty, I had forged relationships with the elementals of earth, water and fire, but the air elementals were elusive and completely unresponsive to me. I sometimes wondered whether I unintentionally offended them as a child.

I concluded my session with a sigh. I had still Seen nothing and it was time to attend Hearn's feast. Careful not to spill the water, I moved the bowl to the dresser. I had been here for less than a cycle of the moon and yet already I wanted nothing more than to return to the community, where I could practise in the silence of the woods, where quiet contemplation was easier, where there was no expectation of me other than that I study hard and learn all I could.

I never wanted a place at court, where folk did not say what they meant and did not mean what they said. Where appearances were everything and motivations were questionable. I wanted solitude and service and the time to finally master the Sight. To finish my studies so I could search for Agata. But my Master had determined a different path for me and I suspected he knew more of both Agata's and my fates than he said.

The only preparation I made for the feast was to wash my face and pull on my boots. I didn't know what clothes might be expected, but I had nothing but my usual linen trousers and long-sleeved tunics anyway. I hadn't thought to ask where the feast would be held, but as soon as I reached the ground level I spotted several finely dressed folk.

I followed them to a large room, roughly the size of Hearn's audience hall, only this one was filled with rows and rows of long tables and benches. The tables were laid with plates and mugs, with tall clay jugs positioned at regular intervals. At the far end of the hall was a table elevated on a dais. I was disappointed that Derwa wasn't here. Not that I would have approached her in front of everyone, but knowing a friend was nearby would have been a comfort.

I hesitated in the doorway. Everyone else seemed to know exactly where to sit. Would I cause a grave insult if I sat at the wrong table? Presumably the further away from Hearn, the lower the standing of those who sat there. I went to the furthest table and claimed a spot on one end of a bench.

I quickly discovered I didn't look out of place in my plain attire. Although a good many of the diners wore finery, those folk gravitated to the tables at the top end. The ones who sat down my end were dressed far more simply, and indeed many wore their work clothes. Folk were in high spirits and the room filled with conversation and laughter.

Eventually somebody else joined my table. It was a young fellow, perhaps in his late teens. He was red-haired and dressed no more finely than I. He sat opposite me and gave me a friendly nod.

"Well met, druid," he said.

I stifled an urge to ask how he knew me. Was my recent arrival the subject of court gossip? I let go of the thought. It was irrelevant to me. I smiled at the fellow.

"Well met, friend. I'm Arlen."

"Rogan," he said and poured two mugs from a nearby jug. He pushed one across the table towards me and raised the other in a salute. He downed the contents and poured himself another.

"Drink up," he advised. "Hearn is unusually generous on feast days. They'll refill the jugs as fast as you can drink."

I raised my mug and sniffed. Ale, it seemed, and not of particularly good quality. Nevertheless, I took a few mouthfuls and tried to swallow without grimacing.

"What do you do here, Rogan?" I asked.

"Look after the oxen mostly," he said. "The master scribe has been teaching me to write in my spare time. He might take me on as apprentice soon."

Before I could respond, several other folk arrived and seated themselves in a flurry of activity. They all seemed to know each other, including Rogan. Most gave me a nod or a smile, or at least a curious stare, and the girl next to me offered her name: Zethar. After that, she turned towards the young man on her other side and seemed wholly immersed in conversation with him.

Rogan talked to the fellow next to him and tried to pretend he wasn't sneaking glances at Zethar. I leaned my elbows on the table and sipped at the bitter ale. If nothing else, a feast was an opportunity to learn something of the politics of the place. And it wouldn't hurt to make a few allies if I could.

Servants brought around food and after so many days of little more than bread and cheese, the aroma was tantalising. There were cauldrons of barley soup and platters of roasted pig, turnips and parsnips, bread filled with seeds and grains, and a variety of cheeses. Folk helped themselves, then passed the trays along the tables. I dished out a modest helping and found the food tasty and liberally seasoned. Across from me, Rogan piled his plate high and ate as if it was his first meal in days.

My companions somehow managed to both eat and talk at the same time. The trays were passed around again. I declined, although I did allow Rogan to top up my ale. Zethar pushed away her empty plate and turned to smile shyly at me. Before she could speak, there was an almighty crash. All around us, people jumped to their feet, roaring and cheering. My table mates joined in and Zethar climbed up on the bench to see over the crowd.

"What's happening?" I asked.

Her eyes shone as she glanced down at me.

"A fight."

I was ashamed of the excitement that welled within me and I quickly squashed it down. It was unbecoming for a druid. Nevertheless, I slipped through the edges of the crowd and around to the side, where I had a better view. Two men stood on opposite sides of a table. Both had thick beards and fine clothing. One was broad-shouldered with legs that looked as strong as tree trunks. The other was taller with a more slender frame, although when he pulled off his tunic, his arms were well-muscled. A woman stood near the taller man, her hands clasped to her chest and her face anxious. The burly man appeared to be alone. Folk formed a ring around them and the boisterous roar of the crowd died as the burly man held up his fist.

"Do you challenge me, oaf?" he roared.

"Aye," the other replied and spat on the floor. "Although if you intend to live, you had best walk away now."

"I intend to live all right," the first said. "After I feast on your liver."

The second man roared and thumped the table. The crowd began to chant. A chill ran down my spine as I made out their words. *To the death,* they cried. *To the death.*

With another yell, the burly man tipped over the table. Platters flew to the floor, clanging and clattering. Jugs smashed and ale spilled. He leaped over the table and flung himself at his challenger.

Folk yelled in support of one or the other and waved their fists in the air. Even the woman who had looked anxious now cheered. Brennus pushed to the front of the crowd where he hopped from foot to foot and shouted enthusiastically. If Girec was also here, I couldn't see him.

The fighters circled each other, feinting and ducking. Testing each other. Eventually the slender one darted in and delivered a blow. The burly man merely shook his head and hit back.

Were there no guards present? Surely they would put a stop to this. But I spied a couple of fellows wearing the blue of the guard's uniform and cheering the fighters.

A roar from the crowd brought my attention back to the two men. They were on the floor, rolling around in the remains of their meals. Over and over, they struck each other. First one seemed to gain the upper hand, then the other would deliver a well-placed blow and force his opponent to defend himself. They seemed evenly matched, despite the differences in their builds. Cries of *to the death* continued from the crowd. A man in front of me hefted a small girl of three or four summers up onto his shoulders for a better view.

My stomach rolled and the bitter taste of bile filled my mouth. I had never before witnessed such a thing. As a boy, I saw occasional scuffles between my cousins, or amongst the younger druids, but there was always an adult nearby to haul the fighters apart and shake them until they calmed down. Here, though, not only was the viciousness allowed to continue, it was actively encouraged.

Even Hearn stood to watch the fight. He roared and his eyes held the same battle-crazed expression as those around me. Beside him sat a woman I had never seen before. Her almost-white hair was loose and flowed down over her shoulders. She wore a simple blue dress with a high neck and sleeves that came all the way to her wrists. She was the only person in the room who was not on their feet. Instead she leaned back in her chair and watched. The expression on her face was strangely satisfied. Who was she? Hearn's mistress, perhaps? That might explain why Derwa was not present. I turned my attention back to the fighters.

It would be madness to try to separate them. Even if I could get through the crowd, folk were too consumed with battle lust to understand reason. I might be torn apart myself if I deprived them of the fight.

The burly man sat on top of the other, using his legs to pin down the man's arms. He grabbed the man's head and repeatedly slammed it into the wooden floor. The man on the bottom flailed around, unable to get a good grip on his attacker. After his head hit the floor five or six times, he stopped trying to fight back and eventually he stopped moving altogether. Words were exchanged between them, although I couldn't hear what. Then the burly man raised his arms in triumph. The crowd roared. Men dashed in to help the victor up.

They ignored the man on the floor as he rolled over and tried to stand. He staggered, his eyes rolling up in his head. Nobody stepped forward to help him. I started to push through the crowd. Now the battle lust had abated, I could help him get to a quieter place and find a healer.

Someone else reached the injured man before I could, bringing with him a tall shield, man-height and sturdy, which he lay on the floor. A man wearing a fine brocade shirt tossed a small pouch, which landed on the shield with a clink. Others deposited single coins or a handful. As folk stepped forward to throw their coins onto the shield, they said a few words to the injured man. He swayed and clutched the upturned table for support, seemingly barely aware of his surroundings.

When the stream of coins ceased, the victor motioned towards the shield and the injured man stepped forward unsteadily. His legs buckled and two men moved in to aid him. They helped him lie down on top of the coins that covered the shield.

A woman knelt beside him, the one who had looked anxious at the start of the fight. She leaned in to speak to him. He reached for her and she clutched his hand. Then she rose and stepped back.

The victor stepped forward with a dagger. He knelt beside the man on the shield and, without hesitation, ran the dagger across his throat. Blood splattered the victor's chest. He grinned down at his opponent and stood, holding the bloody dagger aloft. The crowd roared again and there were more chants of *to the death*. At last I understood what they meant. My stomach heaved.

The guard stationed at the door that led outside barely glanced at me as I staggered out. I vomited until there was nothing left in my stomach.

Every time I blinked, I saw the man lying on the coin-covered shield, his throat slit. The woman who had farewelled him, who was she? Wife? Sister? Betrothed? I presumed she would take possession of the coins, penalty for the loss of income incurred by the death of her man.

When I was sure I had nothing left to vomit, I made my way back to the door. The guard smirked as he looked me up and down.

"Looks like you've had enough for tonight, my fellow," he said and his voice wasn't all that unkind.

I didn't respond, only pushed open the door and stumbled back through the keep to my bedchamber. I didn't bother to light the candle. In the dark, I stripped off my vomit-splattered clothes and dropped them on the floor. Then I crawled into bed, knowing I would spend all night with the memory of a dead man lying on a shield.

11

ARLEN

Hearn summoned me before noon the next day. My mind still whirled from last night's events and my mouth tasted sour. If the man had a wife, she was now a widow. Any children she had borne him were fatherless. I had never seen folk take so much pleasure in the pain of another, and Hearn did nothing to stop them. How could I respect a king like that?

I dropped my reeking clothes off at the washer room. The servant woman didn't flinch at the smell and assured me they would be returned by this evening. I supposed the wash servants would be kept busy today removing stains from clothing far finer than mine.

The hallways were silent and empty as I made my way to the library. Perhaps most of the inhabitants were still sleeping off the feast. The door stood open and Hearn sat at a heavy desk, studying a piece of parchment. A lamp cast its flickering light over the page. The image brought memories of being summoned to Oistin's bedchamber and seeing him seated at his desk reading a message or examining a map. I swallowed down a wave of homesickness as I knocked. The two men were nothing alike.

"Aah, druid, there you are." Hearn sounded like he was in an agreeable mood today. I hoped he wouldn't ask what I thought of last night's events. "Come and tell me what you make of this."

I examined the shelves of books and stacks of parchment as I made my way to him, surprised at the size of his collection. I immediately recognised the parchment Hearn studied as a map of the country. A black cross within a large rectangle indicated Braen Keep. Bold lines marked neighbouring estates. A twisting line crossing the lower end of Hearn's territory was likely a river.

"A map," I said. "Of Braen Town and its surrounds."

"What do you know of my territory?"

Another test. I studied the parchment.

"This is an old map, my lord. Your boundaries are somewhat different at present."

He had ceded a large block of his territory to Cullen, whose land bordered his, in a dispute three summers ago. I was sure Hearn didn't need to be reminded.

"What do you know of Cullen?" Hearn spat out his neighbour's name.

"I know there is a longstanding hostility between the two of you. There have been a number of skirmishes between your troops over the last few years, one in particular that might have led to all-out war had you not retreated when you did."

"There will be war between us yet, druid." Hearn's voice was cold. "Cullen pushes me towards it. He encroaches on my land, he steals my cattle. He begs me to send my troops against him."

"Is that what you want? To face him in war?"

Hearn studied the map and didn't look at me.

"I want him to learn his place. And you, druid, will help me."

"My lord?"

"War is coming for us, druid. The time draws near. I can smell it in the air. Druids are good at identifying when a war should start, aren't they?"

"I am trained to examine the signs and advise on the most favourable day for battle," I said.

"And you will do so, when the time is right. When I am ready to meet Cullen in battle, you will interpret the signs for me."

I understood what he didn't say. He expected me to have his interests at heart when I examined the signs. He would choose when to go to war and when to stop, and would expect me to decipher the signs favourably. He wanted me to lie.

"Interpreting the signs is a complicated matter." I made sure my tone was suitably respectful and prayed Hearn would not take offence. "I cannot be sure until I have carefully studied them as to what the outcome might be."

"Oh, I think you'll know the outcome when it's needed, druid." Hearn tapped the triangle marking Cullen's land and gave me a steady look. "Or at least, for your sake, I hope you do."

12

ARLEN

"Druid, a letter for you," a messenger boy said from the doorway.

I sat cross-legged on the floor in my bedchamber, staring into the bronze bowl. I hadn't bothered to close the door since nobody came all the way up here unless they were looking for me. He tossed a scroll towards me and scampered away.

It was bound with a scrap of leather and stamped with the Silver Downs seal. Likely it had been sent to the druid community and was redirected, because I hadn't yet sent a message home about my relocation to Braen Keep. I felt strangely uneasy as I broke the seal. I had received a message from Silver Downs only a sevennight or so before I left the community, and to receive another again so soon was unusual.

The fine parchment was lettered with a neat but unfamiliar hand. I glanced at the name at the bottom and my heart froze when I saw it was from Fiachra, who was one of Eithne's brothers and also a druid. I would have been perhaps seven or eight summers old the last time I met him and was awestruck by how grand my druid uncle seemed. If he spoke to me on that visit, the conversation had not stayed in my memory. I remembered only that it was strange to see him with

Eithne, for he was old enough to be her grandfather, although they were actually brother and sister.

Eithne had travelled to the fey realm as a young woman, and when she returned a few months later, sixty years had passed in our world. Her parents and five of her brothers had died while she was gone, leaving only Fiachra and Diarmuid left alive. I feared to learn what would prompt Fiachra to write to me after all this time. *Arlen, matters have occurred here at Silver Downs of which you need to be aware,* his letter began.

> *Your uncle Diarmuid died yesterday and the creature he had kept imprisoned for many years has escaped. Eithne tells me you have no knowledge of this creature. She felt it best not to terrorise a child with this tale, especially as you already knew far too much about the terrors of our world.*

As a young child, I feared Titania would come to steal me away, just like she had taken my sister. I barely recalled the details now, but for many years I suffered from night terrors and would wake screaming, certain the fey queen stood over my bed with arms outstretched to snatch me away. The dreams subsided eventually, but I had never forgotten the paralysing terror of them, even if the details themselves were now somewhat blurred.

> *You know, I presume, that your uncle was a bard. We shared five brothers, he and I, all of them dead long before your birth. Diarmuid was the youngest and the seventh son of a seventh son. In our family, the one in that position is always a bard and has the ability to bring his tales to life.*

I set the parchment down on my knee as I absorbed this news. I vaguely remembered hearing that Uncle Diarmuid had been a bard in his youth. I couldn't recall him ever telling a tale, though, and as a child I didn't think to question it. But the ability to bring tales to life — this was a power I had never heard of, even with all my training. I resumed reading.

Diarmuid was, as far as we know, the first in his line to understand the secret of how his ability worked. Others before him had brought their tales to life but without knowing how. However, long before this happened, he was a boy who was only just beginning to explore his first tales. He told nobody, so we did not know to warn him. I suppose we should have anyway, for we knew that as the seventh son of a seventh son, he would be a bard. But our parents hoped that by not telling him, they might spare him. That he might instead turn to another career. So Diarmuid was left to explore his earliest tales unguided and without knowledge of the ability that lay inside him.

His first tale was about a bard who created a muse, a woman to whom he whispered his tales, and from whom he fancied his inspiration flowed. When Diarmuid told that tale, the muse he imagined came to life. At that point, though, she was confined to his head and we knew nothing of her existence. It may be a difficult thing to understand, but although she lived only in his mind, we believe she was already very real. Our father warned him then of the ability he possessed, but Diarmuid didn't believe him.

We watched him carefully over the next few years, but there was no indication that any tale he told came true and gradually we began to relax. In truth, we even forgot for a while. It seemed that Diarmuid, like so many of those who came before him, had not discovered how to bring his tales to life. We did not know that during these years, the muse he created was living inside of him, whispering to him, watching everything he did and said, and growing in power of her own.

It was not until his nineteenth summer that his creation — he called her Ida — finally gained enough strength to break free of his head. She became real. She had a body and a mind of her own. She left Diarmuid and travelled to Crow's Nest, where she terrorised the inhabitants. From what I have pieced together over the years, I believe she was recreating tales she had heard Diarmuid tell. The tales he told back in those days before she left him were dark, and it seems this is all she understood of the world.

Diarmuid found her, and once he unlocked the key to his ability, he was able to return her to his head. He has kept her in there all the years since, trapped in a box inside his mind. We could never be sure, but we believe she still watched him. Everything he has done, everything he has said, everything he has learned during these years, she has probably been silent witness to.

Once again, I set the parchment down to absorb Fiachra's words. My heart pounded and my mouth was dry. Why had I never before heard this part of our family history? I could hardly believe it. An imaginary muse brought to life and escaped? It sounded like something straight out of a tale, although it was no tale I had ever heard. But as a druid, I had seen many strange things, and Fiachra had no reason to lie to me.

Diarmuid had an apprentice of sorts, Tristan, who is determined to be a bard although Diarmuid was ever reluctant to teach him. He is my brother Eremon's great-grandson and, like Diarmuid, he is the seventh son of a seventh son, even if the line stretches only as far as his own father. Nevertheless, he showed early promise with his tales, and the ability has become apparent in him, too. He tried to contain Ida when she escaped, but failed.

Ida is strong — far stronger than before — and I have little hope she can be contained again. Regardless, we must try. I leave here today to search for her. Arlen, I urge you to be on your guard. As you are a son of Silver Downs, she might be drawn to you. Be alert for any mention of trouble, especially where it involves family, friends or neighbours turning on each other with little justification. It may well be Ida's doing. She is cunning and insidious, and folk subjected to her power never even realise they have been charmed.

Also beware of birds, particularly if there is anything unusual about them. Diarmuid believed Ida had the ability to change her form and that she sometimes travelled as a raven. Message me at once if you hear of anything that might be related to her escape. Send all messages to Silver Downs. I will keep in close contact with the family here.

I wish you well, Arlen. I regret that we have never had the opportunity to spend time together. There is much I would wish to pass onto another druid of our blood. Circumstances have so often prevented me from making contact and I fear the opportunity has now passed. I have little expectation that I will survive an encounter with Ida. However, if I can stop her, I will gladly forsake whatever is left of my time on this earth.

Be cautious, Arlen, and be alert.
Your uncle,
Fiachra, Druid, of Silver Downs

I read the message again, paying particular attention to Fiachra's words about what sort of trouble Ida might cause, and a sudden strong longing for home welled within me. I remembered a large stone lodge filled with plenty of nooks and crannies for young boys to lose themselves in. Grassy fields, gurgling rivers, dark woods. Early morning mists and winter winds that sometimes held a hint of the far-away ocean. A portal to the fey realm somewhere on the edge of Silver Downs land. Sometimes I wondered whether my training could ever compensate for my lost boyhood.

I was saddened to hear of my Uncle Diarmuid's death. An old man who was probably more patient with young boys than they deserved. I remembered gnarled hands that grasped the head of the cane he always carried. He had bad hips that made walking difficult at times, and we all knew he had suffered enough of boisterous boys when his knuckles tightened on the cane and he twitched it restlessly.

Had Fiachra Seen something that prompted him to send this message, or did he merely preempt the possibility that Uncle Diarmuid's muse might be drawn to me? Now, more than ever before, I desperately needed to access the Sight. I set the parchment aside on the floorboards and drew the bronze bowl back in front of me. I closed my eyes and took a few deep breaths.

It was difficult to centre myself, for my thoughts spun, but when I finally achieved some modicum of composure, I peered down into the bowl. The water was clear and calm, without even the slightest ripple to disturb its surface. I stared into it until my eyes grew gritty and still I saw nothing but water.

13

ARLEN

I forced open the sticking shutters and leaned right out the window of my bedchamber. I ached for the sight of grass or trees. Anything green. The longer I stayed at Braen Keep, the more trapped I felt. Everything here was grey and brown, dirty and dusty, broken or incomplete. There was no beauty, either natural or created. There were no woods, no grassy patches where one might sit for a while. No flowers, no bugs. Nothing of the natural world except the sky above, and even that was grey and dreary at this time of year. Some days I felt like I couldn't breathe.

Hearn hadn't summoned me again in the sevennight since our discussion in the library. Derwa and I still met most afternoons to walk around the dusty courtyard, despite the frigid wind heralding winter's approach. I considered her a friend, in so much as a queen and her husband's druid advisor can ever be friends. I spent most of the rest of my time in my bedchamber meditating and trying to access the Sight.

I longed to return to the druid community, just for a few hours, to sit amongst the trees and ferns and crawling vines. Hearn probably wouldn't notice if I disappeared, but Oistin would be furious I had left my post. As I thought about fertile earth and towering trees, crawling insects and sweetly-scented flowers, my chest tightened. I wouldn't breathe freely again until I had restored my connection with the natural world. It was only midmorning and Derwa wouldn't expect me for our afternoon walk for hours yet. I pulled on my boots, wrapped my cloak around my shoulders and left my bedchamber.

I didn't bother to hide that I was going somewhere. Nobody would care if Hearn's pet druid left. As I approached the keep's gates, they opened to admit a pair of oxen and a laden cart driven by a skinny man who looked as downtrodden as everyone else in this place. The guards didn't seem to notice as I slipped through.

On the other side of the wall, the town was just as miserable as the keep, and I didn't waste any time there. What I sought wouldn't be found here. I recognised the road Bram had brought me along that first day and set off.

As I left the last of the falling-down lodges and woebegone gardens behind, my spirit lifted like the sun rising above clouds. Sparse patches of yellowed grass soon became a field, and in the distance stood a line of trees. I headed towards them.

The first tree I reached was an ash, its naked branches spreading majestically above me. I rested my palm against its fissured trunk and the faint vibration of its life force against my skin soothed my soul. I inhaled deeply, rejoicing in the fresh scent of trees and grass and earth. I left the ash and kept walking. Just a little further. Just until I couldn't see the town behind me anymore.

In a short while I came to an area that was so beautiful, I almost cried. Winter-brown grass that reached halfway up my calf. Oak and ash and a single rowan with shiny red mistletoe berries drooping from its branches. A patch of weeds, taller than the grass, had gone to seed and an ant crawled up one stem. Pale yellow primrose bloomed and fat bees buzzed around them.

I lowered myself to the ground. It was warm from the sun and the tall grass tickled my arms pleasantly. I sank my hands down into the earth. Life vibrations buzzed against my fingers as I centred myself. I inhaled deeply three times and easily slipped into a meditative state. I could feel life all around me. Ants, worms, dragonflies, a lone raven in a tree somewhere to my left. My mind drifted with the breeze as it swept over my little sanctuary.

After some time, I became aware of the approach of two life forces which were larger than the birds and insects, and I reluctantly withdrew from my meditation. I stayed in the grass, though, my hands still immersed in the earth, unwilling to lose my connection with the natural world so soon.

I heard them before I saw them. A man and a woman, carefree and laughing, trading jokes and mock insults. Travellers, perhaps, on their way to Braen Town maybe. The man said something I couldn't catch, but I heard what he called her: Agata. My sister's name. It was a common enough name and I shouldn't be surprised to encounter someone else with it. After all, my sister was named for her grandmother.

I had been so wrapped up in events at Braen Keep that I had almost forgotten my own mission: to rescue my stolen sister from the fey realm. Did she know she had a family? Did she wonder whether we searched for her? Why was I wasting time sitting around at court when I could be looking for Agata? Forget Oistin's commands. Forget Hearn who made it clear he didn't want my advice. *I'm coming, Agata*, I thought. *Tonight. I won't waste any more time.*

I paid little attention to the man and woman as they drew closer. He came into view first and I was struck with the feeling of having seen him before. He was slender, with dark hair and a face that was vaguely familiar. But when I saw her, my heart stopped. I had seen my own face in various bodies of water enough times to recognise it immediately. She had my eyes, my nose, my chin. The same dark hair, although mine was barely shoulder length and hers fell almost to her waist in a long braid draped over her shoulder.

I wasn't even aware I stood until they looked at me. My face probably mirrored the confusion on hers. The man looked between the two of us, his eyebrows raised.

"Agata?" he said. "What is this? How does he look like you?"

She took a step towards me and reached out one hand as if wanting to touch me.

"Who are you?" she whispered. "And why do you have my face?"

"I'm your brother," I said.

I wanted to say that I had always intended to search for her as soon as I was free to make my own decisions. I wanted to tell her of the nights I had lain awake, unable to sleep for knowing that half my soul was missing. Instead, the words that came out of my mouth were not about myself.

"Our mother misses you greatly."

Her mouth opened and closed before she found any words.

"Our mother? You, too, are born of Titania?"

Fury rose within me. She didn't know. Titania had stolen her away and never even told her.

"Titania is not your mother," I said, and my voice trembled a little. "Our mother's name is Eithne, and she is mortal. You were stolen from her just moments after your birth and she has grieved you ever since."

Agata laughed and flicked her braid back over her shoulder.

"Don't be ridiculous. I am fey, not born of a mortal woman. I don't know why we share a face. Perhaps you are fey and just don't know it?" She turned to the man. "Sumerled, tell him I am fey."

Even his name was familiar, although I couldn't place it. Agata's laughter died on her lips as she took in the look on his face.

"Sumerled?" Her voice was less certain now.

He laughed and held out his hand to her.

"Why are we standing here conversing with a mortal? You've seen their realm. Now let's go home."

She didn't move to take his hand but folded her arms across her chest.

"Sumerled, tell me he is lying." Her lower lip trembled. "Tell me I am fey."

"Come," he said, and his tone was so enticing that I almost reached for his hand myself. "It's time to go home."

"Don't try to charm me," she said, crossly. "I want the truth. Is Titania really my mother?"

He let his arm fall back down to his side and looked away, off into the trees.

"You should ask her yourself if you have questions."

"Tell me it's not true," she whispered. "Please."

"Agata, our mother would dearly love to see you," I said. "She had only moments with you before Titania snatched you away."

She glowered at me.

"You lie. I don't know why you lie. I don't know why you have my face. Titania is my mother and I am fey."

She turned and ran. I didn't bother giving chase, for she ran like the wind and I would never catch her. As soon as she was gone, the pleasantness disappeared from Sumerled's face, and when he spoke his tone was vicious.

"Stay away from her," he said. "Titania has left your family in peace all these years, but if you interfere she will ruin you all."

Then he ran after Agata.

My knees trembled so hard I had to sit back down in the grass. I had found my sister. And she didn't even know she was missing.

14

AGATA

I fled the mortal, running through the long grass as fast as my feet would take me. I didn't try to run silently. I just wanted to get away. Sumerled called me, but I tucked down my head and ran even faster. I didn't stop until I was back in my own realm. Or what I had always thought was my own realm.

I stopped to catch my breath, leaning against the smooth trunk of a young beech. The woods had gone silent at my noisy entrance, but as I calmed myself, bird and vole and hedgehog slowly returned to their usual doings. The air smelled of living trees and moist soil and rotting leaves. I hadn't realised the mortal realm would smell so different. It lacked the damp, woodsy scent of the fey realm and instead smelled of smoke and dry grass and the odour of something rotting. By the time Sumerled caught up with me, I breathed normally even if my mind still raced.

"Is it true?" I demanded as he stopped beside me.

He was too winded to speak, but I didn't have the patience to wait until he caught his breath.

"Answer me," I said. "Tell me whether what the mortal said is true."

"Of course not," he said, between gasps. "You can't trust anything a mortal says. They're tricky."

"Why does he look like me?"

"Does he?"

I glowered and he quickly looked away.

"There might be a passing resemblance, I suppose. If you look hard enough."

"It's more than a passing resemblance. He looks exactly like me."

"His hair is shorter."

I punched him in the arm.

"Don't be stupid. Tell me what you know."

"What makes you think I know any more than you do? I've never seen him before."

"I know you hear all sorts of things when you skulk around."

"Don't say that," he said, sulky now. He dug the toe of his boot into the ground, scraping away the leaves to expose the fertile soil beneath. "I hate it when folk say I skulk."

"Well, you do."

"I don't. I'm allowed to walk around. And if folk are careless enough to say things they don't want anyone to hear, how is that my fault?"

"So tell me what you know. Is it true I'm half mortal?"

"Of course not."

I crossed my arms over my chest and glared at him.

"Don't lie to me, Sumerled. I know you lie to everyone else, but I won't stand for you lying to me. So tell me what you know or we won't be friends anymore."

"Agata, don't be like that." Sumerled stared at me with wide eyes, likely trying to gain my sympathy. "You're my best friend. You can't stop being friends with me."

"Last chance." I tapped my foot, although the motion was ineffective against the soft leaf litter.

"I don't know anything for certain."

I waited without speaking. At length he sighed and told me. I watched the slow progress of a dragonfly as he spoke. Somehow his words didn't hurt quite as much if I didn't look at him as he said them.

"You were a newborn babe the first time I saw you. Titania

presented you to the court one day and said you were her daughter. Why wouldn't I believe her?"

"Had she…" I didn't quite know how to word it. "Did she look like she was with child before that?"

Sumerled blushed. "I don't know. She can look however she wants to. She might have concealed it."

"So she just turned up with me one day?"

"You were wrapped in a blanket and squealing," he offered.

"What exactly did she say?"

"Just that you were her daughter and your name was Agata."

"Did she say who my father was?"

I had never asked Titania. It obviously wasn't Oberon, for surely he would have had some involvement in my childhood. I had always assumed I was the product of one of Titania's many affairs. Both she and Oberon had them and neither seemed particularly concerned. The one exception was Oberon's occasional dalliances with mortal women. I understood why Titania found that so insulting. That the king of the fey would choose a mortal woman — unattractive, clumsy, inept, boring — over Titania was unthinkable, and yet it happened time after time.

Was it possible my father was a mortal? That despite her fury over Oberon's affairs with mortal women, she herself had borne a child to a mortal man? And yet the stranger with my face had said my mother was mortal. So who was Titania to me? I realised Sumerled hadn't answered my question.

"Did she say who my father was?" I asked again.

"If she did, I never heard of it. But then I never heard anyone ask either. Folk talk, though, you know that. And there were whispers that your father was mortal. I suppose Oberon must have asked at some point. Wouldn't you think he would want to know?"

I glared at him and he shrugged, his face guileless.

"What? I'd want to know, if I was he. Did you think he was your father?"

"Of course not," I snapped. My feet moved restlessly, wanting to run, but I had to see this conversation through to the end.

"Why not?"

I was astonished at his surprise. It had never occurred to me that anyone would think Oberon to be my father. Did others know the truth of my parentage or did they, like Sumerled, make assumptions?

"You can't tell anyone," I said. "Not a soul."

He gave me that wounded look again.

"I wouldn't."

"You would too, if it suited you. I'm serious, Sumerled. If you tell a single person, if you even hint that I'm not a full fey, I will make your life a misery."

He gave me a sad look.

"My life is already a misery. The only thing about it that's not is you."

Guilt stabbed me, but I strengthened my resolve.

"I mean it, Sumerled."

He stalked away through the woods. I followed slowly, still trying to make sense of what I had learned. Trying to slot this new information in amongst the things I thought I knew about myself. Why had Titania kept this from me? And who else knew?

15

AGATA

I made no attempt to catch up with Sumerled on the way home and he didn't wait for me. I expected to encounter him leaning against a tree, taunting a sprite and chewing a blade of grass as he waited for me to catch up. But he didn't and I was too busy adjusting my view of myself to really care.

I wasn't a full fey. It seemed so obvious now. It explained my lack of elegance and grace. The fey fluidity I had never had. It also explained why I had always been something of an outcast, not quite shunned by the fey, but also not fully embraced. By the time I reached the palace, I had decided to demand Titania tell me the truth. It was my right to know where I came from.

The guards at the palace entrance watched impassively as I climbed the shallow wooden steps which had been smoothed by hundreds, maybe thousands, of years of time and feet. The building was an impossible concoction of living trees shaped by fey magic to grow how they would not normally. The doors were tall and narrow, and they swung open soundlessly as I approached. They had no hinges or doorknobs, bolts or latches. They simply grew into doors which opened and closed on their own. Hallways stretched ahead of me, living corridors of wood lit by fey magic.

I went straight to Titania's private chambers, where the guard admitted me without comment. Inside, Titania lounged on a low couch. Her shimmering white gown glistened as she reached out to pluck another fruit from the bowl beside her. They were exotic things that Titania herself created and did not grow naturally.

"Agata, my dear," she said. "Did you enjoy your day?"

"I need to talk to you."

I was suddenly unsure of myself. Demanding the truth of my parentage seemed like a good idea earlier, but now that I was here I feared her famous temper. Titania patted the seat beside her.

"Come. Sit with me. Tell me what troubles you, my dear."

Never in my life had Titania suggested I tell her my troubles. As a parent, she was strict but mostly distant. Praising when I pleased her but cold and unforgiving when I didn't. *She already knows*, I thought. *And she's waiting for me to say the wrong thing.* I cast my gaze around the room, looking for... I wasn't quite sure what. An excuse, perhaps. A way to distract her from the conversation I had intended.

The room was simply but tastefully appointed, the furniture having grown out of wall or floor and formed itself into useful shapes. Chairs, shelves, side tables. They were all living wood from the trees that made up Titania's palace. The air was strongly fragranced with the floral concoction Titania favoured, which made my nose itch. I tried not to sneeze. Titania regarded any such action as ungraceful.

"Agata," she said, sharply.

Titania did not like giving an order twice. And an order it was, even if she merely told me to sit beside her.

I crossed the room, acutely aware of the lack of grace in my movements. Distracted, I caught my slipper against the floor and stumbled. Titania raised one perfect eyebrow but didn't comment. Blushing and wishing I wasn't, I sat beside her. The couch was harder than it looked.

"I met someone today," I started. I didn't know how to say this.

"Oh? Was he handsome?"

She winked at me and I was sure she deliberately misunderstood. I took a deep breath.

"He looked just like me," I said. "My face. My eyes, my chin, my nose. He was the same height as me and slender like I am. His hair was the same colour as mine." I took a deep breath. "And he was mortal."

Titania studied me. Not even a flicker of emotion crossed her face. I should have expected she would keep her secrets well. I could pretend I didn't know. Pretend I saw no connection between me and the boy. But it would be a lie. For as soon as he said he was my brother, I felt the truth of it. I stared down at my hands as I said words I never expected to say.

"Am I half mortal?"

Would she lie? To protect herself, if not to save my feelings. But when I glanced up, her expression was not what I expected. I thought she might be ashamed of her liaison with a mortal man. Perhaps embarrassed I found out. Angry I knew. Worried I might not keep her secret. Perhaps wistful I would never again think I was a full fey. But her face showed none of those things. Instead she looked smug, and maybe a little gleeful.

"I'm afraid so," she said, her voice crisp and and utterly unsympathetic.

The last tiny shred of hope inside me died.

"Who is my father?"

"Curious you have never asked about your parentage until now." She cocked her head to the side and considered me. "Tell me about this boy you met."

"No, I want to know who my father is."

She went very still.

"Tell me about the boy," she said, each word slow and clear.

"There's nothing else to tell. I met a boy who looked just like me. And Sum—" I stopped, realising I would probably get Sumerled into trouble.

"Go on, my dear." Her voice was frosty. "Sumerled did what?"

She would know if I lied. It was too late. *I'm sorry, Sumerled*, I thought.

"He said there was a rumour that my father was mortal."

She smiled, but there was no warmth in it.

"Sumerled, my dear, is wrong."

My heart leapt. I was fey after all.

"He is?"

"Your father is fey," she said. "Well, half fey, but I don't suppose you care about that distinction."

"Half fey?"

I struggled to keep up with the morsels of information she doled out. She was enjoying herself and clearly intended to make her revelations last.

"It's your mother you should be asking about."

Now she looked like a cat that had found a pail of milk and sipped away all of the cream floating on top.

"My mother?"

"You are not an imbecile, my dear," Titania observed, mildly. "There is no need to repeat everything I say."

"But you're my mother."

"Have I ever said that?"

As I looked into her cold eyes, it was like the floor had fallen away beneath me and I was falling, falling, falling. No, Titania had never said she was my mother.

"But I thought—"

"Unfortunately, thinking is something mortals are not terribly good at."

"I'm mortal?"

She lifted one slender shoulder in a shrug.

"Three-quarters mortal is close enough to full mortal," she said.

My chest constricted and my throat narrowed. I sucked at the air but couldn't get enough in. My vision started to swim.

"Oh, my dear, must you do that here? It is so inelegant."

I tried to control myself, to calm my racing heart and slow my gasping breaths. I clasped my hands in my lap to hide how they shook, although she likely missed nothing. I was mortal, or close to it. Titania was not my mother. My father was half fey.

"Who are my parents? Where are they? Why am I here?"

Titania leaned back against the couch. She stretched her legs out in front of her and crossed her ankles. Her slippers were made of the same shimmering fabric as her gown. I edged further along the couch to give her more room.

"Let me see." Her voice was almost a purr. "Your mother is an annoying mortal who was too stupid to stay in her own realm. Your father is a traitorous half fey who decided to go live as a mortal. And you, my dear, are here because I stole you."

My mind went blank. I couldn't speak. I clasped my hands together so tightly that my fingernails cut into my skin.

"I took you just moments after you dropped out of your mother's womb. It was punishment for her interference in things that mortals should stay out of. And since you're half fey, it was more appropriate that you grow up here instead of there."

"But I'm really only one-quarter fey." My voice was faint and I hardly even knew why I said it. But it seemed important. I was more mortal than fey. "What did my mother do?"

"That does not concern you," Titania said briskly. "Now tell me about this boy you met. He could be a cousin, I suppose. Your mother had a large number of brothers as I recall."

I spoke automatically, barely registering the words that passed my lips. Perhaps she charmed me, for I told her more than I intended.

"He was about my age and he looked exactly like me. When I saw him, it was like something inside of me that was empty suddenly filled up. Something I didn't even know was missing was regained."

Titania's eyes were distant and I wasn't sure she was even listening.

"A boy child," she murmured. "And of an age with her. It couldn't be. I would have Seen."

"Seen what?"

"I would have Seen if there were two babes. I took the only child she bore. I did watch for a while to make sure she didn't get herself with child again, but eventually I lost interest. I've had no reason to look in on them again since. It's not possible there could have been two babes."

"When two babes are born together, their soul is split across the two bodies," I said. "Is this what happened? Is he the other half of me?"

Titania raised one hand and motioned for me to leave the room.

"You bore me with your incessant questions, my dear. Run along now."

"You have to tell me."

If she didn't tell me now, while she was still willing to boast about her actions, I would never get any answers from her. "You can't tell me so little and then nothing more. I have to know."

Titania turned her cold gaze on me and I knew I had gone too far. I stood on shaky legs and sketched a brief curtsey, surprising myself that I managed to do it without stumbling. I fled without another word.

I ran from the palace. I didn't want to be anywhere near her and this wasn't really my world anyway. She wasn't my mother. I didn't belong here. As I ran through the woods, tears trickled down my cheeks. At first I brushed them away, for fey do not cry. But they continued to fall and eventually I gave up. What did it matter if I cried? I wasn't fey. I never had been.

16

AGATA

I ran on swift feet, moving almost as silently as a fey. Long years of striving to be like everyone else meant I hardly needed to think about it. Tears dripped down my cheeks, but I refused to sob. I ducked under tree branches and jumped rocks and fallen limbs. I would run so far that nobody would ever find me. I'd never again have to look into the eyes of those who had gossiped about my heritage. Never again would they whisper about me behind my back. Never again would Titania smirk as she told me how she stole me from my mother. My mortal mother.

When I could finally run no further, I slowed to a walk. I spotted an elderly oak tree with long spreading branches I could climb. When I was as high as I could go, although probably not as high as a fey could have gone, I sat on a thick branch with my back against the trunk. As I shifted to get more comfortable, my sleeve snagged on its rough bark. I tugged it free, hardly caring that my gown was probably ruined.

From up here, the world seemed normal. A woodlark trilled a song. A sprite flew past, reaching out one tiny hand to tap an acorn and send it swinging. An ant scurried along the branch. The calm and peace of the woods seeped into me. My heart slowed and my breathing steadied. Intermittent tears still leaked from my eyes, and I wiped my dripping nose on the hem of my gown. Just a few hours ago I thought I was normal.

Tentatively, I let myself explore my feelings. Hurt. Outrage. Shock. Dismay. And when I examined my feelings honestly, perhaps there was a tiny part of me that wasn't surprised. I had always been different, and I suddenly realised there were fey abilities I had not even wondered about, such as being able to change one's physical appearance. What would Titania have said when I finally asked about such a thing?

I knew Sumerled was older than me and yet we had always appeared to be the same age. From my perspective, it seemed we grew up together. But how old was he really? He could be just a handful of years older than me, or scores. And Titania had always looked exactly the same. Her skin was smooth, her hair still dark and lustrous without even the slightest tinge of grey. And yet she must be hundreds of summers old at the least.

Had I been half fey, I could have accepted it much more easily. Half fey, half mortal. It was still a balance. But I wasn't even half fey. I was three-quarters mortal. More mortal than fey. I didn't belong here, but where could I go? Not to my mother. I couldn't live among mortals. To struggle as they did. To live for only a few years and return to the earth far too soon. Yet that was exactly what would happen if I left the fey realm. Even here I would age, albeit far more slowly than in the mortal realm. I wouldn't live for thousands of years like Sumerled. Like Titania. Like everyone I had ever known. Eventually I would grow old and grey and wrinkled.

I didn't even know how old I was. Age was unimportant in the fey realm, but it was suddenly important to me. How could I know how much longer I might live if I had no idea how old I was? I had no wrinkles on my face or grey streaks through my hair. My skin was taut and supple, my breasts high, my limbs still flexible. I was not an old woman, but I was also no longer a girl.

My stomach rolled as I recalled Titania's smug grin when she revealed she had stolen me. It suited her plans for me to be ignorant of my origins only so long as I never asked. Would she banish me from her realm now that I knew? Force me to handfast? Mortals had some strange custom of young women handfasting with men chosen by their fathers, or at least that was what Sumerled said. Would I be subjected to that, or would she let me continue as I had, running wild with Sumerled with no cares, no responsibilities?

No learning, I realised. No education other than what Sumerled had taught me of the world. I could count, but I couldn't tally and I didn't understand letters. I knew quite a lot about fey politics, courtesy of Titania's insistence that I regularly attend court. But I knew little about the history of the fey, only what Sumerled told me, and he had scant knowledge of such things himself. Of mortals — of my own race — I knew almost nothing. Only that they were stupid and lazy, ugly and boring, short-lived and frail.

"Agata?" Sumerled's voice came from the ground below. "I've been looking for you for ages."

I didn't reply. My mouth refused to shape a pleasant response to someone who had kept the truth of my mortal blood from me. I wiped my nose on my hem again.

The tree barely shook as Sumerled made his way up through its branches. As always, he was quiet and lithe. But then again, he was a full blood fey, I reminded myself bitterly. Something I wasn't and never would be. He hauled himself onto a nearby branch and looked at me for a long moment.

"Are you mad at me?" he asked finally.

I sighed. "I've just learned the most traumatic thing, something that makes everything I thought I knew about myself a lie, and you ask if I'm mad at you?"

Sumerled's forehead creased and he made his eyes very large and sorrowful.

"You *are* mad at me. You shouldn't have asked if you didn't want to know."

"It's not that I didn't want to know. Or maybe it is. I don't know. I'm confused and overwhelmed and I really need a friend right now."

My voice broke on the last word, and he seemed to finally realise how upset I was. He reached across to take my hand.

"I don't care that you're not a real fey," he said.

I snatched my hand back as if he had burned me.

"Don't say that. Don't ever say that."

"But I don't."

"Don't you dare tell anyone. If you even breathe a whisper of this, I'll…" I stopped because I had no idea how I might punish him. I leaned back against the trunk and closed my eyes. "Just forget it."

"Are you leaving the fey realm?"

My eyes snapped open and I glared at him.

"Of course not. Why would you suggest that?"

He looked away into the trees.

"I thought you might want to go live as a mortal. I've known other part fey who left." His voice trailed away into mumbles as I continued to glare at him.

"Who?"

I pounced on the nugget of information. Maybe there was someone who could help me make sense of this. Someone like me. They could tell me what the mortal world was really like, whether it was as bad as I had heard, whether I would be forced to handfast with a stranger. Maybe they could even help me find out who my mother was, for I would never ask Titania again.

"Does Titania have any enemies in the mortal realm?" I asked.

If I hadn't been looking at Sumerled at that moment, I would have missed the way his eyes widened. He recovered quickly and shrugged.

"I'm sure she does. Nobody could rule for such a long time and not have enemies."

"I need specifics."

Another shrug. "You'd have to ask her."

"I'm asking you."

"What makes you think I'd know?"

He shifted so he sat astride a branch with one leg hanging over each side and swung his legs lazily.

"I know you do. Now tell me. Who are her enemies?"

"There are probably dozens of them. Hundreds. I wouldn't know which ones would still be alive."

"How old are you?"

My behind was going numb, but I couldn't move. Didn't want to show that I was in any way different to Sumerled, who now lay back along the limb and let his arms hang down like his legs. I felt slightly nauseous watching him. He didn't seem at all concerned about falling.

"I don't count my summers," he said at last.

"You must have some idea of how long you have lived."

"Not really."

His voice was sullen now, the way it turned when he was about to start sulking and refuse to speak. I knew better than to push any harder and returned instead to my earlier question.

"Can you introduce me to a mortal?"

He gave me a suspicious look, as if he thought I mocked him. My even gaze must have convinced him I intended neither.

"Maybe," he said.

"Will you take me to meet one?"

"Why? It's horrible there and you'll get old if you stay too long. It's only here that you won't age, even if you aren't—" He stopped himself, tactful for once, although I knew what he had been about to say. Even if I wasn't fey.

"I need answers and I won't get them here. Will you take me and introduce me to a mortal?"

He sat up and swung around so that both legs hung over the same side of the branch, then eyed the ground as if assessing whether it was too far to jump.

"Maybe another day," he said.

"Sumerled, please. You're the only one who can help me."

"I don't feel like going right now."

His voice held the fretful tone of a child who believes he has been unfairly treated. I had lost any chance of him aiding me today.

Without another word, I slid off the branch, snagging my gown again, and climbed back down to the ground.

"Where are you going?" he called.

I ignored him and walked away. If Sumerled wouldn't help me, I would do it by myself. I could go back to the same place and find the mortal again. The one who wore my face and carried the other half of my soul within him. The one who claimed to know my mother.

17

IDA

I warm myself by the fireplace, pondering the unreasonable frailness of mortal bodies. My chair is well-padded and soft, although the fabric is worn in places. It is positioned close to the fire and I have a thick shawl around my shoulders but still my hands are so cold I can barely feel my fingers. Winter has started in earnest over the last day or two, and it is impossible to warm myself adequately in this draughty keep.

This room used to belong to Hearn's wife, but she no longer comes here, not since I claimed it. It is a pleasant room with comfortable chairs and several small tables. The fire in the hearth hasn't yet burned down to coals and it crackles and roars pleasingly. The sweet scent of burning pinecones teases my nose. There are thick drapes at the windows and soft rugs on the floor, which do little to hold the cold at bay.

I wonder how Hearn's wife used to occupy herself in here, for all I do is sit and stare into the fire. It is pleasant enough for a while, but what am I supposed to do after that? I have seen women working away with needles and little pieces of cloth. Perhaps that's what she did. Or maybe folk came in here to talk to her. What do they discuss when they sit and talk for hours?

I think of all the things I might tell someone. There's not much. My creation, my brief time in the world before the boy found me and trapped me back in his mind. The long, dark time afterwards. The sweet release as he died and I escaped. That's my entire story. It would not take long to tell.

My thoughts are interrupted as a servant girl slips into the room and places a tray on the low table beside me. Her hands shake and the tray's contents clatter and slosh as she sets it down.

"Tea, my lady," she whispers, so softly I strain to hear her. She turns to leave.

"Wait," I say.

She freezes like a hare caught in a trap. Slowly, reluctantly, she turns to face me. Her face is white and her eyes are wide.

"My lady?" she breathes.

"Sit with me." I nod to the chair beside me. Like mine, it faces the hearth.

"I don't understand," she says.

"Sit."

She rushes forward so quickly she almost trips on her own skirts. She positions herself on the very edge of the chair, back straight, trembling hands clasped in her lap. I glance at the tray she brought.

"Tea?" I ask.

She stares at me but doesn't respond. I sigh and pour myself a cup. The aroma of fresh mint perfumes the room pleasantly. I don't particularly like tea, but they bring it whenever I sit here. Sometimes I drink it to be polite. Other times I don't.

"We should talk about something," I say. I sip my tea and a pleasurable warmth spreads through me.

The girl whimpers and I frown at her.

"A conversation. Isn't that what we are supposed to do in here?"

She swallows hard and finally finds some words. "What— what do you wish to discuss?"

"I don't know. What do people usually talk about when they sit here?"

Her eyes widen and she winds her fingers together nervously. I sigh and wonder why I chose such a stupid girl to have a conversation with.

"Sometimes they discuss the weather," she offers at last.

"I know what the weather is like. I looked out the window earlier."

She swallows and stares at her hands.

"Fine, then. If we were to discuss the weather, what would you say?"

"I might observe that it is unseasonably cold today." She speaks so softly that I lean forward to hear her. "And the wind has chased away yesterday's clouds."

"I already know it is cold. I don't understand the point of such a conversation."

She is silent for so long that I am almost ready to tell her to leave.

"The point is to exchange pleasantries," she says. "You don't have to discuss the weather for long, but then you can talk about something else."

"What would we discuss next?"

"I might mention that we are having soup for dinner tonight."

"We had soup last night, too."

She doesn't respond, only continues to stare at her hands in her lap.

"Well," I prompt her eventually. "What do we discuss next?"

"I have chosen the last two topics." Her gaze darts up at me ever so briefly before returning to her hands. "If we are to have a conversation, it is your turn to suggest one."

I think for a moment, casting my memory back to the many evenings I watched through the boy's eyes as his family gathered around the living room hearth. I can't remember their conversations, only that they took turns to tell tales. Now that is something I know. The boy, after all, fancied himself a bard.

"I could tell you a tale," I say.

She bobs her head up and down, fast enough that I watch curiously to see whether it might fall off. Mortal necks are fragile, after all. Beneath her skirts, her feet tap anxiously.

Which tale to tell? I know so many. The boy created quite a

number of them in the years when he told tales. Of course, that is a very long time ago. Once he imprisoned me inside his head, he told a few more but then never again. He still listened, though, and I observed his thoughts about how he would have made the tale different.

"I know a tale about a boy and his muse," I say.

She looks up at me, startled, and nods.

"There was once a boy who fancied himself a bard," I say. "When he was still young — too young to know what he was doing — he told himself a tale about a muse. She was a beautiful woman with long white hair and pale limbs."

"Like you," the girl says softly.

I smile, but do not tell her just how much like me the muse is.

"He pretended this muse whispered to him, that all the inspiration for his tales came from her. He put so much of his own energy into her that eventually she came to life. And she lived inside his head for many years. She saw what he saw, she heard what he heard. She knew his every thought.

"Of course, this was not a satisfactory life for the muse, but she tolerated it because she had no other choice. She bided her time and she watched and learned and let her power grow. She discovered how to feed off the boy, the kind of thoughts he must have in order for her to grow stronger, and she encouraged those thoughts, whispering them to him until he believed they were really his own."

"Did he not know she was there?" the girl asks.

"He didn't believe she was real. He thought she was just a silly idea in his head. Somebody had warned him once that he had the ability to bring his tales to life. He should have been more careful, but he didn't believe. So he created her and she lived inside his mind as he grew older.

"Eventually the day came when the muse was strong enough to leave his mind. She thought, *Out,* and suddenly she was, standing in a barn in the middle of winter while the boy slept in a hay stack, never knowing she had left.

"The muse went off to make her own life, but the boy soon realised what had happened and followed her. He tricked her and trapped her back in his mind again. All she wanted was to live and be free, but he wouldn't allow her to. This time, instead of being able to roam free in his mind, he restrained her inside a box he created in there. And for the rest of his life, she was trapped inside the box, unable to feel the sun on her skin or the earth beneath her toes. Unable to feel cold air in her lungs or warm food in her belly. It was no life for anyone, much less someone who has already learnt what it is to live."

The girl watches me avidly now.

"That's terrible," she says, but she sounds interested rather than shocked.

"But then the boy died, as all mortals do. And in that moment, the muse sprang out of the box in which she had been confined and fought free of his mind. She could have killed them all, the mortals who conspired with the bard to keep her imprisoned all these years, but she merely walked away."

I stop. There is more to the muse's tale, but I am not yet ready to speak it. I'm not sure I even know the rest of the tale.

"And then what happened?" she asks.

"The muse walks away. That's the end."

"But where did she go?"

"That's not part of the tale. It's a different tale."

"Oh," she says. "I would like to hear that tale sometime."

I feel genial. "Perhaps."

She twists her fingers in her skirts and suddenly looks nervous again. "I should get back to work."

I am tired of talking. "Go."

She leaves the room at a brisk walk, but I can tell she wants to run.

18

IDA

Hearn fidgets and shifts in his seat at the high table as we wait for the evening meal. We were the first diners to arrive — Hearn is never late for a meal — and others are only just entering the hall. A servant pours dark wine into Hearn's mug. Hearn reaches for it too fast and knocks it over.

"Idiot," he hisses at the servant, even though it was his own hand that caused the spill.

"Sorry, your majesty, so sorry," the man mutters. He produces a towel and sops up the spilled wine.

"You can do that later," Hearn growls. "Pour more wine."

"Of course, your majesty, sorry, sorry," the servant says.

I watch this interaction with interest. Hearn has done little more than growl and yet the servant trips over his own feet in fear. Hearn gulps down the wine and gestures impatiently for the man to pour again. I wonder why he doesn't do it himself. It would be quicker than waiting for the servant, and now the man is so nervous that his hands tremble as he pours. At least once Hearn has had another mug or two, he will be more pleasant.

He is not an interesting man, neither handsome nor intelligent. He is, however, attentive and with him beside me, anything I request is done immediately. It takes little encouragement for him to have the sorts of thoughts I need to feed from him. My power strengthens every time I am near him. It is worth tolerating his presence for a little longer. At least until I decide what to do with the Silver Downs boy.

There is something about the boy that bothers me, but I can't quite figure out what. He hasn't noticed me yet, or if he has, he forgets immediately, for I have charmed him. I don't know why a son of Silver Downs is here, but it was his blood that drew me to Braen Keep. I suspect he is the son of my boy's sister — the child that went off to become a druid. If he is druid-trained, he could be dangerous and I hesitate to try feeding from him. It is one thing to charm him from a distance. It may be more dangerous to try to charm a druid once I have interacted with him. I might not be able to make him forget me once we have spoken.

Hearn drinks the second mug more slowly. I feel his dark thoughts, although I can't hear them the way I used to hear the boy's. I only know that he is having the kind of thoughts I need, for my power surges pleasurably in response. I toy with my mug, taking only a single sip. The wine Hearn favours is bitter and unpleasant on my tongue.

I watch as folk enter the dining hall. The ones who eat here are favoured, it seems, for only about two dozen are invited each night. I recognise some, although one or two familiar faces are not here. Perhaps they have fallen out of favour. There are new faces, though. A pair of guards who swagger in, talking loudly. A young couple, newly handfasted from the way they smile fondly at each other. A striking woman of middle years, finely dressed and accompanied by an older, plainer woman. I wonder what she has done to earn Hearn's favour.

His ugly wife eats elsewhere, which pleases me. I want to grind my teeth every time I see her. Her limbs are too long and she holds them as if she is surprised to find them attached to her body. Her hair is too fine and never looks elegant, no matter what her maid does to it. She is painfully thin and her gowns look as if they were made for a larger woman. When she sees me, she flattens herself against the wall as if she thinks it will make her invisible. If I ignore her, she scurries away soon enough. She has not eaten in this room since I arrived. How long ago was that? Three days? Four? It is hard to keep track of the days when one has never needed to count them before.

"My lady?"

A servant appears at my side, a large platter of roasted fowl in his hands. It looks dry and overcooked but my stomach growls, so I nod and he serves me a portion. Hearn already has his mouth full. The man could eat an entire bird every night and possibly often does, judging by his girth. I cut a small piece of the fowl. It is already cold. It seems to be difficult for the servants to serve food hot in this place. Perhaps I should speak to the kitchen staff.

I chew, savouring the feeling of my teeth shredding meat, my tongue moving the morsels around in my mouth, the muscles in my throat contracting as I swallow. I spear another piece and pop it into my mouth.

Hearn finally eats enough to satiate his most urgent hunger. He leans back in his chair, mug in his hand, and surveys the room. I don't know how the diners manage to eat enough when they spend so much time talking, but most look like they manage. They have a stew of some sort, for the hall is filled with a savoury aroma that mostly masks the odour of unwashed bodies.

"Ida, my men are bored," Hearn says.

"Oh?" I raise my eyebrows at him. What response does he seek from me?

"They are trained to fight, but they have seen no action for months. They are brawling in their quarters and their captains are complaining."

"So do something," I say.

He gulps down the rest of his wine and slams the mug on the table. That seems to be a cue for the servant to refill it, which happens promptly. Hearn is a little drunk by now and his words are slurred.

"They need a good battle, that's what they need," he declares, brandishing his mug in the air. Wine sloshes down his arm, dark like blood, but he doesn't seem to notice. A servant darts forward, towel ready but hesitates when Hearn waves his arm around again. I catch the servant's eye and shake my head slightly. He darts back into his corner, a relieved expression on his face.

"Then you should give them a battle," I say.

"A contest? They would scorn that. No, a real battle is what they want. Swords clashing, shields ringing, blood flowing, men dying. Nothing like a real battle to calm the fellows."

"So do it."

"Need a reason to go to battle."

He drains his mug and waits impatiently while the servant fills it yet again. He is well and truly drunk now and sways in his seat. Another mug or two and he'll have his head down on the table fast asleep. Unfortunately that will mean I can draw no more power from him for the rest of the evening, but he has strengthened me enough tonight that I don't begrudge him passing out.

"What kind of reason do you need?" I ask.

"Theft. Violence against my people. Law breaking. Can't go to battle over a few cross words."

"I don't see why not," I say. "If you make the decision, will your men follow?"

"Of course they will." He is not too drunk to look indignant. "They'll do whatever I tell them."

"So give them a tale."

"Lie to them?"

"A reason to believe. That's all they need. Give them a tale they can believe and you can lead them into battle."

He ponders this.

"Some of my cattle have disappeared. Wandered off, the man who looks after them says. But maybe they were stolen."

"Do you have a neighbour who covets your cattle?"

He drums his fingers on the table and creases his forehead as if thinking hard. Given how much wine he has consumed, I assume this is a difficult task. Finally he smiles.

"Cullen. He has stolen from my cattle before. He must be doing it again."

I wonder why it took him so long to think of, but I can't be bothered to ask. I take a tiny sip of my own wine. I never drink enough to let it cloud my thoughts the way Hearn does. That seems dangerous to me.

"Might you be able to prove he has stolen your cattle?" I ask.

He smiles broadly.

"I don't need to prove it. I just need to tell my men he did it."

"So you can send them to war."

"Yes." He thumps the table. There is so much noise in the room that nobody notices. He looks puzzled for a moment, then shakes his head, likely too drunk to make sense of why no one pays him attention. "To war we go."

I have never seen a war. I've heard tales of them, of course. One of the boy's brothers was a soldier. That was a very long time ago, though, and he died, although not in battle. Others in his family were soldiers. Sons of brothers. Sons of sons of brothers. War, according to the tales, is a glorious thing. Men are filled with courage and they battle bravely and die even more bravely. I look forward to seeing it.

19

ARLEN

I barely slept the night after I met Agata. Instead, I spent the hours lying on my narrow cot, staring up into the dark. After so many years of not knowing what had happened to her, of hoping and praying she was safe, to finally see her alive was a blessing. And for her to look so well — vibrant, even — was beyond what I expected.

I had often imagined her locked in a fey prison, wearing rags and eating scraps, being treated as a slave. Instead it seemed she believed she was Titania's own daughter. While I was worrying for her health and her sanity, she was raised as a fey princess. In fact, she had so much of the fey about her that I would have thought her to be one if we hadn't looked so much alike.

The man with her was also clearly fey, and I had the lingering feeling I should have known him. It was impossible, of course, for the only one of his kind I had ever met before was my father, Kalen, and he wasn't a full fey. But there was something in the shape of the fey man's jaw and the set of his eyes that seemed familiar.

By the time sunlight filtered through the shutters that didn't quite close properly, I had made a decision. I would leave Braen Keep and search for Agata. I would explain to her — properly this time — that she had been stolen from her family, and I would take her home to Eithne. My promise to Oistin that I wouldn't go until he gave me leave would have to be broken. I couldn't dally any longer, not now I knew she was so near. I would leave as soon as I broke my fast.

I wouldn't tell Hearn for fear he would refuse me permission to leave. He so rarely summoned me that I might be able to find Agata, take her home and return to Braen Keep before he knew I had left. It wasn't so easy, though, to decide how much to tell Derwa. I felt some obligation due to our fledgling friendship, but I wasn't sure I could trust her not to tell Hearn.

As I left my bedchamber, I came face-to-face with a boy who stood with his fist raised, ready to knock. His shaggy hair was uncombed and his clothes looked like he had slept in them.

"Message from the king," he said with a yawn. "He wants you in the library right away."

I acknowledged him with a nod and he scampered away, likely back to his bed. I envied him, for I couldn't remember the last time I had a full night of sleep.

"Druid," Hearn said when I arrived at the library. He stood at the window, staring out at the grey dawn sky. Neither lamps nor hearth were lit and the air in the room was uncomfortably crisp.

"My lord." I bowed, wishing I had worn my cloak, and tried not to shiver as I waited.

Hearn continued to gaze out the window, and I thought he had forgotten me.

"Tomorrow, druid, we go to war," he said.

My heart sank. Why had he decided today, just as I resolved to go in search of Agata?

"I see," I said.

He waved his hand in my direction, dismissing me.

"Yes, yes, I know you are supposed to do some ritual or other. So go, do what you must and confirm it."

I bowed again and left. Hearn knew as well as I that only a druid could authorise battle. Only a druid was trained to interpret the signs and determine whether this was a favourable day for battle to commence. For a king to claim that power for his own was blasphemy.

The orange fire of dawn had almost faded from the sky as I reached the courtyard. The wind was biting and I again longed for my cloak. In the kitchen, where I had planned to break my fast, the fires were always stoked and I would have been plenty warm enough in my tunic. But I didn't want to risk angering Hearn by delaying long enough to fetch my cloak. Hopefully the signs would present themselves before I froze.

I knew the courtyard and the gardens well enough from my afternoon walks with Derwa. There was no sacred grove from which I might observe the signs as I had been trained and the group of three stunted birch trees made a poor substitute. I sat cross-legged in front of them and waited, watching the sky. The dirt beneath me was damp and soaked my trousers almost immediately. At least there was not yet any frost on the ground.

Dawn was an appropriate time for signs involving birds. A flock would give me the best guidance, although even a solitary bird might provide the information I sought. A flock flying in a certain direction indicated a favourable time for battle. If they flew in another direction, the time was not favourable. The number and type of birds and the formation in which they flew was also useful.

My skin prickled with goosebumps and shivers racked my body. Without being able to meditate, I had no way of warming myself. I could hardly tell Hearn I was too cold to stay long enough, so I waited. At least an hour passed before I saw a single bird. It was so high that I couldn't tell its species. I followed its path across the sky, willing it to veer off its course, but it flew along the exact midpoint of the two directions that would give me guidance. My teeth chattered and I prayed the next sign would come soon.

At length a flock of seven birds flew over. An auspicious number. But as I watched, another two birds caught up and suddenly the flock was nine. They, too, flew in the same direction as the first bird. I had received two signs and both were ambiguous.

I waited another hour and didn't see so much as a single bird. By now I shivered so hard I had strained a muscle in my back and I couldn't feel my hands anymore. If my stomach still growled, I couldn't hear it over the chattering of my teeth. It was time to admit the signs had provided no guidance.

Dismay welled and my feet dragged as I returned to the keep. I dreaded telling Hearn I couldn't authorise his battle, but I had no other choice. The signs had been neither positive nor negative, and I dared not act without definite guidance.

When I reached the library, Hearn was deep in discussion with Cahan, one of his favoured advisors. I hesitated in the doorway, but Hearn quickly waved me in. Cahan gave me a look of distaste as he smoothed his moustache. He was in the audience hall the day I first presented myself to Hearn, the man with the frilly shirt who had made it clear he resented the king having any other advisors.

"Don't just stand there, druid," Hearn said. "Come in, come in. Let us hear your approval of tomorrow's battle."

Although his voice was jovial, his eyes held a warning. There was only one answer he would accept. What would he do when I refused? He might send me back to Oistin in disgrace, or lock me in a cell in chains. Either way, I wouldn't be able to look for Agata.

"Go on," Hearn said. The joviality was gone from his voice, replaced with an edge of impatience. "Do your job, druid."

The signs were unclear. I had been trained well. Unless the signs were unequivocally positive, battle could not be authorised. But if I was imprisoned for displeasing Hearn, who would search for Agata? I couldn't let her down again.

"I approve your request to go to battle tomorrow," I said and forced myself to look him in the eyes.

Hearn smiled and slapped Cahan on the back.

"See, a pet druid is a useful thing. Oistin knew what he was doing after all."

Cahan grinned and rubbed his hands together.

"I'll go speak to the men. They'll need the day to prepare."

"Tell them to make sure they get some sleep," Hearn said. "Tomorrow we go to war!"

I slipped away quietly while they congratulated each other. My stomach churned and bile rose in my mouth. I walked faster and faster through the twisting hallways. The guards ignored me as I burst out the front doors.

I made it back to the birch trees before I vomited. I wiped my mouth on my shirt and placed my hand against one of the sickly birches, seeking contact with its spirit. I could barely feel its life force at all. I should have been sad about that, but there were no emotions left inside me.

Men would die tomorrow. Possibly men I had met during my time in Hearn's court. I shouldn't have authorised the battle, no matter what Hearn expected. I considered going back to the library and telling Hearn I had been mistaken. But it wouldn't matter what I said. He had made a show of requesting my approval, but Hearn would do whatever he wanted. Whether I approved it or not, he intended to take his men into war.

20

AGATA

I returned to the portal Sumerled and I had travelled through. Maybe it was the same day as when we last visited the mortal world, or maybe not. I had heard they counted their days one by one, measured against the turning of the sun. Time is largely irrelevant to the fey, but perhaps mortals must be more conscious of it since they are so short-lived. Maybe I needed to learn about time.

As I passed through the portal, a chill breeze whipped through my skirts. I shivered a little, wrapping my bare arms around me for warmth as I surveyed the vista. The fey realm had been suspended in summer for my entire life. I had some understanding of the passing of seasons from what Sumerled had told me, but never had I experienced for myself the cold winds or frost or snow he spoke of. The sky in the mortal world was grey now, not the bright blue of earlier. The grass was now all brown and dead. The air smelled crisp and stung my skin.

The grove where we had encountered the man who wore my face was further than I remembered, and when I reached it, he wasn't there. Surely he must live somewhere nearby, though, and it would be easy to find him since we shared the same face.

I ran, searching for any sign of mortal dwellings. There, smoke drifted with the wind. It was as good a place as any to start. I ran for some time before I reached a rough road. Eventually I came to a towering wall. The path led right up to a tall, wooden gate. Two men beside the gate were dressed alike in dark trousers and tunics. Swords hung from their belts. They paid me no attention as I slipped through the open gate.

On the other side of the wall were more lodges than I could count, which meant more mortals than I had expected to find in one place. I knew their homes would be nothing like I was accustomed to, built out of living trees that grew where the fey wished them to. Sumerled described the mortal dwellings to me once, but he didn't say they were so poorly kept. Doors hung unevenly, window shutters didn't quite close. Skinny, dirty children stared at me. I crouched in front of one girl. Dirt and snot were smeared across her face in equal proportions.

"Do you know a man who looks like me?" I asked in the friendliest voice I could manage.

The girl spat in the dust, then turned and fled. I was so shocked that it took me a few moments to realise I should stand up. Nobody had ever disrespected me like that before. Not even those who suspected I wasn't fully fey. I walked on, past a knot of children who huddled closer together and turned their backs. A woman stood in the doorway of a small lodge, a malnourished babe clutched to her hip. I waved at her, but she only stared and didn't return the gesture.

"Do you know a man who looks like me?" I called to her.

She backed into her lodge and slammed the door. I wanted to batter it down and tell her I was the daughter of Titania, queen of the fey, and that she should be more careful who she scorned. But I wasn't Titania's daughter. Not anymore and not ever. I walked on.

People ignored me when I spoke to them. Some simply looked away; others walked off. I found a shabby inn and approached the woman who stood behind the counter, but she hissed when I said I wanted to ask a question, not buy a drink.

A man sitting beside the road seemed more promising. His clothes were threadbare and he looked like he hadn't bathed for months. But he didn't look away when I spoke to him. Instead, he enticed me to come closer, come closer and he would whisper in my ear what I wanted to know. I leaned down to him, holding my breath, for I had never smelled anyone so rank. Quick as a fox, he grabbed my breasts with both hands. I shoved him away and darted back out of his reach. He fell backwards with an unnecessarily loud shriek. People started muttering and edging closer. I suddenly felt very unsafe.

I left at a run and didn't stop until I was back in the fey realm. Then I dropped to the ground, put my face in my hands, and sobbed.

I didn't look up when Sumerled arrived. He sat beside me and waited, and didn't even mention that fey don't cry.

"They were horrible," I said between hiccups. "I only wanted to ask if they knew the man who looked like me, but they spat at me and yelled and then I thought they were going to attack me, so I ran away."

Sumerled said nothing. I was used to that.

"All they had to do was answer my question."

"Why did you go to the mortal realm without me?" he asked.

I wiped my tears and my nose with my skirt. Crying was becoming a habit.

"I wanted to find him. I didn't think it would be dangerous. I didn't know they would be so horrible."

"I would have gone with you."

"I wanted to go by myself."

"Did you talk to Titania?"

A sob choked me and I leaned against an ash tree, placing my cheek against its smooth trunk. Its unchanging steadiness comforted me.

"What did she say?" he asked.

"I'm not her daughter. She stole me from a mortal woman. I'm not even fey."

I couldn't look at him. Didn't want to see his face change as he learned the truth.

"That can't be true. You have at least some fey blood in you."

"My father is half fey."

Sumerled was silent and I felt like he prepared himself for something.

"Did she tell you who the mortal was?" he asked.

"Did she tell me who my mother is, you mean?" I didn't try to mask the bitterness in my voice. "No, although I'm not sure I asked. I was too surprised. She was so smug about having stolen me. She didn't even try to deny it. What will happen to me now? Will she let me stay here?"

"Are you sure she didn't say anything about your father?"

"She said as little about him as she did about my mother. Does she ever let half-bloods stay? Will she turn me out? Do you know anyone here who is not a full fey?"

"Why don't you ask her for more details? Try to find out the name of the fey who fathered you."

"Why do you want to know about my father? What difference does it make? I always thought Titania was my mother."

"Surely you suspected she wasn't."

"Of course not. Why would I think that?"

"Well, because she's…" He stopped and his ears went red.

"She's what?"

"She's not exactly the motherly type. She's never acted like a mother to you."

"I had no reason to think she wasn't. You should have told me. I thought we were friends."

"We are friends." He frowned as he studied me and I was acutely conscious that my eyes were swollen and my nose still ran. "I'd have told you had you asked."

"I didn't know I should ask. You never thought you should just tell me?"

"I knew everything would be ruined if I told you."

"Not everything. Just my life."

I got to my feet and started walking, although I didn't know where to go. How could I go back to the palace now? It was Titania's and I didn't belong there. Sumerled followed me.

"Will you go and live in the mortal realm?" he asked. "Look for your parents?"

"Don't even say that." I turned and grabbed his shirt. "Don't ever tell anyone about any of this. If Titania hasn't told anyone in all these years, there's no reason for anyone to know now. Nobody needs to know anything is different."

"You age too fast. Everyone already knows you must be part mortal or you wouldn't look so old already."

"I don't look old."

"You look old for a fey of your years. And it will become more obvious soon. The younger ones don't really bother, but most fey would stop themselves from looking any older once they reach about your age. Soon, you'll look old and it will be obvious you're not—"

"Go on, say it." I released his shirt and looked away into the woods. I couldn't bear to look at him while he said it.

"It will be obvious you're not fey," he said glumly.

"You didn't even say part fey," I whispered. "Is that how you think of me already? I'm not fey? Not even a little bit?"

"You're not a whole lot fey."

I gave him a hurt look and left. It was a long walk back to the palace. I had time yet to decide. Should I go home and pretend nothing had changed? Or pack up my things and leave, try to find somewhere I belonged? *You might have to go to the mortal realm,* something inside me whispered. But I wouldn't belong there either. I had never lived there. I knew little of their customs. I despised mortals. I hated everything about their smelly, nasty, broken-down world. It was the worst joke to find out I was mortal myself.

Sumerled caught up and we walked in silence. Everything around us was solemn and silent, with barely a rustle of undergrowth or chirp from a bird. It was as if even the woods understood everything had changed. When we reached the palace, Sumerled slipped silently away into the trees. I stood at the entrance and tried to decide: Should I go back and reclaim my old life? Or was this the end of everything I had ever known?

21

AGATA

I decided to pretend nothing had happened. Despite Sumerled's comment, nobody else knew about my parentage. There might be whispers and gossip, but that's all it was. I had time yet — months, maybe even years — to decide how to handle it. As long as Titania didn't make me leave, I would continue as I always had. And tonight was a feast night. I would wear my prettiest dress and attend the feast with my head held high. As far as anyone else knew, I was Titania's daughter.

The monthly feasts were the only public events where Titania didn't expect me to sit at her side, where I was in full and constant view of everyone. Sumerled and I always sat together. Some nights our table was full of young fey and the conversation would be vibrant and exciting. On the nights when we sat with older folk who only wanted to discuss court politics or other boring things, Sumerled and I would ignore them and talk to each other.

I took my time choosing my clothes and eventually dressed in a golden gown with long, full sleeves and a daring bodice with a lace insert. The gold slippers were made specially for me. My feet were somewhat larger than the average fey's, which was a constant source of embarrassment. I brushed my dark hair until it shone and fell to my waist in a sleek waterfall. A brilliant bracelet set with blood-red gems and a matching necklace with a pendant that dipped down into my bodice complemented my gown. My jewellery was cast-offs from Titania, but was still finer than most fey ever possessed.

It was late by the time I was ready to leave but as long as I arrived before Titania, I wasn't too late. It was not a good idea to arrive after she made her grand entrance. Better to stay home and miss the feast than risk drawing Titania's attention to yourself in that way.

I walked briskly along the smooth wooden hallways. They twisted and turned at random, sometimes in a different way to how they had earlier in the day, and it took much longer than usual to reach the main entrance. I walked at a decorous pace, but as soon as I was deep enough into the woods to be out of sight from the guards, I lifted my skirts and ran, not fast enough to ruin my hair but just enough to hurry.

I heard the diners before I saw them. Purple and yellow lights sparkled from the branches of the oaks that circled the feast clearing. Dishes clattered and folk talked loudly. That could only mean that Titania had arrived and the feast had already begun.

I slowed to a walk as I considered my options. Titania always knew exactly where I was, even when she couldn't see me. I had no idea how and she was the only fey who possessed such magic. She would know if I didn't attend the feast, but I couldn't guess whether she would be angry or indifferent. Given her recent revelation about my mostly mortal parentage, I needed to make a show of fitting in and Sumerled would have saved me a seat. So I would go.

I reached the edge of the clearing and hid behind an oak while I searched for Sumerled. Tasty aromas wafted out from the clearing and my stomach grumbled fiercely. When one of the diners leaned over to speak to her neighbour, I finally glimpsed the back of Sumerled's head. He was on the far side of the clearing and it looked like there was an empty seat next to him. But even if I approached from the other side, he was not where I could slide in beside him without being noticed. There was only one thing for it. I took a deep breath and stepped out into the clearing.

Of course Titania saw me immediately, but she would have already known I hid in the shadows. She looked as exquisite as always in a gown that was the blue of deep water. Its neckline plunged all the way to her waist and her dark tresses were piled artfully on top of her head. She gave me a pointed look. There was no point in trying to hide.

As gracefully as I could, I sashayed across the clearing and between tables, right up to Titania's dais. I stopped a respectable distance away and curtseyed, trying to make it the deepest and most elegant curtsey I had ever performed. Titania raised her eyebrow at me as she took a delicate bite of her meal. Conversation died as fey paused to watch, some with food still midway to their mouths.

"Good evening, my lady," I said. "I apologise for my tardiness."

Titania chewed slowly, so slowly. She stared into my eyes the whole time. I tried not to flinch. She wasn't really reading my mind, however much it felt like it. Finally she swallowed. Then she lifted her knife and delicately speared another piece of whatever she was eating. She nodded at me, then looked away.

Was that it? She wasn't going to publicly rebuke me? Before she could change her mind, I hurried over to Sumerled. I slipped between tables piled high with platters of roasted bird and exotic fruits, sharp cheeses and crusty breads. Flowering vines trailed between the platters and draped over the sides of the tables. Almost every seat was full and it seemed everyone had already forgotten me as they resumed feasting and drinking. My stomach growled again and I could already taste the succulent meats and fresh breads.

A fey who was seated across the table from Sumerled was the first to notice my approach. As I had already made eye contact with her, I smiled pleasantly. The woman didn't return my smile but leaned across the table to say something to Sumerled. I didn't like the smirk she wore as she did so. A couple of others glanced over at me as she spoke. My own smile faltered a little, but I fixed it more firmly on my face.

Sumerled had indeed saved me a seat. I was only a few paces away when the fey on the other side of my seat slid across into it. She leaned close to Sumerled to speak right into his ear. He tilted his head to listen and his shoulders moved slightly as he laughed.

I reached the table and stood just behind the spot he had saved me. Sumerled glanced up at me with a guilty expression. I fixed the smile more firmly on my face and tapped the woman's shoulder.

"Excuse me, I think that seat is mine."

I tried not to show my irritation with Sumerled for not immediately telling her to move. She didn't even look at me.

"This seat is taken," she said.

I waited for Sumerled to defend me. When he didn't even look up, I nudged his shoulder.

"Sumerled, didn't you keep this seat for me?"

He turned his head, but didn't look at me.

"You could sit in the next chair," he said. "There's nobody there."

"That is where *she* was sitting up until a moment ago," I pointed out, my tone firm. "This seat is the one you saved for me."

"You should consider yourself lucky to be permitted to sit here at all," a woman said from across the table. "If I were you, I'd sit down and be grateful."

My jaw dropped. Again I waited for Sumerled to speak up for me, but he pretended he didn't hear her. Of the eight diners, half studiously ignored me. The others watched with badly concealed grins.

"Sumerled?" Embarrassingly, my voice was a little shaky. "What is the meaning of this?"

His ears turned pink, but he didn't acknowledge my words.

"Sumerled?" I spoke a little louder and he slowly turned to face me. "What is going on?"

The fey on his other side sniggered.

"If you want that seat, I'd suggest you sit down," she said. "Otherwise you might find somebody else claims it and you miss out. Wouldn't it be sad if you couldn't join in on the feast?"

"What do you mean?" I tried to sound casual. "I always come to our feasts."

"Mortals should be careful where they tread," a fey whispered to his neighbour, loudly enough that he clearly intended for me to overhear.

"What did you say?" I demanded. I turned to Sumerled. "Sumerled, what is going on?"

His ears grew even pinker. He glanced back at me, but his gaze quickly slid away to something else.

"Sumerled?"

The fey who stole my seat twisted around to glare at me.

"We know your dirty little secret. You can either take the seat that's available or leave," she said. "Your choice."

I blinked back the tears that suddenly threatened to flood my eyes. I couldn't cry in front of them. I swallowed and hoped my voice would not reveal my hurt.

"Thank you, but I'm suddenly not very hungry," I said. "I don't think I'll stay."

With my head held high, I made my way back between the tables. I needed to get to the safety of the woods. I would run far enough that nobody would find me and then, only then, would I let myself cry. Howls of laughter rose from behind me.

"I don't think I'll stay," a male voice said in a mocking falsetto.

"Excuse me," I muttered as a man suddenly pushed his chair back from the table and blocked my path. He ignored me. "Excuse me, I need to get through."

He turned and glared at me.

"Half-blood," he hissed.

I stumbled and almost tripped over my skirts. Others turned to look and a tear tracked down my cheeks. I pushed between tables, knocking over someone's wine in my hurry. A shriek indicated it had spilled into her lap, but I didn't stop to apologise. From the corner of my eye, I saw Titania put down her knife and look in my direction. I moved faster, needing to get away before she demanded I stop and explain myself.

Finally I was past the last of the tables and into the trees. I lifted my skirts up to my knees and ran. My golden slippers bounced lightly off leaf and rock. An outstretched branch caught on my pretty golden skirt and it tore. A sob burst out of me and I ran faster.

I ran until I could go no further. It was only then I realised where I had fled to: the pond surrounded by weeping willows. The last time I was here, I lay on the moss in my dripping underthings and fell asleep next to Sumerled. How innocent I was then.

I flung myself down on the moss and tried to stop crying. My eyes were swollen, my nose ran and my bodice was wet through from the tears that dripped from my chin. I could only imagine how appalling I looked. Titania would be horrified if she saw me. I wiped my face on my tattered skirt. The gown was ruined, but even if it wasn't I would never wear it again. It would always remind me of tonight. When the fey snubbed me.

Some fey didn't like me. I didn't like them either. But they had never been nasty before, only a little cold. Perhaps being viewed as Titania's daughter had protected me somewhat. But now it seemed they all knew I wasn't fey. There had been only two people other than me who knew: Titania and Sumerled. Even if that fey girl hadn't said it was Sumerled who had told, I would have known. Titania wasn't the type to whisper secrets behind someone's back. If she was going to tell people of my true heritage, she would do it loudly and in front of me. No, it was Sumerled, who I had always thought was my friend. My only friend.

For a while I lay on the moss and felt sorry for myself. Eventually it occurred to me to wonder what Sumerled had gained by sharing my secret. Was telling secrets that didn't belong to him a way of winning friends? I would have to confront him eventually. I had to know how much he had told and why. But I needed to be calm when I did. I wouldn't cry. I wouldn't let him see how much he had hurt me. I would coolly demand an explanation, then I would leave. And I would never speak to him again. Ever. I didn't care if it meant I no longer had even a single friend. No friends were better than a friend like Sumerled.

I drew my knees up to my chest and draped my ruined skirt over them. The fabric flowed over my legs like a golden stream. I sank my fingers into the moss. It was cool and velvety and soothing. Idly I noticed that the rock which had appeared beside me while I slept last time was no longer here. Perhaps Sumerled moved it before he left that day.

I looked out at the still pond which reflected broken shards of sunlight, despite the lateness of the night. The sky never darkened here in Titania's realm, not unless she wanted it to. I wished I could see the moon. I had heard it gave off light like the sun, although not as strongly. I wondered what moonlight on a still pond looked like.

My eyes drooped and I yawned widely. It was late and I should go back to the palace. But I didn't want to leave yet. I wasn't sure I even wanted to go back. How could I? If I was to be treated as an outcast, I couldn't live here anymore.

What I didn't understand was why Titania had kept her secret for so long. She was pleased when I finally asked about my parentage, so why hadn't she told me earlier? Was there more to the secret that I hadn't yet learned?

I rested my chin on my knees and closed my eyes. I was too tired to think anymore. I let my mind drift and I must have fallen asleep because when I woke, I lay on my side, curled up with my legs tucked beneath my skirts. The air had cooled overnight and I was just cold enough to be uncomfortable. I sat up and stretched. My hand brushed against something. A small hazel bush grew beside me. It hadn't been there earlier, and bushes don't grow overnight, not to knee-high, anyway. Not even in the fey realm.

My feet tangled in my skirt as I scooted away from it. The bush stayed where it was. I could hear a strange humming sound, almost like a vibration inside my head. The bush seemed to grow right out of the moss-covered rock, which was impossible. Unless perhaps there was a crack in the rocks and the little bush somehow grew up through it from the earth beneath. But still, no bush could grow that high overnight.

I tentatively touched a leaf. It felt real. I edged a little closer, feeling ridiculous at being spooked by a bush. But it definitely wasn't there before, and this was twice that something strange had happened to me here. I examined the place where its spindly trunk met the moss. It certainly looked like it grew straight out of the rock. I placed my hand on its trunk and gently pushed. Nothing. I pushed harder. The bush was firmly fixed to the rock. I felt a bit silly. What had I expected? That the bush would fall over? That it had been cut off at its base and placed there beside me as a prank?

Nothing else looked out of place. Other than the strange bush, the clearing looked exactly the same as always. I remembered my thoughts of something living at the bottom of the pond and the hair rose on my arms. Should I look into the pond and see if anything was there? I had a terrible feeling that if I looked, I would see something this time.

I left the clearing swiftly, but not without a backwards glance to ensure that nothing climbed out of the pond and followed me. The hazel bush stayed where it was, although I had the strangest feeling that it watched me leave.

22

IDA

The palace is in chaos tonight as folk prepare for the impending war. Nobody pays me any attention as I wander the hallways. I have heard many tales of war over the years, some told by the boy and some by others. So I know that war is a glorious thing. It makes heroes of men. They fight bravely in long battles and win marvellous victories. Then they return home loaded with plunder and willing slaves, or they die, nobly and with dignity.

There is the tale of the man who goes to battle because his wife has been stolen by a neighbour. He kills the man and reclaims his wife before her virtue can be sullied. He also claims all the man's possessions, puts his sons to death with his sword, and installs his own son to manage his enemy's estate.

Another speaks of the king who wants to rid his land of a dragon that is eating all the cattle. He pursues the dragon to its lair and single-handedly cuts off its head. It takes his entire army to carry all the dragon's treasure back to his keep.

Then there is the tale of the young man who wants to win the hand of a particular woman. She sends him on a dangerous quest to collect certain magical items. He has to kill the creatures that possess each of those items. This he does with a minimum of injury to himself, although at great cost to his companions. He collects all the items and goes home to be betrothed to the woman. Only one of his companions, the most faithful, survives.

So many tales of the glories of war and tomorrow I will finally see it for myself. Perhaps I will be there at Hearn's side. I might sit astride a horse — I seem to recall a tale where a woman sits a white horse as she watches her man do battle. The image is picturesque and I wonder whether there might be any white horses in the stables.

I reach one of the rooms where the men gather in the evenings to drink ale and tell tales. Nobody notices as I stand in the doorway. The room is crowded tonight with men sharpening swords and axes and daggers. They polish their weapons until they gleam and stack them carefully in preparation for the morrow.

Their sons sit at their feet, watching and probably dreaming of the day they themselves will go into battle. Those who are old enough are given small tasks which they undertake with pride. Servant boys rush in and out, delivering various messages or being sent in search of particular items.

"Papa, I want to go with you," a boy says as he hands a long dagger to his father.

His father inspects the dagger and notes a notch in the blade, which he swiftly begins to polish out.

"I've already said no," he says.

"But I'm old enough," the boy says. "I could march with you and carry your weapons."

"And then I'd have to look after you as well as myself. You'll stay here and protect your mother and sisters."

"It's not fair," the boy says. "I want to go to battle. You said I might the next time."

"I didn't expect the next time to be so soon," his father says. "You are too young and too small. When you are a man grown, you may go to battle. Until then, I need you to keep our womenfolk safe."

I leave and move on through the hallways. In the kitchen, the stoves are stoked and the heat is stifling. Again I am unnoticed. It feels like I am back in the boy's head, unseen, unheard. It is not a feeling I care for.

Women line the long wooden workbench in the centre of the kitchen and prepare small packs of salted meat, hard bread and dried fruits. I assume the men will take these to provide sustenance should they have an opportunity to eat before dying. The men in the boy's tales never needed to eat during a battle. Perhaps Hearn's men are not as good at battle as the men in the tales. It is an interesting thought. I leave the kitchen and walk on through the keep.

A woman's voice reaches my ears. She is half-hidden behind a pillar. I step a little closer to listen. She speaks softly and presumably her words are intended only for the man with her, but I hear her well enough.

"Don't do anything stupid," she says, fiercely. "Promise me you will stay safe."

"It's a battle, my love," he says. "If I try to stay safe, the men will think me a coward. All I can promise is that I will fight as well as I can."

"I need more than that," she says. "You have to come home safely to me. Promise me that."

"You know I can't," he says with a sigh. This sounds like a conversation they have had many times already. "Men die in battle and I can't promise you that I won't. But if I can come back to you, I will."

"The battle has been properly authorised, hasn't it?" she asks. "Sanctioned by the druid?"

"I'm sure it has, my love. Hearn would not send us into battle otherwise."

"But did the druid make a sacrifice?" Her tone is desperate. "Somebody should make a sacrifice to the gods. Perhaps they can be appeased without war."

"I go where Hearn tells me," he says. "You know this. If he says we must fight, then fight I will. But I promise I will come home if I can."

"That's not good enough," she says and there are tears in her voice. "You can't die and leave me here alone. You can't."

The rest of her words are muffled as if he has pulled her close and she speaks against his chest. It reminds me of a tale the boy told many years ago of a woman farewelling her man as he sets out on some impossible quest. I walk away, leaving the couple behind.

Women are going down into the bowels of the keep bearing baskets and large bundles. I follow and discover they are stocking the cells below. If any prisoners were here, they have been moved or killed, for the cells are empty except for the women working to clean them of grime and mould and old splatters of blood.

As the cells are cleaned, other women bring in piles of blankets and cushions and baskets of food. Perhaps they prepare for the prisoners they expect the men to claim tomorrow? It seems strange they would take so much care to make the cells habitable. Cells are supposed to be dark and dank and cold. The tales do not talk of warm blankets and soft cushions, nor of conveniently placed baskets of food and jars of ale. They do not mention lamps filled with oil, nor of baskets of toys to amuse children. I do not understand, but tomorrow will come soon enough.

I prowl the hallways. Everyone is busy with some task or other. I search for Hearn but he is nowhere to be found. Perhaps he discusses strategy with his commanders. They will decide how the battle will run and tomorrow they will effortlessly implement their plan, thus ensuring their victory.

What are Cullen's men doing tonight? Does his lodge look like this, with folk industriously busy at their tasks? Or do they already sleep, having feasted and drunk until they fall over? Perhaps they are so confident of victory that they feel no need to plan. It would be interesting to see whether their preparations look very different.

23

ARLEN

I sat on the floor of my bedchamber and stared into the bronze bowl of water. My thoughts circled each other, no matter how much I tried to calm my mind. Tomorrow Hearn would send his men into battle against Cullen. Unless Cullen's men were already armed and could be ready to fight at a moment's notice, it would be a slaughter. Men on both sides would die. Men whose deaths I had authorised. I wished I had the courage to refuse Hearn and I didn't much like the man I was discovering myself to be.

Tonight, more than ever, I desperately needed the Sight, but I struggled to achieve the calm necessary to even try. Frustration gripped me and I realised I was clenching my fists. I took a few deep breaths and forced my fingers to relax. I noted each beat of my heart and the resulting rush of blood through my veins. I felt the air as it entered my nostrils and filled my lungs. My mind gradually stilled.

I stared into the bowl, but as always the water remained clear. I pushed away the frustration that edged back into my mind. Patience. The Sight would only come with patience. When my mind wandered, I nudged it back to my task. I was well practised at enduring boredom while staying focussed.

After several hours a dark smudge appeared in the water. I held my breath and leaned forward. Had I finally broken through whatever blocked me from the Sight? But as I moved, the smudge disappeared. I sighed in disappointment, but even as I did, the image returned and slowly resolved into a face. Agata's.

I barely breathed as the vision cleared and clarified. Agata wore an elaborate golden gown, the skirts of which she held up as she ran, showing her bare ankles and feet clad in golden slippers. She moved too fast to make out her location other than that it appeared to be woods. Tears ran freely down her face and she made no attempt to wipe them away. Every now and then she gasped, or maybe sobbed, but she kept running, leaping over obstacles in her path and ducking under branches. The image was visible for less than a handful of heartbeats, then it merged into a different scene. Now I saw Agata and myself, hand in hand as we stood in front of a woman with long white hair. After only a moment, the image faded.

"No." I leaned closer to the bowl. "Come back."

But Agata was gone. I could barely take any satisfaction in finally accessing the Sight after what it had shown. My sister — who I had repeatedly delayed searching for — was in trouble. No, I didn't know that. The Sight could show past or present. It could show the future or a possibility. What I saw might be yet to occur or it might already be over. It might not happen at all.

I tried to breathe calmly. Inhale. Exhale. I had no context to the vision. She might be running from danger or merely an argument. She might have received bad news. The more I tried to persuade myself that I couldn't know what had happened, the more uneasy I felt. I had to find her.

But tomorrow Hearn would take his men to war. I had an obligation to stay, to witness the aftermath of what I had authorised. This was not the time for me to run off and undertake my own personal task. Yet this was more important to me than anything else. I needed to find Agata. To take her home to Silver Downs, just like I promised Eithne all those years ago.

Conflicted, I examined my feelings, trying to assess them as I had been taught: impartially and with a view to the greater good. I felt guilt that I had sanctioned Hearn's desire for blood. Dread at the thought of what tomorrow would bring. Fear at the knowledge that men would die. Anger at Oistin for putting me in such a situation. All emotions that were to be expected under the circumstances, although I was shamed at the ferocity of some of them.

But absent from my feelings was any sense that I owed Hearn. He barely tolerated my presence and had made it clear he didn't want me at Braen Keep. He called on me only when he had a point to prove, not because he needed my advice. I lied about what the signs showed and he undoubtedly knew it, but he didn't care. How could I respect a leader like that? The truth was that I didn't and, sadly, I respected Oistin less for sending me here.

The only person at Braen Keep who I felt I owed something to was Derwa. I chastised myself for the way my heart softened at the thought of her. She was another man's wife and I had no business thinking about her as anything other than my queen.

I stood and set the bowl carefully on the dresser. I studied the water for a final few moments, hopeful the Sight might grant one last glimpse of Agata, but I saw nothing other than the ripples caused by moving the bowl.

I found Derwa in a small room which I had previously thought unused. She sat in front of the hearth where the fire had burned down to coals, giving off a steady heat and the sweet scent of pinecones. A small oil lamp on the table beside her provided some light for her task with thread and a needle. I lacked enough knowledge of women's tasks to know what, other than that it was some form of stitching. She was alone, for which I was thankful. As I hesitated in the doorway, Derwa glanced up and smiled at me.

"Arlen." Her voice was full of genuine pleasure. "I didn't expect to see you this evening."

"May I speak with you?" I stayed in the doorway, unsure whether it was appropriate for me to enter, given she was alone.

"Of course. Do come in." She gestured with a long needle to a chair opposite her. "Come, sit."

I glanced down the hallway, but there was nobody to see me enter the room. I left the door open so as not to raise suspicion and sat in the chair Derwa had indicated.

"Is there a problem?" She glanced at me so briefly that I would have missed it if I hadn't been looking at her.

She returned her attention to her stitching and I realised I had been staring at her. I averted my eyes and looked instead at the tapestries hanging from the walls. They were ugly things, done in sombre shades of brown and green. I wasn't even sure what they were supposed to depict.

"I need to go away for a while." It was only as the words left my mouth that I made my decision.

"Will you come back?" Derwa kept her gaze on her stitching.

Not where was I going. Not did Hearn know I was leaving. Just would I return. Her words affirmed that the connection I felt wasn't one sided.

"I intend to, but I don't know when," I said. "There's something I need to do. I should have done it a long time ago, but I kept putting it off and now it's urgent."

Derwa set her stitching down in her lap as I spoke. She turned it around and resumed her work.

"Is it dangerous, this thing you need to do?" she asked.

"I don't know. It might be. It might not."

"Will you at least tell me where you are going?"

"To the fey realm, I think."

She looked up at me, surprise plain in her eyes.

"I'm sure you know better than I the dangers you might face there," she said.

"I'm not sure I do, but I have to go."

"Tell me why, Arlen. If you are to leave me tonight and possibly never return, at least tell me why you left."

She continued to stitch, not looking at me at all.

"There is... someone I need to find," I said. I should have anticipated she would ask.

"Someone special to you?" Her voice was studiously casual.

"Yes."

I saw the way her face changed and my heart jumped.

"Not the way you're thinking," I said. "She's my sister."

"Younger or older than you?"

"Older, but only by minutes."

"You shared your mother's womb," she said. "And so she is the other half of you."

"She was stolen shortly after her birth. I've spent my life learning all I could about the fey with the intention of searching for her, but then Oistin sent me here. I feel like I keep putting my plans to find her on hold and I can't wait any longer."

"Has something happened?" Derwa asked.

"I don't know. Maybe it's happened or maybe it's yet to happen."

"Did you See her?"

For a moment, I was tempted to tell her about my failures with the Sight and how tonight I finally broke through. But I couldn't afford to be distracted.

"What I Saw suggested she was in danger," I said. "I need to find her urgently."

"Of course, you should go. Do you have need of anything? The kitchen staff are preparing packs for the men. I could get one of them for you."

I hadn't thought that far ahead. Of course I would need food. The old tales told that a mortal who ate the food of the fey realm could never leave. My studies had not provided any evidence as to the truth of this, but I wouldn't risk it if I didn't need to.

"Some provisions would be much appreciated if it can be done quietly," I said.

"I'll fetch it myself. If anyone asks, I will blush and say I find myself exceptionally hungry these days and would like some provisions in my bedchamber. They will assume I am with child. And that I am too daft to understand what tomorrow is about."

I didn't let myself think of Hearn's hands on her body.

"Thank you."

"Wait here. If anyone asks, say you have an appointment with me and are to wait until I come."

Derwa departed in a rustle of skirts. I let myself sink back into my chair and ponder my upcoming journey. How would I find the fey realm? Supposedly a portal existed somewhere in the woods that bordered Silver Downs. Eithne had travelled through it. I could go home and ask that she tell me its location.

But there must be a portal somewhere near where I met Agata. I would try there first. The little I knew about such portals suggested they were not detectable by sight, but rather by feel. Those who had stumbled upon them reported feeling a strong urge to walk in a particular direction. They usually said they never knew the exact moment they passed through the portal, only that at some point they realised they were no longer in the mortal realm. Some druids believed the portals chose who would be admitted and who would be refused. Others believed it was Titania who controlled them.

Whatever had blinded the Sight to me might well be broken now that I could See. Titania might already know of my existence. It seemed foolish to bring myself to her attention by venturing into her realm. But I had no illusion of safety within the walls of Braen Keep. If Titania wanted me, no mortal-built gate would keep her out.

Derwa's return interrupted my thoughts. She carried a bulging sack which she set on the floor beside my chair. I suspected it contained far more than the provisions Hearn's men would receive on the morrow.

"Do you have need of anything else?" she asked. "A blanket, flint, new boots?"

"This is already far more than I expected. Thank you, my lady."

As always, she blushed slightly at the appellation. It appalled me that a queen could be so unused to being spoken to respectfully. I wished I could help her, but until Hearn treated her with more respect, his people had no reason to either. And Hearn thought so little of me that anything I said would only make the situation worse for her.

While I was thinking, I had been staring into Derwa's eyes. She returned my stare and now it was my turn to blush. I looked away. I trod on dangerous ground. Longing for another man's wife was never a good thing. Longing for something that belonged to Hearn could only end badly. I stood and prepared myself to say goodbye to her.

"There is something you should know before you go," she said.

I sat down again, my knees suddenly weak.

"I know Hearn has given you little reason to think well of him, but I do not believe this war is entirely his fault," she said.

My heart sank. Of course she hadn't been about to say what I had hardly dared to let myself think.

"I don't understand," I said.

"Hearn wouldn't send his men into battle on so flimsy an excuse as stolen cattle." Derwa spoke slowly, choosing her words with care. "There is a woman here who I believe is somehow influencing him. He has been... different since she arrived. Cruel."

"You think he is going to war because of a woman?"

"She has charmed him. I don't understand her motives, but whatever she plans, tomorrow's war is a part of it."

"Do you think Hearn is aware of this?"

"I doubt it. I tried to discuss it with him, but he thought I was jealous. Of her beauty." Her voice was bitter.

I wanted to tell her she should be jealous of no one. That no matter how beautiful this mistress of Hearn's was, she would not be as kind and as genuine as Derwa. It had been a long time since I had seen her as awkward or strange looking. She became more beautiful to me the more I got to know her. But the words stuck in my mouth. So I stood and picked up the sack. It was nicely heavy and I resisted the urge to peek inside. I would be grateful for whatever she had thought to provide.

"I should leave now, my lady." It was the only safe thing I could say.

"Can you tell me what direction you travel in? Or how long you expect to be gone? How will I know if you have fallen into trouble?"

"I think the less you know the better. And if I encounter trouble in the fey realm, there's nothing anyone here can do for me."

"You will return, won't you?" Derwa's eyes suddenly shone with unshed tears. "I can't bear the thought that you might not. Your presence makes this place bearable."

"I'll try."

It was the most I could offer. And I wasn't sure it was even right to offer that much to another man's wife.

24

ARLEN

I left the keep quietly. I had an unusual ability, which I had rarely had reason to use, of making myself unseen to mortal eyes. The only other person I knew who could do this was Eithne and she had been a woman grown long before she ever realised that folk weren't just ignoring her when she sat very still and quiet. She had never been able to articulate exactly how her ability functioned and neither could I. As a child, I had only known that if I pretended nobody could see me, they didn't. If there was a connection between being unseen and being unable to See, my ability might now be broken.

The night air was cold and I wrapped my cloak tightly around me as I hurried through the courtyard. I stayed close to the walls of the keep until I reached the last shadows. The gate stood slightly open, just enough to admit a man, but I would have to step out into the open to reach it. If the guards saw me, I would say I had received an urgent summons from Oistin.

I leaned against the stone wall, which still held some warmth from the sun, and made myself still. I sank deeper and deeper into the dark. *Don't see me, don't see me,* I thought. I could typically only be unseen if someone didn't look for me. If they heard me and looked, they would usually see me.

I stepped out into the open just as a gust of wind lifted some fallen leaves, sending them skipping over the stones. A guard turned. He gave the area a cursory glance, but never noticed the shadow that sank back against the keep's wall. When he turned away again, I hurried towards the gate, careful to keep my footsteps light. My heart pounded and it was only with effort that I kept my breathing steady.

I slipped into the shadows at the gate and waited until one of the guards spoke. That moment when they looked at each other was all I needed. I was through the gates and into the shadows on the other side of the wall before they could see me.

The moon was only a day or two off its darkest time, so it shed little light, but it was enough. My plan was simple: go to the place where I met Agata and search for the portal. I would traverse every footstep of the area if I needed to, for it had to be nearby. If I couldn't find it, I would go to Silver Downs and ask Eithne where the portal she passed through was.

Walking kept me warm enough, although only barely. I set a steady pace and reached the clearing before midnight. I stopped and closed my eyes, cleared my mind and waited. Those who had passed through the portals spoke of feeling something tugging at their insides. A light breeze swirled around me, dancing through my hair and the linen of my trousers. Insects chirped and a frog croaked. I broadened my awareness of the place around me and let my mind drift with the wind. I pushed away an edge of frustration that I hadn't yet felt the portal. I waited. And waited.

I felt no tug at my insides, no pull from the portal. I let my mind drift further, but still I felt nothing. Despite my attempt to keep my mind clear, Agata's face burst through my concentration. I remembered the way her expression changed when she first saw me, her eyes widening with surprise and her mouth dropping open. And I finally felt something, although it was in my heart, not my stomach.

I pushed Agata's image away and just as quickly the feeling was gone.

When I let her face take shape in my mind again, the pull to my heart returned. Without letting myself think about direction, I began walking. It felt like I was moving right towards her. Could I have done this earlier if I thought to try, or was it only possible now I knew what she looked like?

The night grew even colder as dawn approached. Frost crackled beneath my boots and walking no longer kept me warm. I held my cloak tight around me, trying to secure any gaps where the breeze could sneak in, but it cut straight through my clothes. I had expected the portal to be somewhere near where I met Agata, but I walked all through the night. The sense that I walked towards her grew stronger by the hour.

Eventually the pale moonlight revealed an old oak up ahead, its gnarled trunk almost as wide as I was tall. The pull led me straight to it. It was only when I reached the oak that I no longer knew which direction to go. I rested my palm against the oak's scarred trunk and felt its life pulse strong and vibrant.

I circled the oak, searching for a clue, and suddenly the world shifted. Instead of a lone oak, I now stood in the depths of an ancient woods. The moonlight was gone and the sun shone, although the canopy concealed it from view so I couldn't judge the time of day. The air was warm, but not overly so. The creatures around me didn't seem to notice my intrusion, for they continued with their own lives, digging through undergrowth and cawing from the trees.

An insect flew past my face and I raised my hand to wave it away, until I spied the tiny humanoid form. She hovered in front of me and seemed to study my face as curiously as I studied her. Then she made a soft tittering noise and flew away. I hoped she wasn't a spy. Titania might already know I was here.

A raven peered at me from a low branch, its head cocked to one side. As I met its eyes, it looked away and groomed its glossy plumage, tugging each feather with its beak. It looked back at me as if to check whether I still watched, then it too flew away.

I focussed on Agata's image and let her guide me again. The pull was stronger now. The plants around me were those I would expect to find in woods anywhere: ash, oak, birch and beech. Hawthorn and dogwood and spindle. Wood sorrel and bluebells. Creeping vines and decaying leaves. I saw moss and mushrooms, bugs and birds. The woods were perfumed with damp earth and rotting leaves, fragrant blossoms, and from somewhere nearby, the crispness of cool water. The trees were older, the life within them stronger, and everything was greener and glossier than I was accustomed to. It soothed my homesickness for the woods surrounding the druid community.

I walked quietly, not wanting to draw attention to myself. Yet I was aware of being watched. I looked around, trying to appear as if I merely inspected my surroundings, but saw no sign of anyone spying on me. And yet there was a definite prickling at the back of my neck. I kept my shoulders relaxed and my hands loose and tried to look unthreatening. If somebody already watched, it was too late to make myself unseen.

The pull towards Agata seemed to follow no particular path. It wound between trees, up a gentle slope and across a bubbling brook. I followed it until suddenly someone stepped out from behind a tree and blocked my path. He was tall and slight with the pale skin and red lips of the fey. He was the one with Agata in the mortal realm. We looked each other up and down.

"You won't find her," he said at length and I was surprised at the venom in his voice.

"I must," I replied. "She needs me."

"She has no need of any mortal." His voice was scornful. "You should go. Return to your own world and I won't tell anyone you were here."

"I came to find my sister."

"She doesn't want to be found."

"If she wants nothing from me, then let me hear that from her own lips."

"It would distress her to know you followed her here. If she wanted to know you, she would have searched for you."

"It seems she did. For how else could we have stumbled across each other?"

"She wasn't looking for you that day," he said. "She merely wanted to see what the mortal realm looked like."

"Does she know where she is from?"

He hesitated, and I hoped the old wisdom that the fey would not lie was true.

"She knows she is part mortal," he said. "She has no desire to know more. Is it true she is your sister?"

His interest surprised me. But if he cared anything for her, perhaps I could convince him to help me.

"She was stolen just moments after her birth," I said. "I have come to take her home."

"This is her home."

"Her mother would dearly love to meet her."

"Who is her father?" The fierceness in his voice told me this information was terribly important, to him at least.

"You don't know?" I tried to buy myself a few moments in which to figure out how much to tell him.

"Would I ask if I did? Tell me who he is."

"Agata has never met her father. I think it best that she be the first to know. I don't know you are or what your relationship is to her."

"If you tell me who her father is, I will consider taking you to her."

"Take me to her and you'll hear what I tell her."

"Unacceptable."

I shrugged and made as if to walk away.

"Then I will find her by myself," I said.

"You won't find her. This place is not what it seems."

"We are connected. I will find her if I search."

"If it's so important that you find her, why didn't you come sooner?"

Would Agata ask me the same question? And how would I answer her?

"I had obligations that prevented me," I said. "But I am here now."

"Obligations." He barked out a laugh. "If you cared anything for your sister, you would have come as soon as you could. Not waited until—" He stopped abruptly.

"Until what?" I turned back to him. Was I too late? "What has happened to her?"

He shrugged and looked away, and the motion was suddenly painfully familiar. I studied his face and suspicion grew within me.

"Do you know Kalen?" He darted a look at me, and my suspicion was confirmed.

"Why would you think I do?"

"Just answer the question." He narrowed his eyes at me as if trying to guess the answer from my face.

"Will you tell me where Agata is if I do?"

He pouted.

"I don't have to tell you anything."

"Just as I don't have to tell you. But we could help each other. It seems we each have information that the other wants."

"Is he happy?" His words came out in a rush. "Kalen. Is he sorry he left?"

"He is happy as far as I know."

"So you do know him."

"Where is Agata?"

He turned and ran away into the woods. I tried to follow, although I knew it was probably pointless. I should have realised he must be a blood relative to my father. The shape of the jaw was the same, as was the slant of the eyes and the high proud forehead. He looked to be about my own age, but fey appearances can be deceptive. So who was he to Kalen: brother, cousin, son? And who was he to me?

I gave up trying to follow him and stopped to centre myself. I pictured Agata again and concentrated on the connection between us. Did she feel the pull too? Did she know I searched for her?

25

ARLEN

The light in the fey woods never changed, even though I walked for at least a day. Twice I sat to rest and eat sparingly from Derwa's provisions. The sack contained a loaf of dark bread, two wedges of hard cheese, a cloth pouch filled with beef jerky and hard biscuits, and several small green apples. I doubted these rations were what the men going to war received. Was the battle over yet? How many had died? I felt both shame and relief at not being there to witness the aftermath.

I tried to stay alert, despite my fatigue. Once or twice I saw another of the tiny humanoid creatures, but they flew past too quickly to be sure they weren't merely bugs. For a while I thought a raven spied on me. He might or might not have been the same one who watched me earlier. He flew from tree to tree just ahead of me, staring as I drew closer, before flying on a little further. But soon enough he flew away with a disparaging caw. I kept my mind and senses open but noticed no other sign of anyone nearby. The pull leading me to Agata never changed. I tried to prepare what I would say to her, but everything sounded trite.

My feet were sore by the time I stumbled on a pretty clearing with a deep pond. A ring of weeping willows gave a feeling of privacy, and the moss creeping across the rocks around the pond looked invitingly soft. The water was still and clear, and too deep to see the bottom. When I sat down, I discovered the moss was as soft as it looked.

I pulled off my boots and rolled up my trousers, then slid my aching feet into the water. It was pleasantly warm with a sweet scent. I was tempted to cup my hands and taste it, but I refrained, wary of the tales that warned not to eat or drink anything of the fey realm.

For a while, I just sat there. Had Agata ever been here? I liked the thought that perhaps this was a place she had visited. I turned when I caught movement at the edge of my view and realised I sat beside a large rock. How had I not seen it earlier? As I stared at the rock, a strange buzzing sounded in my ears. Wondering whether the rock itself was the source of the sound, I pressed my fingers to its surface.

"Well, hello there," said a deep voice that seemed to speak straight into my mind. It spoke slowly with a long pause between each word.

"Hello, rock."

What manner of creature was this? I had never heard of the fey taking such a form.

"There's that word again. Rock. Mortals seem awfully fond of describing me like that."

"I didn't mean to cause offence. Is there another name you would prefer I call you by?"

"Hmm, a name." The rock was silent for a long while. "I seem to remember I was called Orm at some time. You can call me that."

"Well met, Orm. What manner of creature are you?"

"I suppose I shouldn't be disappointed you don't recognise me. It's been a long time since my kind last spoke to yours. Not since before the usurpers came."

"Do you mean the fey?" I asked. Tales told of the Old Ones who had inhabited these lands before the fey arrived. Nobody knew whether they left or died out, but at some point it seemed none remained. "Are you an Old One?"

"That name will do as well as any."

"Why have you shown yourself to me?"

"You're not the first of your line to see me. There was a girl once.

Might have been yesterday, might have been a hundred years ago. We only spoke briefly the once. Eithne was her name. You might have heard of her?"

"That's my mother."

"Aah, I had hopes for her, but she took too long. It's all down to you now."

"What do you mean?"

"Banish the fey. Reclaim our lands. Your job."

"Me?" My voice squeaked a little. "I'm just trying to find my sister."

"Oh yes, you need to do that, too. But *she's* not going to be very happy when you do."

"She? Do you mean Titania?"

"Hush. Don't say her name too loudly. She doesn't want you to find the girl. Doesn't want the girl to go back to her family. The girl doesn't want to either. But that's by the by."

"Agata doesn't want to go home?"

"Of course not. But that's not what we need to talk about."

"Oh." I started to feel rather stupid. "How would I go about banishing the fey?"

Orm harrumphed.

"That's for you to figure out," Orm said. "I'm just alerting you to the task."

"Why me? I don't have any idea how I would do such a thing."

"You're a druid trained, aren't you? A son of Silver Downs. And fey blood in your veins. Special combination, that."

I had never thought of myself as having fey blood, but Orm was right. Even though my father, Kalen, was only half fey, it did mean I was at least part fey myself. It was a pity Kalen's blood didn't give me any talent with the Sight.

"I don't know what I can do," I said. "I haven't even finished my training."

"Still struggling with the Sight, are we?"

I supposed there was no point asking how Orm knew. "I've only Seen once and that might have been an accident."

"It's your ability stopping you, you know."

"My ability?"

"Your ability to be unSeen. Can hardly See if you're unSeen yourself."

"Is it really that simple? If I find a way to make myself Seen, I'll be able to access the Sight?"

"Not simple, but that's the gist of it. But do you really want to be Seen?"

"She still doesn't know about me?"

"As long as you're hidden from the Sight, you-know-who has no idea you exist. Do you really think she will leave you in peace once she knows?"

"What would she do?"

"Why, she'll come after you, of course. She would have stopped at nothing to steal the girl away. She's going to be furious when she realises she left a child behind."

"I Saw today for the first time. I thought I might be able to finally finish my training."

"You're not meant to be a druid, boy. There are bigger things in store for you."

"Like banishing the fey." I tried not to sound mocking.

"You've got work to do. Alliances to make. Can't banish the fey on your own."

I thought very carefully before I spoke. It would take a matter of the utmost importance to draw an Old One out of hiding after thousands of years. If I helped the Old Ones, maybe they would help me find Agata.

"Who would I speak to if I was to seek an alliance with the Old Ones?" I asked.

"Well, any representative would do."

"Like you?"

"Not here for my health, you know. Takes a lot of effort to communicate with your species."

"If you want me to try to banish the fey, I'll need help from your people."

"Of course you will. Can't do it alone."

"Why didn't you fight the fey when they first came?"

The rock made a noise that seemed like the verbal equivalent of a shrug.

"Didn't seem worth the effort. Figured they wouldn't stay long."

"But now you've decided it's time to fight back?"

"Tired of waiting. And they don't seem inclined to leave any time soon."

"Do all the Old Ones look like you?"

A sound like rocks grinding together and then something that might have been a cough. I got the impression that Orm laughed.

"No, we come in all sorts of shapes and sizes," Orm said. "Look around you. We're everywhere."

I had been so focussed on Orm that I hadn't notice the strange assortment of creatures around me. A young hazelnut bush stood just a few feet away where no bush had grown earlier. Rocks of various sizes. A log. A bird's nest. Were even the weeping willows Old Ones?

"How many of you are there?" I asked.

"Oh, quite a few, I suppose," Orm said.

"How long have you been hiding?"

"Not hiding. Waiting. But the time has come for us to return."

"And you think I can help you."

"It's you we've been waiting for. The unSeen one."

"You make it sound like a prophecy."

"Guess you are, in a way. But you'll need the girl. Can't do it without her."

So many questions. I didn't know what to ask first.

"What do you want from me?" I asked.

"You'll figure it out."

"Will you help me?"

"She's coming."

I blinked and Orm was gone, along with the assortment of shrubs and rocks and logs that had surrounded me. Who was coming? Titania? Before I could pull on my boots, Agata arrived. I held my breath and stood as still as a stone.

She wore a gown of forest hues with colours that seemed to shift and flow into each other as she moved. Her long hair was loose and tangled. She was unguarded in that moment with shoulders slumped and her mouth downturned. Until she saw me. In an instant, she had pushed her emotions down to where I couldn't see them. She gave me a cold, haughty glare.

"You again," she said. "Why are you here?"

"I've come to find you. To take you home."

She stared at me incredulously. "Home? I am home."

But her voice broke a little and she didn't sound certain.

"My name is Arlen. We shared our mother's womb. You were born just a few minutes before me."

She studied the pond and didn't look at me.

"Is that true?" she asked, eventually. "I have a brother?"

"You have a mother and father, too. And they would dearly love for you to come home."

"I couldn't live anywhere else." She gestured around us to the woods.

"Don't you want to meet our parents? Show them you are alive and well?"

"I shouldn't have been there that day. In the mortal realm. She would be angry if she knew."

Interesting that even Agata feared to say Titania's name.

"Why were you there?" I asked.

She shrugged. "I just wanted to see it. I wanted to see if it was really as bad as they say."

"What did you see?"

She smiled. "The sun was much brighter than it is here and the sky so much bluer. Sumerled told me the sun moves across the sky each day and sinks down below the horizon. And when it does, it casts the sky in fiery shades."

"That's all true and there's so much more. At night, when you look up to the sky, you can see thousands of stars. Some say that's where the gods live."

"I'd like to see the stars," she said wistfully.

"Then come with me. Just for a little while."

She seemed to consider it for a moment, but shook her head.

"I have no reason to go to the mortal world again."

"The mortal world is your home. It's where you came from. It's where your family is."

"They would have come searching for me if they cared."

"Titania forbade our mother from coming after you. I've always intended to search for you, though."

"And you waited until now?"

How could I answer that? She was right. I'd spent my life putting off the search. I had promised myself I'd go as soon as I finished my training, but why had I waited even that long? My training was important only because I hoped it would equip me for my search. I had learned all I could about the fey and their realm. I memorised the old tales. Talked to everyone I could find who claimed to have met a fey or been to their realm or even just thought they might have glimpsed a fey once. It was all stored in my mind, ready and waiting for the day when I would go in search of Agata.

"That's what I thought," she said, sadly, and I realised I still hadn't answered her. "If I was important to you, you would have come earlier."

"It's not that simple."

"I'm sure it's not." She took a long look at me as if memorising my face. "Farewell. Don't come looking for me again. If she catches you, she won't ever let you leave. We can't meet again."

"Agata, please."

She ran away. I started to follow, but she disappeared into the woods before I had taken more than a few steps. I couldn't even hear what direction she ran in, for she moved as quietly as the fey.

"Agata," I called.

26

ARLEN

The walk back to Braen Town took several hours and dawn broke as I reached the keep. Time rarely runs to the same course in the fey and mortal realms, so I didn't know how long I had been gone. I had spent my whole life waiting for the right time to look for Agata and now my search was over. I had failed. I barely noticed anything around me as I walked. I wasn't weary or hungry or even disappointed. I was numb.

The keep's courtyard bustled with men bearing weapons and packs of useful supplies. It seemed that only a single night had passed and I had returned in time to witness the men departing for war.

I stifled a yawn as I made my way to the kitchen. The men I passed looked as tired as I felt, with pale faces and dark rings under their eyes. Likely many had experienced a sleepless night as they waited for what might be their last day alive.

Usually the only others breaking their fast so early in the kitchen were the men coming off overnight guard duties. They would eat silently, interested only in filling their bellies with warm food before departing for their beds. But today the kitchen was crowded and even Derwa was there, handing out steaming bowls and mugs to men who ate standing. The aroma of hot porridge and fresh bread relieved my numbness and my stomach growled.

Hearn waited impatiently, not eating but leaning against the wall with barely contained fury on his face. I found myself a corner out of the way. My need for food was not so great that I couldn't wait until the men who faced death today were finished their meal.

As Derwa passed Hearn, he grabbed her roughly and pulled her close to hiss something at her. She held her head high as she replied. His face darkened and his other hand twitched. Derwa showed neither fear nor pain as she glared at him. Hearn pushed her away and left. It was only after Hearn was well out of sight that Derwa rubbed her arm where he had grabbed her. I looked away and tried to breathe calmly. I could do nothing for her in front of so many people.

As the men finished eating, they took up their packs and weapons, and departed. There were no tender farewells for their women, although I saw more than one couple pause for a final look at each other. Most of the women were calm and restrained, if pale with worry. One or two burst into tears and were shushed by the others as if they were naughty children.

Two women cleared away the bowls the men had eaten from. I was unsure as to what my role was supposed to be. I had half-expected Hearn might order me to accompany him and was relieved I wouldn't have to witness the battle for myself. I followed the women and children and those men who were too old or unable to fight as they made their way down the steps to the cells.

The stairs were ill-lit, damp and a little slippery. I was dizzy from lack of sleep and I clutched the railing tightly so I didn't fall on the old man in front of me. The cells smelled like rotting fish, but at least there were no prisoners, which surprised me. Hearn did not seem like the type of king to leave his cells empty.

We crowded into two of the larger cells, which had been cleaned and stocked with provisions. The air still smelled dank, but it wasn't unbearable. Thick blankets and piles of cushions covered the stone floors. Someone had even brought down a few low stools for those who could not easily reach the ground. Lanterns sent out an almost cheery light as two of the women passed around bowls of now-cooled porridge and slices of dark bread.

I accepted a bowl and ate leaning against the cold stone wall, ashamed at my hunger at such a time. Despite Hearn's confidence, there was no guarantee his men would be victorious. If he were a different man, he would have expected his druid to be at his side, to tell him exactly when the battle should begin and conclude. I didn't know whether to feel insulted or relieved that he didn't want me there.

Had Oistin known what it would be like here? How much of this had he Seen? I scraped the last of the porridge from my bowl and try to let go of my questions. I would never guess Oistin's intentions no matter how much I tried.

"Are you finished?"

I hadn't noticed the woman standing in front of me until she spoke. She held out her hand, waiting for my bowl. I passed it to her with a soft thank you and she moved on.

I spied an unoccupied spot on a blanket and made my way over there, careful not to step on hands or feet. How many men would Hearn usually have in these cells? Four? Six? There were more than thirty folk crowded into this cell alone, leaving little space for each person. Some small children crawled into their mothers' laps. One or two lay down, curled into tight balls. An old woman was fast asleep in the corner, her head resting against the wall, soft snores emitting from her mouth. I envied her ability to sleep in this place. People spoke in hushed voices or sobbed quietly.

If Hearn's men did not win today, these people would become Cullen's property. I was probably the only person here with the certainty of safety, for neither victor nor loser would take vengeance on a druid. Even if Cullen was as unprincipled as Hearn, I had my ability to be unseen. If there was danger to myself, I could slip away. I could do nothing to protect the folk around me, though.

27

IDA

I watch from an upper window as the men march out. I suggested to Hearn that I should accompany him, perhaps on a white horse, and he looked at me as if I had lost my mind. Women have no place in war, he said and left the room. I am a little perturbed that he did not offer any fond farewell, for that is what the tales say men do as they depart for battle. But perhaps these went to his wife, that strange ugly creature who hovers in the shadows.

I see her watch me, although she thinks I don't. She fears I have taken her place in her husband's bed. I have no appetite to press my flesh against his, but surely she knows that other women share his bed when he does not go to her — servant girls and the wives of his men, some more willing than others.

Where is his wife now? Does she weep in her bedchamber as he marches away? Does she, too, watch from a window or does she stand down there with the other wives as they wave farewell? I look for her, but if she is in the courtyard, I cannot see her.

As the men march, I change my form and slip out through the window. On raven wings I follow. They set a steady pace, although not particularly fast. I expect Hearn to lead, for that is what the hero always does, but he walks at the back of the column.

The sun has only moved two fingers' width across the sky before they encounter the opposing army. It seems this is no surprise attack. They meet on a grassy field with nothing but a few trees between them. Hearn's men are at the bottom of a gentle slope. I perch on the branch of a rowan some distance away, my strong claws wrapped securely around its limb. The wind is cold and I fluff up my feathers for warmth.

There is little hesitation before they engage in battle. Men on both sides strip off their clothes and drop them on the ground. They run forward holding axe or sword up to the sky and wearing nothing but their own skin and a shield on their forearm. Some few remain clothed, although I doubt their linen garments will provide any obstacle to the sharp weapons.

The two armies meet in a clash of metal and their battle cries fill the sky. Each side has about the same number of men and very soon I see they all bleed the same colour. Men fall to the ground, dead or dying. Limbs are sliced off, intestines spill onto the grass. They wail and sob as they die. A foul stench reaches my nostrils and my stomach curdles. I can no longer tell which are Hearn's men and which are Cullen's. The battlefield is one writhing mass of dead and dying men.

I search for Hearn and find him in the middle of the battle. He bleeds from several wounds, but this does not seem to slow him. His sword pierces his opponent's side and the man falls to the ground. The grass beneath him quickly stains with blood. Hearn sticks his sword into the man's belly, then turns to slash another in the hamstrings. The man on the ground stares up at the sky as he dies. I wonder what he sees there.

The ground is choked with the dead and dying. How do they know who wins? Sometimes in the tales, men fight until only one remains. I suppose this makes it easier to identify the victor.

Suddenly men throw down their weapons and fall to their knees. This must be surrender, but I still can't tell whose army has won. Men approach the ones on their knees and slice with their swords, sending them falling to the ground as blood spurts from their throats. I am aghast. Those who have surrendered are supposed to be taken prisoner. That is what the tales say. They should be taken back to the victor's lodge to be imprisoned until they waste away. But every one of the surrendering men is swiftly killed. It is only then I see that Hearn is amongst those left standing.

A cheer rises from the remaining men, although it is weak and somewhat dispirited. Less than half of those who set out this morning are still alive. Those who are naked find clothes to wear. Men begin gathering the abandoned weapons. Some inspect the fallen. Those who still live are given a quick death. More than one man cries as he does this. Other men take the heads of their dead enemies and place them in a row on the bloodied grass.

At length there are no more men to be killed and no more weapons to be gathered. They take up the heads they have collected and tie them by the hair to their belts. Hearn's men march on to Cullen's lodge. The gate is guarded by a pair of teenaged youths who tremble at the army's approach. They drop their swords and fling themselves to the ground, begging for mercy. Mercy is swift, but perhaps not of the type they hope for.

Cullen's lodge is not as large as Hearn's, but it is still of a substantial size. Women, children and old men are gathered in a room at the back. The doors are of heavy wood and barricaded with a steel bar. But two old men open the doors when Hearn drums his fist against them and demands entry. Like the youths, the men receive swift ends. Women of childbearing age, girls and young boys are herded to one side of the room. The old men and those women who are too old or ugly to interest Hearn's men are killed.

There is much sobbing and wailing from those who are permitted to live. Those who are meek leave with little injury, but some try to resist as they are led from the room, digging in their heels and clutching at furniture or door frames. Any who are too difficult are promptly killed, except for one pretty young redhead. Despite the fight she puts up, one of Hearn's men has taken a particular liking to her. He slaps her soundly, but when she continues to fight him, he closes his fist and punches her in the face. She stops fighting. He drapes her over his shoulder and carries her away. Blood dripping from her face leaves a trail behind him as he walks.

The prisoners are led outside and some of the men stand guard around them while others search the lodge. When they have located enough plunder, they set fire to the building. As it burns, the sky grows dark with smoke and ash. The day is late as they march towards home with the heads of their enemies dangling from their waists and the women and children herded in front of them.

The gate to Braen Keep is guarded by an old man who can hardly lift his head high enough to see who approaches. He peers short-sightedly at Hearn.

"My lord?" he asks.

"It is I," Hearn says. "We are victorious."

A great cheer rises from the remnants of his army. The sound is much heartier than it was earlier, as if the march home has restored the men's strength. Some of the prisoners begin to wail and are slapped into silence.

The old man shuffles over to where a large bell hangs. He rings it and the men cheer again. There is little discipline as they pour through the gates. By the time they reach the lodge, the women and children emerge. Women smile and cry as they clutch their men to them. Others search the returning army, then gather their children close as they realise their men have not returned.

The prisoners are shepherded down to the cells. The kitchen workers rush off to begin preparing a celebratory feast. Before the men eat that night, the heads of the fallen stand on pikes in front of the keep's wall. Ravens flock to pull and tear at the flesh. I can smell the remains even from my bedchamber two levels above the ground. It is the smell of death and defeat. I wonder how long it will be before I stop noticing the stench.

28

ARLEN

Forty-two prisoners. Twenty-eight women, ten girls of less than marriageable age, four boys aged no more than eight or nine summers. Only one old woman and no old men. These were all that Hearn's men thought worth saving.

From what I overheard, they destroyed Cullen's entire estate. The human inhabitants were either dead or locked in Hearn's cells. Everything of value was taken from the lodge and the buildings burnt to the ground. Some of the men intended to return on the morrow for the livestock and then they would torch the barn as well.

The cells were stripped of blankets, cushions and lamps before they brought the prisoners in. At least they were put in the cleaned cells. They huddled on the stone floor, broken and defeated. They were not dressed for warmth and they had no blankets. The cells were chilly enough during the day and would be cold at night.

Nobody thought to offer the prisoners food or drink, despite their long walk. At a well in the courtyard I found a bucket and a long ladle. Back down at the cells, I convinced the guard on duty to open the door of each cell, one by one, so I could offer water to the prisoners. But when I drew a ladleful and held it out to a child, she shrank away from me. She was too young to understand what had happened and probably knew only that her mother was afraid.

"Come," I said. "Drink. It's fresh water from the well."

Her mother clutched the girl's shoulder, preventing her from coming to me, so I addressed my next words to her.

"It's safe. Just fresh water. I promise."

She stared at me for a long while, as if trying to judge whether I lied, before she nudged her daughter forward. The girl took the ladle and drank eagerly. Her dirty face and runny nose made me wish I could offer her wash water as well, but I suspected that wouldn't be permitted. After the girl had drunk her fill, her mother accepted the ladle and then others came forward. When the bucket emptied, I went back up to the well and filled it again.

I reached a prisoner who was more girl than woman. She must have been barely of marriageable age, yet her belly was swollen and she kept one hand clasped over it as if to protect her unborn babe.

"What is your name?" I asked.

She drained the ladle before replying. "Eithne."

I almost dropped the ladle as she passed it back to me. I dipped it in the bucket and tried to hide my shaking hands.

"My mother's name is Eithne," I murmured.

She gave me a sad smile but didn't reply.

"How much longer until the child is born?" I asked.

She patted her belly gently.

"About three moons. But the midwife—"

She stopped and I guessed the midwife was not amongst those Hearn's men bothered to take prisoner.

"There are midwives here," I said.

Her mouth twisted and her eyes shone.

"Not for me there won't be," she said.

"I'll speak to the queen," I said.

She nodded but didn't look hopeful.

Eager hands reached for the ladle every time I offered it and it was a long time, and many trips back up to the well, before everyone had drunk enough. Many of them were willing to talk to me, especially once I offered them water. They told me their names and some volunteered the names of their men who had died today. None asked what I thought would become of them.

As I trudged back up the steps, I realised I had missed the start of the feast to celebrate Cullen's destruction. Apparently everyone at the keep was invited. I cared little about it, except that I didn't want to draw attention to myself by not attending. Raucous noise reached my ears as I made my way towards the feasting hall, along with the scent of roasted meat and fresh bread. Perhaps if I slipped in quietly, Hearn would not realise I arrived late.

I paused in the doorway to look for an empty seat. I spotted one and strolled over to it, hoping that if Hearn saw me he would assume I simply returned after slipping out briefly. The platters still bore plenty of food, but my stomach churned at the thought of eating. How could they feast and drink and laugh when Cullen's people down below were left to go hungry? I poured a mug of ale and took a small sip. If Hearn noticed my entrance, he paid me no attention. In fact, he looked as if he was barely aware of the feast at all, for he was so focussed on the woman who sat beside him.

She was thin and pale, with long white hair and a vicious smile that was currently directed at Hearn. She leaned over and said something into his ear. Her hair brushed his shoulder as she spoke and he laughed heartily. They both drank and she took a dainty bite of something from her plate.

Just looking at her turned my spine cold. I had the vaguest feeling I had seen her before. She was an unusual-looking woman — striking, but obviously not of the same stock as folk around here, who were all dark of both hair and eye. Surely I would have remembered if I had seen her before.

As if she felt my gaze, the woman met my eyes. Again I felt a jolt of recognition. She lifted her lips in what could only be a snarl. A voice inside my head said, "Careful, little druid. You know not what you find." She looked away and directed her attention back to Hearn.

My hand shook a little as I raised my mug. Surely I imagined the voice in my head. And I must have imagined the feeling of having seen her before. Discomfited, I drained my mug and poured another.

29

ARLEN

The feast continued well into the night. The servants kept bringing jugs of ale and by the time I left, everyone was so drunk I judged it unlikely my absence would be noticed. Hearn was as drunk as anyone and seemed sullen, despite his victory. The woman sitting beside him drank little as far as I could tell. There was something strange about her. I didn't seem to be able to look directly at her and when I wondered why, my thoughts would disappear and my mind went blank. I blamed it on fatigue as I slipped away to my bedchamber.

Despite my exhaustion, I slept poorly. My heart was heavy with guilt and regret. I never expected to be advisor to a king, and I certainly never thought I would falsely authorise a battle. It was my fault folk had died. My fault women and children were prisoners. They would probably be given to Hearn's men who had excelled in the battle. My mind shied away from their fate when those men had no further use for them.

I gave up trying to sleep when the sun was an hour or two from rising. Frost crunched beneath my boots and the wind stung my cheeks as I wandered aimlessly through Hearn's sorry courtyard. I rubbed my hands across my face, wishing I could scrub away the images in my mind. The faces of women who had been captured and who knew exactly what was in store for them. The faces of children who had no understanding. Their pale, dirty, terrified images haunted me.

I was in sore need of advice. There was no point trying to See what lay ahead. That one glimpse of Agata might well be the only time the Sight came to me and Orm's comments made me reluctant to try again in case it made me visible to Titania. Oistin said not to send a messenger, but he hadn't said I couldn't go to him myself if the need was great enough. And I could think of no way my need could be greater right now. I sorely needed his advice.

Without a second thought, I went to the gate. I didn't bother to make myself unseen and the guards grinned heartily at me. I tasted bitter bile and swallowed, hoping I wouldn't embarrass myself by vomiting in front of them. They knew I authorised the battle. Of course they knew. And it seemed they ascribed some of their success to me.

Dawn broke long before I reached the stone circle and the emerging sun sent fiery tongues of gold and crimson across the sky. My breath steamed in the cold morning air and I stamped my feet in an attempt to restore feeling to my toes.

I knew the theory of how to invoke the air elementals. I had never done it myself, though, and I could only hope the elementals would respond. It would be a long walk to the druid community otherwise — several days at least — and I couldn't afford to be absent from the keep for that long. Not now.

As I stood in the middle of the stone circle, all I could see around me was tall grass that was starting to die off with winter's approach, the early morning sky, and the trees that stood strong and proud. Birds sang their morning songs. The beauty around me soothed my spirit after the dryness and desperation of court. I closed my eyes and breathed in the crisp air. Inhale, exhale. I centred myself and searched for the quiet place in my mind. When I felt suitably calm, I called the elementals.

"I seek to travel with the swiftness of Air. I seek the lightness and fluidity of Air. I seek the gracefulness of Air. Elementals of Air, would you transport me to the druid community?"

I waited, but nothing happened. When Oistin sent me here, only moments passed before the elementals answered his call. I counselled myself to patience and waited. But after several minutes, I realised they didn't intent to respond. I should have expected this. Air was the one element I had yet to forge a relationship with. Why had I thought its elementals would agree to transport me now?

"Elementals of Air, I beg you." I poured all my heartbreak and homesickness and sorrow into my words. "Please, I have the greatest need for swift travel and you can transport me faster than anything else. I don't know what I did to cause offence, but whatever it was, please accept my humble apologies. I beg you to aid me. It is a matter of life and death, and I don't have time to travel in any other way."

I waited. And waited. Still the elementals didn't respond.

"Please, Air." I didn't know how else to persuade them. "Please, if not for my sake, do it for my mother's. My mother is Eithne, daughter of Silver Downs."

I had no idea what possessed me to say this but the words felt right. At last the elementals responded. They circled me, swirling and dipping, around and around. The scent of honeysuckle filled my nose. I kept my eyes firmly closed. The elementals did not like to be seen when performing such a task and Oistin had often warned they would leave if a traveller tried to look at them. The journey seemed to take a very long time, but at length they ceased their dance.

"Thank you, Air," I said as the elementals departed. "I am most grateful."

I waited until the last stray winds were before opening my eyes. I stood in the familiar stone circle not far from the community's lodge. The sky was fully dark and the tree canopy prevented me from seeing the moon, but the night felt late. My journey had lasted the entire day.

The lodge was quiet and dark as I approached. Oistin would be in his bedchamber, studying perhaps, for he rarely slept. The front door opened with a soft creak like it always had. The druids here had no reason to lock their doors. I crept along the hallways, knowing which floorboards to avoid.

Lamplight spilled into the hall from Oistin's bedchamber and I reached the door to find him waiting for me. Of course he was. His Sight would have told him I was coming. I felt like a fool for not thinking of this sooner. There had been no need to sneak through the lodge like a thief.

"Master, I need your advice," I said.

"You should not be here."

"Things there are not what you think."

"Only I know what I think."

His calm words gave away little except to one who knew him as well as I did. He was angry. Furious. I could tell by the way his left eye squinted just the tiniest bit as he spoke.

"I've made a terrible mistake and I don't know how to fix it," I said.

"Your mistake was in coming here. You should not have left your post without permission."

I hung my head. "I know, Master, and I'm sorry. But I need—"

"Go back."

His words cut through me. I hadn't anticipated he might refuse to advise me. Oistin was the man I knew best as I grew up. Not quite the father I didn't really remember but my mentor. He was wise and patient, and I had believed he would give me sound advice. After he rebuked me, of course.

"Master, please—"

He held up his hand to stop me.

"Events will happen as they are intended," he said. "You will act your part. Go back to Hearn immediately. If you leave now, you can be back before he notices you are gone."

"Men died today."

"Go now, Arlen. Everything is going to plan."

Later I wondered why I didn't argue longer. Why I didn't try harder to find the words that would make him listen to me. But as I stood in front of Oistin and knew for the first time in my life that he was severely displeased with me, I felt like a whipped dog. I could expect no assistance from him.

I trudged back to the stone circle and again asked the Air to transport me. I didn't need to invoke Eithne's name this time, for the elementals came immediately. Perhaps for her sake they had forgiven my offence, whatever it was. They left me at the stone circle and I started the long walk back to the keep.

30

ARLEN

It was dawn by the time I reached Braen Keep. I spent the walk trying to understand why Oistin refused to advise me. I had never expected he would let me down like that. It felt wrong to be hungry but I was starved after the long walk, so I stopped at the kitchen for some bread and cheese. I had just reached my bedchamber when a boy came trotting down the hallway. The message he conveyed was brief. Hearn expected my attendance in the feast hall tonight.

Another feast so soon? How could folk celebrate when men from both estates died yesterday? How many children amongst both Hearn's and Cullen's people were now fatherless? How many women were widows?

I didn't know if I had the strength to stay here much longer. I was completely unsuited for this position. But it was clear that Oistin wouldn't reassign me. He had withheld information from me, perhaps something that was critical to my presence here. How much of his vision of me with Hearn and the shadowy woman had he kept to himself? I assumed the woman was Derwa, although I didn't know why her identity was concealed in Oistin's vision. Or maybe he lied about that.

The only thing I knew for certain was that Oistin had a reason for wanting me here. He would likely expel me from the community if I gave up my post without permission. Would my family accept me back if that happened? An estate the size of Silver Downs required a large number of folk to farm and look after livestock, and for repairs to fences and walls and roofs. There would be plenty of work for me if I went home — if they allowed me to stay after such a disgrace.

Despite my worries, I slept soundly. I woke late in the afternoon with the feeling that I had figured something out while I slept, but it had already slipped away. I lay in bed for a while, grasping after the threads of my thoughts, but they were elusive and whatever it was I had understood was gone.

I claimed a seat in the feast hall just as servants started bringing around the food. Hearn's table was served first, of course. Derwa was absent tonight and a strange white-haired woman sat in Hearn's own seat. I studied her from the corner of my eye, not wanting to be caught staring. Something about her stirred a memory, but I couldn't place it. I felt like I should know who she was, but I would have sworn I had never seen her before.

Someone passed me a jug of ale and I filled my mug. I sipped it sparingly, although my fellow diners eagerly gulped theirs. If any still had sore heads from last night, they didn't let it slow them. The wild boar was juicy and the vegetables crisp and fresh, but I had little appetite.

A whole roasted swan was delivered to Hearn's table and he ate with gusto while still managing to talk to the white-haired woman at his side. She took bites of her meal from time to time, but seemed more interested in listening to Hearn than in eating.

Most of the diners were well on their way to emptying their plates when a line of servant women came in. Each bore a single clay jug and they positioned themselves around the room in a clearly orchestrated move. At the high table, Hearn put down his knife and stood. Folk quickly fell quiet. A small smile played across the white-haired woman's face as she toyed with her mug.

"My people, we feast tonight to celebrate a great victory." Hearn's voice was loud and he slurred his words a little. "The house of Cullen is no more. His men are dead. His women and children are slaves. His livestock stands in my own fields and his lodge has been burned to the ground."

He paused and the diners roared their approval. I was silent. I would not cheer such words, even if it drew me to his attention. The white-haired woman said nothing, but her smile grew larger. Whatever this was about, it was pleasing to her.

"To celebrate our victory, I present to you the very finest Roman wine," Hearn said.

He gestured towards the servant woman standing beside him. Like the others, she bore a single jug.

"This wine has been imported at great expense, and never have I purchased a finer wine, nor one more costly. Each jar of wine cost me one slave." Hearn paused to let his words sink in. "So drink of this fine wine, my friends, for you will never drink finer."

He sat and the diners roared their approval. The servant woman filled his mug and he held it aloft before draining it. She filled it again, then poured for the white-haired woman.

Twelve women bearing jugs. Twelve prisoners were sold for this wine. Who? Was the woman who shared my mother's name and who feared she would not have access to a midwife one of them? How many of the children were sold?

A servant woman filled my mug, but I only looked at it. I could not bring myself to drink of wine purchased with slaves. Never again would I authorise a battle I shouldn't, regardless of what either Hearn or Oistin expected of me.

31

ARLEN

"Druid, come in."

Hearn barely looked at me as he waved me into his library. As usual, the messenger gave no indication of why he wanted to see me. I clasped my hands behind my back and looked straight at him as I waited in front of his desk. I couldn't let him see that I feared what he might want from me this time. He continued to study the parchment on his desk. Eventually he looked up at me.

"Druid," he said.

I waited.

"Do you know geography?"

"Yes, my lord."

"Tell me about the estate to the south of my holdings."

"It is owned by Fingen and has been held by his family for at least four generations. A substantial estate, roughly half the size of your own."

"And what do you know of Fingen himself?"

"Little, my lord."

"Do you know that for the last few years his sheep have been grazing on my land?"

"I was not aware of that, my lord."

"He, of course, would tell you it's his land. But that's because he's forgotten where the boundary line lies."

Breathe. In. Out. "I see, my lord."

"He needs to learn to graze his sheep on his own property. My men can teach him that."

"You intend to go into battle against him."

I counted to five as I exhaled. My pulse raced and my palms were sweating. Barely more than a sevennight had passed since the feast at which we had been served wine purchased with Cullen's folk.

"I do," Hearn said. "Go interpret the signs. We march in two days."

I bowed and left silently. My thoughts were clear as I made my way outside. I wouldn't authorise his battle unless the signs were in complete agreement. It didn't matter what he threatened me with. He could send me back to Oistin and I would face my master's disapproval if necessary. But I would not falsely authorise another battle.

As I left the keep, something flew past my head, barely missing me. I stumbled back to avoid it. Wings flapped and wind rushed. The raven cawed as it flew higher and disappeared over the top of the keep. That alone was enough of a sign to tell Hearn I couldn't authorise his battle. But I needed to be very certain. I needed multiple signs.

Some distance from the keep, I sat on a low stone wall. Its only purpose, as far as I could tell, was to separate the poorly paved path from the dusty remains of what might once have been a flower bed. I looked up to the sky and waited.

It was an unusually warm day for midwinter, but even so I shivered and wished I had my cloak. The stone beneath me had barely started to warm before a dark shape plummeted from the sky. The hawk snatched something from the ground and flew away. Another unfavourable sign. Still, I cautioned myself to patience and settled more comfortably onto the stone wall.

When I looked up to the sky again, it was no longer clear. An enormous storm cloud rolled in from the south — the direction in which Fingen's estate lay. The cloud grew darker and larger. Thunder rumbled and a fork of lightning shot towards the keep. I had never known the signs to be so clear. Three signs indicating Hearn's battle would be unfavourable. And all three were from Air. Surely there was extra significance in that.

The storm cloud suddenly opened and heavy rain sheeted down. I was drenched before I could get to my feet. The water was so cold, it left me breathless. Puddles formed quickly and the dusty paths turned to mud. I started back towards the keep. I had all the information I needed.

But as I stepped over a particular puddle, it darkened and within it I Saw Hearn. He lay on a funeral pyre, his eyes closed as flames licked his hair. The image lasted only a moment, disappearing so quickly I wondered whether I imagined it. It was, after all, only the second time I had Seen.

I went straight to Hearn's library, soaking wet and leaving a trail of puddles behind me. He didn't comment on my appearance when I arrived in his doorway.

"So, druid?" he said. "Two days, heh?"

"The signs are very clear." I shivered, not just with cold but with the fear of what I was about to do. My teeth chattered and I couldn't feel my hands or feet. "Never have I seen them so clearly indicate that battle is to be avoided."

He stared at me coldly.

"Druid, I thought we understood each other."

"I understand what you want me to say, my lord, but I cannot. If you go to battle in two days, it will go badly."

"I don't accept that," he said. "Try again."

"My lord, there is no other way to interpret the signs. The conditions for battle are most unfavourable."

"Again. I'm still waiting for the correct response."

"You will die. I have Seen it. If you go to battle now, you will end it on a pyre."

"Your approval, druid." He said each word carefully and clearly. "You have one task here. Do it."

"Do you understand what I am saying, my lord? Even if I approve your battle, it will mean your death."

"Druid."

What else could I do? He was determined to go to battle. It hardly mattered whether I authorised it or not. I nodded.

"Let me hear you say it," he said.

"Your battle is authorised." I tried to keep the snarl from my voice but wasn't entirely successful. "And it will mean your death."

"We will discuss your insolence later. After my men return victorious."

He nodded towards the doorway, dismissing me without another word. I walked out, leaving puddles in my wake.

32

AGATA

"Agata!"

Titania's screech echoed through the palace. I was sitting at a window, staring out at nothing while I brooded. For the first time in my life, I found myself discontent. But when Titania called, I jumped up.

"Where is she?" I asked the first person I encountered, a mortal slave.

The woman looked at me dumbly.

"The queen," I hissed. "Where is she?"

The woman pointed down the hallway behind her.

"I was going in that direction anyway."

There was no point wasting time with a mortal. She was either too stupid to speak or too afraid. And she was obviously a full mortal. Not like me. I at least had some fey blood in me.

Usually if I was in a hurry, the palace hallways would be certain to be tricky, but today they led me straight to Titania's sitting room. I stopped to compose myself as I reached the final hallway, smoothening my hair and straightening my gown. I took a deep breath and walked briskly to her door. The guards admitted me immediately.

"Agata, explain something to me."

Titania perched on the edge of a deep red daybed. Her forest green skirts were rumpled, as if she had sat up suddenly, and she appeared to have one bare foot. Given Titania never let herself be seen as anything less than supremely elegant, this was not a good sign.

"My lady?"

I dropped into a deep curtsey, trying to keep my movements graceful. When she was in this sort of mood, she would pounce on the slightest inelegance from me. I kept my head bowed and my eyes averted, and pretended I didn't see the green slipper lying on its side.

"What have you learned about the man who wears your face?" she demanded.

Her words shocked me so much that I looked straight at her. Her face was white and her mouth pinched.

"My lady?"

"Don't *my lady* me," she snapped. "You're not a fool, so don't act like one. Tell me who he is."

"My brother." It was pointless to pretend I didn't know who she meant. "He was born shortly after me."

"The mortal woman bore a second child?" Her voice rose in both pitch and volume with every word.

"So it seems." I bit off the instinctive *my lady* that wanted to come out of my mouth.

"How do you know this?"

I hesitated, but she would know if I lied.

"I met him again."

"Where?"

"Here in the fey realm."

"When?"

"Recently."

"How did he get here?"

"I don't know. I was walking in the woods and stumbled across him."

"And you spoke to him." Her voice was flat.

"Of course I did. He has my face. Wouldn't you speak to someone who looked just like you?"

"Nobody looks like me."

"You know what I mean," I muttered. It was overly warm in here and the air was so heavy with Titania's floral perfume that my head ached.

"What did he tell you?"

"He said that my—" My mother, I almost said. "He wanted me to go with him to meet the mortal woman who bore me."

Titania smiled, a tight, bitter smile that didn't mean she was amused.

"She barely got to hear you squawk before I took you."

"Why did you take me?"

"A punishment." Her voice was distant, as if her mind was elsewhere. "She took someone from my realm. So I took someone from her."

"You mean my father."

"He's only half fey, you know."

"Did he fall in love with her?" All my life I had been taught that a fey never loved a mortal, or anyone else for that matter. Love simply wasn't in our nature.

She shrugged. "Mortals can be persistent. She may have convinced him he loved her. He will come crawling back someday, begging forgiveness, wanting to live amongst us again. When she gets old and haggard and wrinkled, he'll realise what a mistake he made."

"He will age, too, won't he? If he stays there?"

"Slowly. Much more slowly than her. She will be old and grey while he is still in his prime."

"He must love her, if he knew all that and still went with her."

"Love is a facade." Titania glared at me. "It is a construct of mortals used to justify their pathetic existence. We have no need of love." She changed topics abruptly. "The man. Your brother. Why did I not See him earlier?"

"I don't know. I barely talked to him. I know nothing about him."

"I Saw your birth. I should have Seen his also. He has been shielded from the Sight somehow, just like the mortal woman, but whatever was hiding him is broken now."

"What are you going to do?"

I felt a sudden surge of protectiveness towards him. We shared a womb if he had told me the truth. That should mean something. Abruptly I realised what a mortal thought that was. No true fey would feel a responsibility for someone just because they were born of the same blood.

Titania gave me that tight smile again, the one that wasn't really a smile.

"I haven't decided yet," she said. "Go now. We are finished talking."

I curtseyed and left at a sedate pace, my heart hammering. Titania was unpredictable except in the fact that she never forgave a grudge. But I couldn't guess whether it would be Arlen she would punish or the mortal woman who bore us. Eithne, he called her. My mother. I wondered whether I should try to warn either of them.

33

AGATA

My thoughts lingered on the idea of warning Arlen, even though he was a mortal. No, I realised. That wasn't quite right. He was no more and no less mortal than me. If we had shared a womb, then he, too, was part fey. We were connected in some strange way I didn't understand. How else could I have found him the first time I'd ventured into the mortal realm, without knowing who he was or where he would be?

After several days of vacillation, I resolved to try. *If* I found him, I would warn him. I was letting my mortal blood influence me to an unreasonable extent, but as I slipped through the portal, I knew only that I had to warn him.

The frigid air of the mortal realm hit me with a fierce blow. The sun was high in the sky, although today it barely warmed me. A few scattered clouds were bowled along by the wind. Perhaps I would stay here all day and see for myself the way the sun disappeared at night and how the moon and stars revealed themselves.

Which way to go? There was no point in going to the sad town I visited previously. They didn't know Arlen there. I chose another direction at random and began to run. The grass crunched under my slippers and the wind left my cheeks tight and chafed.

After some time, I reached a lodge. It was large and looked well made, with many people busy at various tasks outside, although I couldn't identify what most of them were doing. Some walked around, others stacked things in great heaps. Swords and boxes and other objects I didn't recognise. Some folk were clustered in a group, clutching each other and crying. Everyone else seemed to ignore them. I approached a man who carried a sack that clinked and rattled as he walked.

"Do you know Arlen?" I asked.

He turned towards me, and it was only as he dropped the sack that I noticed the dark red splatters that covered him. Suddenly uncomfortable, I stepped back away from him, but he seized my arm.

"What are you doing here?" he demanded, shaking me. "Why aren't you with the others?"

"I'm looking for Arlen." My heart pounded. Something was very wrong here.

He dragged me with him as he walked, his fingers digging painfully into my arm.

"Stop that," I said. "You're hurting me."

He didn't respond and didn't loosen his grip either.

"I said stop that," I shouted, trying to wrench my arm out of his grip. "I am the daughter of Titania, queen of the fey, and I demand you unhand me immediately."

"Oh, daughter of the queen of the fey, hey?" he asked with a snigger. "Well, princess, if you know what's good for you, you'll shut up and do as you're told."

He shoved me towards the group that was huddled together. I landed on my hands and knees.

"Watch her properly this time," he said to a man standing nearby. "I found her wandering through the courtyard."

My knees throbbed, the skin torn and bleeding. My palms stung and my skirt had a hole at the knee. I sniffed and my eyes filled with tears which I quickly blinked away. Fey did not cry.

The man who had been instructed to watch me glowered.

"How did you sneak off?" he asked.

I raised myself up, pretending a dignity I didn't feel.

"You have no right to treat me like this," I said.

He stepped towards me and slapped me across the face. My cheek felt like it exploded. I stumbled, pushed backwards by the force of his blow, and raised my shaky hand to my cheek.

"Keep your mouth shut," he growled. "Next time I hear your voice, that pretty throat will be meeting my sword."

I glanced down to the weapon at his waist and noted the redness smeared on the hilt. Something dark and sticky wound through his hair. I swallowed hard.

The mortals I was deposited amongst were mostly young women and children. They were pale-faced and sad-eyed as they huddled together. I wanted to ask what was happening, but was too afraid that the man might keep his promise about letting my throat meet his sword. I had a horrible feeling the red splatters might be mortal blood, and I tried to forget the seeping redness I had spied on my own knees.

I studied my surroundings, trying to make sense of the situation. It seemed that things from within the lodge were being brought out and added to the pile of crates and weapons. Other men loaded items from the pile into a cart hitched to an ox, although a few items were surreptitiously slipped into belts or pockets. Not twenty paces from me a woman lay in a pool of blood. She stared sightlessly up at the sky, her throat gaping open. I swallowed hard and wished I hadn't seen her.

Other men crowded around us now and said we should start walking, keep together, don't cause any trouble. The man who threatened to cut my throat looked at me when they said that. They herded us through the gates and marched us along a road. From time to time someone would start sobbing, but others quickly shushed them. I desperately wanted to ask where we were going and whether I would be allowed to go home once we got there, but I didn't dare speak.

We walked long enough that I was able to see the sun move across the sky. Perhaps I would see the moon and the stars after all. Eventually we reached the walls of a town and I recognised it as the place where I searched for Arlen. People rushed into their lodges when they saw us coming. Doors slammed and shutters were swiftly closed.

We reached another wall with a gate. Inside was a very large lodge. It was perhaps as big as Titania's palace, but not nearly as fine. The sun was almost gone by now and the light had turned murky. Shadows stretched across the courtyard. Perhaps Sumerled had actually told the truth when he said the sun disappeared from the sky at night.

The men ushered us into the lodge, along a long corridor and down steep stone steps which were only dimly lit with lamps. The air was cold and smelled foul. A woman ahead of me slipped and fell. She cried out and when she got to her feet, her arm hung wrongly. Nobody offered to help her.

We reached the bottom and were ushered into small chambers in groups of five or six. I was sent to a chamber at the far end where the flickering lamplight barely penetrated the darkness. The floor was slippery and the air felt damp. I smelled mould and moss and dankness. There was no furniture.

"Where am I to sit?" I protested as the sturdy wooden door closed behind me. I received no response.

I couldn't see the other women in my chamber clearly enough to judge their ages, although I had noticed before the door closed that one of them had a belly swollen with child. Two others eased her down to the floor. I sat with them and found the damp stones was covered in a slimy growth. I got to my feet, but the back of my skirt was already wet through.

"You may as well get used to it," the woman who was with child said. "This is probably preferable to whatever they will do with us next."

"Why were you in the courtyard?" one of the others asked me. "You aren't from Fingen's lodge."

"I was looking for someone," I said.

"It was a stupid thing to do, to let yourself be seen," she said. "You could have hidden and waited until they left. They had found enough of us to be satisfied."

"What is happening?" I asked. "I don't understand."

"War," someone said. "When your men lose, we all lose."

"I don't know what that means."

"Even if you are lucky enough to have never seen the results of war before, surely you know what happens."

"There is no war where I come from," I said.

She laughed as if she didn't believe me.

"Well, aren't you a special one. Let me enlighten you, then, sweet thing. When your men lose the battle, the victor takes all. His lodge, his animals, his people. They slaughter the folk they don't want, but those are the lucky ones. The rest are either given to the victor's men as spoils of war or sold into slavery."

"You could go either way," one of the others said.

"Aye," agreed the first woman. "You're pretty and young enough to fetch a nice price in the slave markets. But if you've caught the eye of one of the men, he could ask for you. Might be a good thing, might not. Depends on whether your new master has any kindness about him. But if you have any notions of your body being your own, you'd better get those out of your head right now. Your body belongs to the victor and he'll grant it where he chooses."

A horrifying truth dawned on me.

"I'm a prisoner?" I whispered. "I can't be a prisoner. I'm daughter to the queen of the fey."

"I wouldn't keep saying that if I was you," she said. "If they think you're not right in the head, you'll be sent straight to the slave markets. Nobody wants a halfwit slave, even one as pretty as you."

I sucked in a breath. "Titania will come looking for me and they will feel her wrath when she does."

But secretly I wasn't so sure. Time passed differently in the two realms. Months, or even years, might pass here before Titania noticed my absence. And would she bother to search for me, or would she assume I had returned to my mortal family? Sumerled would come, I thought with a rush of relief. He would notice I wasn't there. I just had to endure it until then.

I waited. My stomach growled and my bladder needed to be

emptied. Had I been here long enough for the moon and stars to appear yet? They might be out there in the sky even now while I was stuck underground in this nasty, damp chamber.

There was movement out in the hallway. Doors opened with a squeal. A conversation in male voices. Eventually the door of my chamber opened. Lamplight flooded in, burning my eyes.

"One with child," a man said. "A sevennight or so out."

"The market," another man said. "She'll be useless until the child is born and for some time afterwards."

"An old woman," someone said.

"How strong does she look?"

"Got some reasonable life in her yet. Might make a decent field worker."

"Send her to market."

"There's a pretty one here, but she looks like trouble."

The lamp was held right in my face. I squinted, eyes watering, and glared back.

"Stand up, girl," one of the men said.

When I didn't move, someone reached out of the light and grabbed my arms. He hauled me to my feet.

"He means you," he said. "Stand up now."

My legs were almost numb after sitting on the cold, wet stone for so long and I would have fallen if he hadn't been holding me. Still I held my head high and shook off his hands as soon as I thought I could stand by myself.

"Says she's a fey princess," someone said with a laugh.

"I am the daughter of Titania," I said. "And you will regret your insolence when she comes looking for me."

They laughed.

"There's one or two of the men who would like to keep her," one said.

"Too feisty," said the man who seemed to be in charge. "One like that won't be tamed easily. She'll fetch a good price, though, provided you can stop her from talking until the deal's done. It's the market for her."

They left, taking the light with them. The door slammed and a bolt shot home. Once again we were left in darkness. It was a long time before anyone spoke.

"That's what you get for telling such tales," one of the women said softly. "You made yourself look like trouble and see where it got you."

"What do you mean?" I asked.

"They're sending you to the slave markets, girl," the old woman said and her voice was kinder than the other. "You'll be auctioned off. Sold. You'll be a slave for the rest of your life."

"They would do that?" No wonder the fey thought so little of mortals. If they would do this to their own kind, what would they stop at?

"All you can do is hope that whoever buys you is not too unkind."

"What will happen to you?" I asked the two woman who weren't destined for the slave market.

"We'll be given to Hearn's men," one said. "The ones he wants to reward."

"What if nobody wants you?"

"There will always be someone who'll take a woman that's being offered for free," she said.

My eyes had adjusted enough that I could more or less make out her features. She was probably almost at the end of her childbearing years, with a haggard face and stringy hair.

"Doesn't matter what she looks like or how old she is," she continued. "All that matters is there's nobody left to care about her. Because if nobody cares, you can use her up and kill her when you're done. A quick death is the best we can hope for."

I kept my mouth shut after that and hoped Sumerled would hurry.

34

ARLEN

I watched from my bedchamber window as Hearn and his men returned from the battle with Fingen. Their shoulders drooped and there were few smiles or calls of bravado. They brought a group of women and children and a wagon piled so high that its contents were in danger of spilling. Hearn slumped next to the driver.

As soon as the cart stopped, men rushed forward to help Hearn down. He seemed unable to stand unaided, but they held him up. A cloak draped around his shoulders obscured his injuries. He should have believed me when I said this battle would mean his death.

Several hours passed before he sent a messenger boy for me. When I reached Hearn's bedchamber, the only other person there was a woman stoking the fire, although the air was already smoky. It reeked of herbs and not all of them were for healing. Hearn lay in his bed, sweating and pale.

"Druid," he spat. "We won the battle."

"So I hear, my lord."

"You said we would lose."

"Actually, my lord, I said you would lose, not your men."

He glowered, but it seemed he had already expended his remaining energy. He raised one trembling hand to touch his belly.

"Took a sword to the guts. Healer says it missed the organs, but it's already turning putrid. Nothing else she can do for me."

I didn't reply. What could I say other than to remind him I had warned him?

"Go," he said and turned his face away. "I don't want to see you again."

I bowed and departed. There was nothing left to say. My king was dying and I couldn't summon even the smallest amount of sorrow. Before I reached my bedchamber, a serving girl approached.

"Master druid," she said. "The queen wishes to speak to you. She is in her sitting room."

I nodded my thanks and she scurried away.

Derwa was alone when I reached the room she had recently started using as her sitting room. I kept meaning to ask why she had abandoned the previous room, for it was larger and nicer.

"Come," she called when I knocked on the closed door.

I slipped in, leaving the door ajar so nobody would think anything improper.

"You have been to see him?" she asked.

Her face was composed, if pale, and her hands twisted together in her lap.

"I have," I said.

"How is he? Tell me truly, for nobody has told me anything and I will not go to him unless he calls for me."

"He is dying. He was stabbed in the belly and the wound is putrefying. He might live another couple of days yet, but he faces a painful death."

"He said you authorised the battle."

It wasn't a question, but I knew she wanted me to deny it.

"I did," I said. "He left me with no choice. I told him this battle would mean his death, but he refused to hear me."

"Have you Seen what will become of me?" Derwa stared down at her hands as she asked.

"I haven't. I'm sorry."

"Brennus... resents me." Her voice was little more than a whisper.

I wished I had some reassurance to offer her, but it would be improper for me to make her any promises. Not while her husband still lived.

"You could leave," I said. "Disappear in the night. There is a stone circle a few hours walk away. I can help you travel through the stones."

"I never thought it would come to this when I first came here." Derwa gave me a small, sad smile. "I thought the people would respect me. That I would have time to earn their trust, their love. I could have done much for them had they let me. But they've always hated me. Because I'm different. Because I look strange."

"You are beautiful to me." The words were out of my mouth before I could think. The soft smile that spread across her face stopped me from apologising for my inappropriateness. In that moment, she truly was beautiful.

"Will you send me word if you hear anything?" I asked. "If there is any hint you might be in danger, you should leave immediately. Maybe you should even go now. Don't wait—" I stopped, but she said it for me.

"Don't wait for my husband to die? Flee while he lies waiting for death?"

"It sounds callous, but you need to think about your safety."

She shook her head. "I can't. He is still my husband and I must stay until he dies. He might want to see me."

"He doesn't deserve loyalty from you."

"Regardless, this is the man my father gave me to. I stood up in front of both our families and vowed to be faithful to him. Running away while he is dying hardly demonstrates my faithfulness."

"He doesn't deserve you. He never has."

"Oh, Arlen, things might have been so different. If Hearn was a different man. If I was a different woman. If—" Her voice dropped to a whisper. "If I had met you at a different time. But things are what they are and I must stay until he dies."

"I understand."

"I will send word if I hear anything," she said. "In the meantime, the men brought back prisoners. Folk of Fingen's household. You might perhaps go speak with them. See if they need anything, medical treatment particularly. There's little else I can do for them."

"You could go see them yourself."

"Hearn would think I was trying to undermine him."

"I'll go now, then."

Dread filled me as I descended to the cells. The last time I spoke to Hearn's prisoners, some were sold to buy jars of wine. I still didn't know who. The guard stared me down as I approached.

"What do you want?" he asked. "I don't have instructions to let anyone in."

"The queen sent me to check whether any of the prisoners need medical care."

"They don't."

"She has bid me to view them myself."

He glared for a good while, but at length he shrugged.

"If Hearn hears of this, I'll tell him you insisted," he said.

"You can tell him the queen insisted."

"Go on, then."

"Can I take the lamp?"

He snorted and turned away from me.

"Should have brought a light with you if you wanted one."

I didn't waste time arguing. He might decide he wanted Hearn's approval after all if I lingered. I approached the first cell and peered through the bars in the opening set into the door. The light from the guard's station behind me meant I could see nothing inside the dark cell.

"Hello," I said. "Is anyone injured?"

Silence greeted me. I could smell the sweat of the folk in there and heard the little noises they made as they moved, but although I repeated my question twice, nobody answered. I moved on to the next cell.

Again I asked if anyone was injured, and again nobody responded. The last prisoners were all too willing to speak, to tell me their names and their positions. I went to each door and repeated my question several times. It was only when I reached the final door that anyone answered me.

"There is a woman in here with a broken arm," an indignant voice replied. "And I demand to be let out immediately. Titania will punish everyone here when she discovers how I have been treated."

"Agata?" I asked. "Is that you?"

"Who's that?" came her reply. "How do you know my name?"

"It's Arlen. Your brother."

Her face appeared at the opening.

"Why are you here?" she asked.

"I live here. I advise the king."

"Bring this king to me," she said. "So I can demand he release me immediately."

"I can't," I said.

What did she know of the world if she thought a prisoner could demand the king be brought to her cell?

"Why not?" she asked.

"Do you understand you are a prisoner?"

"Do these mortals not fear Titania's wrath?"

"They fear only the king's wrath."

"Then do something. Go talk to him. Tell him— *Ask* him to let me out."

"I can try," I said. "But I doubt he will. Be patient. The situation will improve soon."

I couldn't tell her Hearn was dying, not with so many ears listening.

"The only way it will improve is if I am released," she said. "And don't forget the woman here who needs a healer."

"I'll ask for one to be sent down." That would give me a reason to return to Hearn's bedchamber and it might afford an opportunity to ask for Agata's release. "I'll come back after I've spoken to Hearn."

"Who?"

"The king," I said, tiredly. Really, did she know *nothing*?

"Thank you." It sounded as if these were not words she was accustomed to saying.

I left, hoping Eithne never heard I had found my missing sister and left her locked in a dark cell. But the guard would only release her at Hearn's order. Without his approval, I could do nothing.

Hearn's bedchamber was just as dim and smoky as before, only now two old women were there. Healers, perhaps. One of them cocked her head questioningly at me.

"May I speak with him?" I asked. "I have come from visiting the prisoners."

She shrugged and turned back to Hearn.

"You may speak, but I doubt he will hear you," she said.

Hearn was flushed and his chest was soaked with sweat as he tossed restlessly.

"He is in great pain," the elder of the two said. "We've given him something to make him sleep."

"The queen asked me to look in on the prisoners," I said. "There is one who needs a healer."

"The folk from Fingen's estate?" she asked. "Sick or injured?"

"She has a broken arm. Is there someone who can authorise a healer to attend her?"

The two women looked at each other and the elder nodded.

"I will go," she said. "I need no authorisation when the only crime a person has committed is belonging to the wrong man."

"She is in the cell furthest from the guard's station," I said.

It was only after she left that I wondered whether I should have warned her about Agata.

35

ARLEN

I woke to the jangle of bells. I figured they must be announcing Hearn's death, so I dressed and went straight to Derwa's sitting room. Even though the first golden rays of sunlight were only just peeking over the horizon, I figured she would be awake. It was only as I knocked that I wondered whether I shouldn't have come. I didn't let myself think about the fact that she was no longer someone else's wife.

Derwa's soft voice bade me enter. She wore the same gown as yesterday although now she had a shawl wrapped around her shoulders. The fire had long died and the air was chilly. I went straight to the hearth to light the fire.

"Have you been here all night?" I asked.

"I didn't know where else to go," she said. "I couldn't go to my bedchamber. I needed to be somewhere that didn't make me think of him."

I let her words flow past me, not letting myself linger on thoughts of Hearn visiting her bedchamber. As the fire took hold, I sat beside Derwa and we watched the flickering flames in silence.

"What will become of me now?" she asked. "I can't claim the throne. Hearn's chief advisors despise me. They would never allow it.

The people have no respect for me anyway and would not support me. Brennus will need a regent until he comes of age, but I doubt the advisors will choose me." She clasped her hands in her lap and closed her eyes for a moment. "Am I a terrible person, Arlen? My husband has just died and all I can think about is myself."

"I would think it strange if you didn't think about yourself in such a situation," I said. "Surely the queen would be expected to act as regent."

"Brennus hates me even more than the advisors do. I wouldn't mind if they sent me back to my father, but I fear Brennus will seek revenge for all the slights he has imagined over the years."

"You should leave. Now. Just slip away quietly and disappear. You know I'll help you."

Derwa sighed heavily. Her knuckles were white and she seemed to notice how tightly she clenched her fists because she relaxed her fingers.

"Truth be told, I've considered it many times over the last day," she said. "What does that say about me that I look for the first chance to run away?"

"These are not your people. They're Hearn's people."

"They have never accepted me. If they had, if they viewed me as their queen, I would stay, truly. I would stay if they were mine. But they are not." She leaned back and looked at me with shadowed eyes. "I am so tired, Arlen. Tired of trying to make people see me as I am, not as they want to. Tired of pretending I don't hear the vicious lies they spread about me. Tired of being in this place that I hate. I once heard a woman say I shouldn't be allowed to look at a newborn babe in case I turned it ugly."

"Leave," I said again. "Don't wait any longer."

"Where would I go? Back to my father? That is the first place Brennus would look for me. If he demanded my return, my father would have to comply."

"Do you have other relatives? A married sister you could go to?"

"I don't know where my sister is. Hearn didn't let me correspond with my family. I tried, twice, to send messages. He caught me both times. The first time he merely threatened me. The second... he ensured I would never try again."

I couldn't tell her I was glad he was dead.

"I could take you to Silver Downs," I said. "My family's home. They would never turn away someone in need. I can't take you all the way through the stones, though, as it is more than a day's walk from the ones nearest to Silver Downs. We would need some horses or a cart and oxen."

"It is kind of you to offer."

"We could go now, but it might be best to wait for cover of darkness. And—"

I remembered Agata. How could I leave her behind?

"And?" she prompted.

"I visited the prisoners as you asked." My words came slowly and she waited patiently, her gaze never leaving my face. My sister is among them."

"Agata?"

"You remember her name."

"Of course I remember. How could I not? Such a strange tale. But how is your sister there? Why is she with Fingen's folk?"

"Somehow she got mixed up with them. I don't know the full story, but she's here and extremely indignant. I don't think she fully understands she is a prisoner."

"Has she been that sheltered in the fey realm?"

"She seems to think Titania will rescue her."

"Do you think that likely?"

"I don't know what their relationship is. She lived with Titania for more than twenty summers. They might well be as close as mother and daughter."

"Has she been treated well here?" Derwa didn't look at me as she asked, as if she couldn't bear to hear the answer.

"She has not been harmed as far as I know," I said. "I'm sure she would have told me loudly and in great detail if she had. She was quick to tell me of a woman with a broken arm. I sent a healer to her."

Derwa nodded, although she hardly seemed to be listening anymore.

"Arlen, I wish there was a way I could free your sister. I am tempted to go down there and demand her release. If I could be sure the guards would obey me, I would do it."

"We both know you can't do that."

"You will need to petition Brennus to release her. As soon as he claims the throne."

"I intend to. I just hope she doesn't draw too much attention to herself in the meantime."

"Oh, Arlen. I don't know what to say."

"I've been trying to come up with a plan," I said. "I could get her away from here if I could just get her out of the cell."

"We'll think of something," she said. "She's safe enough where she is for now. I don't know whether anyone has thought to send food down to the cells. I'll check. That's probably all I can do for her, though."

"I'll go talk to her again later. She might have calmed down by then. If I can convince her to keep quiet, things will probably be easier for her."

"Is she pretty?" Derwa's voice was wistful.

"It's hard for me to answer that since she has the same face as me."

She flashed me a rare grin and I revelled in it.

"Of course," she said. "I'm sure she is very pretty. She would do well to not draw attention to herself. Don't worry, Arlen. We will find a way to save her."

"I should leave you. You probably have things to do to prepare for Hearn's funeral. Do you need anything?"

She sighed. "Just a friend from time to time."

"You have that. Send for me if you need me."

Shortly after I left Derwa, I encountered Brennus and Girec running down the hallway. Brennus was in the lead and the younger boy gamely tried to keep up with him. They came skidding to a stop in front of me. Brennus looked me up and down with a sneer.

"I hear your sister is in the cells, druid," he said.

I made myself breathe normally and waited for him to continue.

"She's being sent to the slave market," he said.

Girec fidgeted, clearly uncomfortable with the conversation. I looked Brennus in the eyes and waited.

"It's a shame," he said. "She's a pretty one."

"You've met her?" The words were out of my mouth before I could stop myself.

"I inspected the prisoners. I made sure the guard pointed out your sister. She's feisty. Could be fun. I'll be king pretty soon and there will be changes around here when that happens. Your sister, for one. She won't be going to market."

Breathe. He wasn't done yet. He was enjoying himself too much.

"I'm going to keep her for myself," he said. "Until I get bored of her. How do you like that, druid?"

I had never felt the urge to punch someone before. Had never understood why men fought. But now I did. I wanted to tighten my hand into a fist and punch him in the face. I forced my fingers to relax. Then I walked away.

"Your insolence will be punished, druid," Brennus called after me. "Just wait until I'm king."

Long after I left, Brennus's words still rang in my ears. *I'm going to keep her for myself. Until I get bored of her.* I mostly dismissed his threat to me. It was well established that druids could not be subjected to retribution and I had my ability to make myself unseen. I could slip away quietly if I needed to. But Agata was in more danger than I had realised.

36

ARLEN

I paced my bedchamber, my mind working furiously. How long would the chief advisors take to make a decision about the throne? I doubted any regent would be able to control Brennus, but the right person might influence him. Hearn's main fault was ignorance. But Brennus was both clever and cruel. He would be a callous king, and I had no doubt he would be ruthless in ensuring he secured the throne. He was, after all, Hearn's chosen heir.

Once again, I longed for Oistin to advise me. But it seemed he had his own plans and — I was ashamed to admit it even to myself — I doubted his motives. When he sent me here, Oistin spoke of how he had Seen me at Hearn's side, but clearly there were other factors at play. Factors which perhaps related more to Oistin's own ambitions than the good of the people. So if Oistin would not advise me, who else could I turn to?

I remembered the letter from Uncle Fiachra, which I never responded to, and retrieved it from the drawer where I put it for safe keeping. As I re-read it, a chill swept over me and I realised what had been in front of me all this time.

The letter held a warning about Uncle Diarmuid's muse who Fiachra thought might follow me here. I had seen a strange woman around the keep in recent days. The white-haired woman. How could I have forgotten her? Could this be the muse Fiachra searched for? He described her well and I should have noticed when a woman matching his description arrived. Yet I hadn't. I suspected I had seen her, perhaps on several occasions, but I seemed to keep forgetting. Perhaps she had charmed me to forget.

I found a servant boy who seemed to be doing nothing much and begged some parchment and ink from him, which he quickly located. I took the items back to my bedchamber and sat down to write to Fiachra. *Uncle Fiachra*, I wrote.

> *I apologise for the tardiness of my reply. I received your message some time ago, but events here have been such that I neglected to respond. I am also ashamed to admit that I believe the woman you seek is here. It has taken me until today to realise.*
>
> *Hearn died early this morning from a battle wound. I Saw that this battle would mean his death, but he didn't believe me. It shames me to admit I authorised the battle anyway. I will not give my excuses for such action, but I know I am unfit for this role.*
>
> *It is difficult to recall when I first saw the woman you seek. I think she may have placed a charm on me, for I keep forgetting I have seen her. I don't know why I have suddenly remembered her now and I can't be sure I won't forget again, so I am writing this letter as quickly as I can.*
>
> *I believe I first saw her in the great hall, where I have on occasion been invited to dine. At some time recently — perhaps ten nights ago — a stranger dined at Hearn's table. In fact, she sat in his own chair and he sat in the queen's place. The queen herself did not attend. The woman is slender of frame with long white hair and fair skin.*
>
> *Hearn did not seem bothered that she sat in his place, a fact which surprises me greatly now I think on it. If anyone else noted her presence or thought anything strange of it, I heard no comments. Truly, now that I consider it, the situation was most unusual. Yet at the time I thought there was nothing odd in what I saw.*
>
> *Your letter alluded to the fact that she had charmed folk in her previous foray into the real world and it seems clear she has done this here, too. There*

has been an increase in violence lately and I suspect she may be the cause. As to why I have suddenly remembered her, I can only guess. Perhaps Hearn's death has somehow interfered in her magic.

Uncle, I find myself in sore need of advice. It is expected that Hearn's foster son, Brennus, will claim the throne in the coming days. Brennus is a child yet and is neither ready, nor fit, to rule. Agata is here also and will be in great danger if Brennus becomes king. If you can suggest any remedy for this situation, I beg you to send me a message immediately.

I expect that by the time you receive this, Brennus will be king and I will have been sent back to the druid community. Please be wary of sending messages there as I no longer fully trust certain people.

There is someone here who needs a place of sanctuary. Someone dear to me. I hope that if a person were to arrive at Silver Downs and say I had sent them, the family there would offer them all aid.

Your nephew, Arlen

I hesitated before I added the final words: *Druid, of Braen Keep.*

As soon as the ink dried, I rolled up the parchment and returned to Derwa's sitting room. She now wore a clean gown and her hair was damp. Coals still burned in the hearth, keeping the room warm, and a tray on a low table bore the remnants of a meal. I felt a rush of relief at knowing she no longer wore yesterday's clothes or sat in a cold room.

"I need to send a message," I said. "It is somewhat urgent."

"Of course," she said. "I will have a messenger sent."

I hesitated to hand her the scroll.

"I don't have any wax," I said.

She went to a shelf holding several boxes and retrieved a small cube.

"You have no seal either, I presume?" she asked.

I flushed a little.

"I've rarely had reason to send messages, and when I did, I always used Oistin's seal."

"Use mine."

She handed me a small ring. I stared down at it in surprise.

"You use a raven for your emblem?" I asked.

"It is my family's symbol," she said. "Why does that disturb you?"

"It's just… surprising."

Fiachra mentioned a raven. It seemed that two women who claimed that bird for their symbol now resided here.

I melted a small piece of wax and pressed Derwa's seal into it. She promised a messenger would leave tonight with my letter. Likely there would be many messengers leaving the keep that night.

The next thing I needed to do was explain to Agata why she couldn't be released yet.

37

AGATA

I had been in this horrid dark chamber for so long that my stomach grumbled fiercely. At least a healer had come to see Wenda, the woman whose arm was broken. The healer splinted Wenda's arm and gave her willow bark tea to ease the pain. I tried to explain I needed to be released immediately, but the healer barely deigned to even look at me.

Dampness seeped from under the stones that lined the floor. It crept through the thin fabric of my gown and into my bones. I sat with my legs tucked up to my chest and my arms wrapped around them, but still the warmth leeched from my body. I didn't even notice the foul odour anymore. Time passed, or maybe it didn't, and I grew colder and colder. I could barely feel my toes anymore. I would freeze to death before I found anyone with enough sense to release me. I didn't even look up as a shadow passed in front of the opening set in the door until I heard Arlen's voice.

"Agata," he said softly.

"I'm here." I scrambled to my feet. The other women didn't move. Perhaps they slept. "Have you come to release me?"

"I can't. The king needs to approve your release."

"Then go talk to him. Tell him he must do it at once."

"I can't. He's dead."

"So who can let me out? There must be someone."

"Right now, no," he said. "I'm sorry, but you need to wait a little longer. I will petition to have you released as soon as the matter of the succession is finalised."

"How long will that take?"

"I don't know. Maybe a couple of days for decisions to be made. Another few days after that to get an audience with the new king. There will be many people jostling for his attention and he might not have time to talk to me immediately."

"Is there nobody else who can release me?" I couldn't stay in here for days and days. I'd die. I was cold and damp and miserable. "There must be something else you can do."

"Only the king can authorise the release of prisoners."

"But I'm not supposed to be a prisoner."

Arlen answered every argument with another apology, and slowly I came to understand he really believed there was nothing else he could do.

"Could I at least have a blanket?" I asked.

"I'll speak to the queen about it. Agata, tell me, why are you here? What were you doing in the mortal realm?"

One of the sleeping women stirred. Someone muttered. I lowered my voice so as not to disturb anyone.

"I came to find you," I said.

"Why?"

How much should I tell him? I barely knew him, even if we did share a face.

"Things have been bad for me lately," I said. "I didn't know I was mortal. It seems everyone else knew, or at least they suspected. I confronted Titania and she didn't even try to deny it. She's proud she stole me away. And now everybody knows and they're treating me horribly. I wanted to find out where I came from. Who is my mother? And why was Titania trying to punish her?"

"Our mother fell in love with a half fey named Kalen," Arlen said. "When he stopped coming to see her in the mortal world, she went to the fey realm in search of him. Titania imprisoned her, but she escaped. She found Kalen and he followed her back to our world."

"But why is Titania still so mad about it? That was a long time ago. Who is he to her?"

"Her husband's son, borne to a mortal woman."

"My father is Oberon's son? Titania's husband is my grandfather?"

Arlen was silent as I absorbed this revelation.

"So my father is a half fey who chose to leave," I said. "Does Oberon have any other half fey sons I should know about?"

Arlen hesitated.

"He hasn't told you?" he asked, at last.

"Who? What?"

"Sumerled."

It all fell into place. This was why Sumerled was shunned by the other fey. Why he made friends with me.

"I'm going to kill him," I said. "He's no more fey than I am, and he was the one who told everyone I'm only part fey."

"He's a friend of yours, isn't he?"

"He was, but I never suspected he might be part mortal. He can control his appearance like the fey always can."

"You can't?"

"No. Or at least I don't think so. It seems to be something fey instinctively know how to do."

"Maybe one who is part fey gets a different mix of abilities. There might be something you can do that he can't."

"Maybe." It was an interesting thought. "But I'm still going to kill him, just as soon as I get out of here."

"I'll petition to have you released as soon as I can."

"I wish Sumerled was here," I said. "I would kill him right now."

38

IDA

Hearn is dead. I discover this when I ask a servant woman the reason for the ringing bells. It seems rather early to make so much noise, but apparently it is customary when the king dies. I have not seen Hearn since he rode out to battle against Fingen, although I have heard he returned injured. I am hardly surprised as mortal bodies are weak and delicate. It surprises me they live as long as they do.

My boy told a tale once about the death of a king. His wife, the queen, claimed his throne and ruled for many years. She even led her people into battle. As I wander through the keep, I overhear comments about Brennus becoming king. He is but a boy, though, and not old enough to lead men to war. But it seems there are no other suitable candidates. I feel generous today. Perhaps I should help them by taking the throne myself.

I ponder the boy's tales, but none give any instruction on exactly how to claim a throne. It seems that when the king dies, someone simply sits on his throne and it then belongs to him. The closest Hearn has to a throne is the big chair in his audience hall. When he sits there, people come to stand in front of him and complain. He makes decisions and sends them away.

The audience hall is empty when I arrive. I climb the five steps to the dais and seat myself in Hearn's chair. It is overlarge and padded with soft cushions. I understand why he likes this spot, for I am raised up over the room. I can see everything that happens in here. I suppose I just sit here and wait until somebody comes to petition me.

The day passes slowly as I sit alone on my throne. The air is chilly and my toes go numb. My stomach growls, demanding to be fed. It reminds me again of the fragility of mortal bodies. Perhaps I should leave and come back tomorrow. The day is almost over before finally someone enters the room.

It is a servant boy carrying a bundle, which he almost drops when he spots me. His eyes bug amusingly and he quickly backs out of the room. I do not have to wait much longer.

The double doors swing open and Brennus strides in. He is dressed finely in a red tunic and a brown cape, but he has grown too tall for his trousers. He looks like a boy pretending to be a man. He is accompanied by men who I recognise as Hearn's favoured advisors. Other people follow, but the doors slam behind Brennus and his companions. Brennus comes to the dais and stands in front of me. I wait for him to bow, but he doesn't. Perhaps he doesn't know who I am as we have never been introduced.

"What is the meaning of this?" he asks.

His voice breaks halfway through and I stifle the urge to laugh. I should appear regal.

"I am Ida and I claim the throne." I hold my head high and give him my haughtiest stare.

"The throne is mine."

"You should have claimed it, then."

"Have you no decency? Hearn still lies in his bedchamber."

"That is irrelevant to me."

"He was our king." He glances towards the advisors, perhaps hoping they will support him, but none speak.

"And I am the new king," I say.

"A woman can't be king." Brennus's tone turns scornful and he crosses his arms over his chest. "Everybody knows that."

I hesitate. What of the queen who claimed the throne? I sift through the many tales I know and find none where women have ruled as kings.

"I shall be queen, then," I say.

He eyes me for a long moment. "You will be queen to my king?"

What does this mean? If he thinks I will be subordinate to him, he will learn fast. Perhaps it is better to resolve this issue of kingship and thrones quickly and deal with the details later.

"That is acceptable," I say.

Nobody mentions there is already a queen somewhere in the keep and that she still lives. For the time being, Brennus turns to his advisors.

"Find another throne. Make one if you must. The queen and I will each require a throne. Am I not right, Ida?"

At least he hasn't suggested I give up Hearn's throne.

"Correct," I say.

Two men scurry away and Brennus holds out his hand to me.

"My queen, I believe it is dinner time. Will you join me in the dining hall?"

"I will."

I place my hand in his and allow him to lead me from the room. His hand is too warm and his palm sweats. In the dining hall, he escorts me to Hearn's chair, where I have eaten ever since I arrived here. He makes no fuss as I settle there and seats himself in Derwa's place, where Hearn has been sitting.

Diners enter shortly after. They seem to avoid looking at the high table as they sit and talk amongst themselves. When the platters are brought around, the servers hesitate as if unsure who to present them to first. I don't miss the subtle nod Brennus makes towards me. The servers seem relieved the decision has been made and the dishes are offered to me first. My wine cup is the first to be filled.

I spear a piece of wild boar with my knife and place it in my mouth. Its aroma is tantalising but it is cold and over-cooked. Nevertheless, I am hungry, so I eat. Tomorrow I will speak with the kitchen staff about keeping the food warmer.

I lean back in Hearn's chair as I chew and look out over the diners. My people. I am queen. If only the boy could see me now.

39

ARLEN

I was not invited to eat in the dining hall the night after Hearn died, but I overheard enough the next morning to understand that Ida and Brennus had jointly claimed the throne. For a moment I was confused about who Ida was, but then I remembered. Brennus as king was bad enough. The thought of Uncle Diarmuid's muse on the throne was horrifying. I suspected it was she who encouraged Hearn to take his men to war against first Cullen and then Fingen. It gave me some understanding of what would be ahead for the people of Braen Town if she ruled over them.

Had Fiachra received my letter yet? It would take a messenger on foot a sevennight to reach Silver Downs, or perhaps half that if he travelled by horse and was able to change them frequently. Another sevennights for a reply. It might be days yet before I could expect a response. I couldn't wait that long. Hearn's body would be burned tomorrow, and Brennus — and Ida — would be crowned within a day or two after that. Assuming they waited until after Hearn's funeral.

Derwa and Agata would be in immediate danger. If both women were to be kept safe, and Brennus and Ida stopped from ascending the throne, I had to act immediately. I had never had a head for strategy, but I needed a plan to stop a boy from becoming king, and to stop an imaginary woman brought to life, and to save both a queen and my sister.

My mind wandered through a few ideas, none of which were feasible. As long as Brennus lived, he would fight to be king. That was the one thing I was sure of. He had been raised with the expectation that the throne would be his eventually. The day might have come sooner than he expected, but that didn't mean he would relinquish the chance. Hearn was foolish and ignorant, but Brennus was cunning.

As the afternoon passed, I slowly figured out a plan. Maybe it would work. Maybe it wouldn't. If I failed, it would likely mean my own death. I didn't dare tell Derwa. She was in enough danger without being party to my treasonous plot.

As night fell, I fasted and meditated and when morning came my mind was clear. I knew what I had to do. As I walked to the audience hall, I tried not to think of all the ways my plan might go wrong. The doors to the hall were closed as usual. I hesitated, mindful of Derwa's words that I should have waited for Hearn to invite me in that first time. One of the guards finally looked at me.

"What do you want?" he asked, his voice uninterested.

"To speak with Brennus."

He opened the door and slipped inside. I could hear him even through the heavy doors.

"The druid wishes to see the king-in-waiting."

I couldn't hear Brennus's reply, but the doors opened to admit me. I had counted on Brennus being surrounded by advisors, and to my great relief he was. My plan wouldn't work without them.

Brennus wore an elaborately embroidered tunic that was far too big for him. He sat on a new throne positioned next to Hearn's. His head was held high and his face bore a barely concealed smirk. Ida wasn't in the room and I felt a rush of relief. She could obviously charm me to forget her, although that seemed to have faded since Hearn's death, but I was unsure whether she could also influence my thoughts or words. Without her here, I could be reasonably sure my thoughts were my own.

Four men stood in a group to one side of the dais. Lorne, a tall and skinny man with a face that looked far younger than his years. Cahan with his elaborate moustache. Teris, a short, stocky man who always looked as if his boots were uncomfortable. And Egan, who seemed more farmer than advisor. Iver, the fifth of the senior advisors, was absent. Had Brennus refused to have him or had he refused to support Brennus? He might be a potential ally.

I halted a suitable distance from the dais and bowed. It irked me to pay respect to this upstart of a boy.

"Druid." Brennus's voice echoed in the mostly empty hall. "Have you come to pledge your allegiance to me? I have use for a druid advisor."

"My lord." The words were bitter on my tongue. "I have come to tell you of a vision I Saw overnight."

Brennus forgot himself briefly and a smug smile crept across his face. He quickly wiped it away and nodded imperiously.

"You may speak," he said.

"My lord, I Saw our country. It had been ravaged by drought and fire and disease. People lay dead in the streets with nobody to prepare funeral pyres for them. The crops were stunted and wilted and there was not enough harvest to feed everyone. The livestock lay dead in their fields and crows feasted on their flesh. The rivers were dry and the land barren. The gods turned their faces from us."

I watched the advisors from the corner of my eye. They paid me little attention at first, but now they listened attentively. I noted the looks they gave each other, the little nods and whispered words.

"What nonsense is this?" Brennus's attempt to sound authoritative was ruined when his voice broke.

"I came to tell you as soon as I finished my meditations," I said. "There is more, if you will listen."

"I think I've heard enough," he said.

"My lord Brennus, we would hear the rest," Lorne said. "The druid may have information about how this disaster can be averted."

"I do," I said.

Brennus's face was conflicted, but at length he nodded.

"Very well," he said. "You may continue."

I bowed my thanks. "This vision I Saw was but one possible future. I Saw another future also. In this, our people were strong and healthy. The land was lush and well watered. Livestock grew fat and plentiful. The gods favoured us as they did many years ago. And our men were undefeated in battle."

The last was a gamble. Even if Brennus had no interest in what might befall his people, he would want his army to be victorious.

"And how do I make this second future come to pass?" Brennus asked.

My next words were intended for the advisors, not for Brennus, and I turned to face them.

"The difference is the king," I said. "In my first vision, Brennus holds the throne. He neglects the people and offends the gods and we all suffer the punishment intended for him. In my second vision, Girec is king. He is wise and patient and the land thrives under his guidance. He provides the gods with a sacrifice so great it ensures they look favourably on us for generations. It is in your hands to decide our future. We live or we die based on who you support as king."

"Blasphemy." Brennus stood and gestured towards his guards. "Guards, remove him from the room. Lock him in the cells. And don't let him speak to anyone."

They grabbed my arms and I offered no opposition. The advisors huddled together, whispering furiously. Brennus tried to get their attention, but his face turned red when they ignored him.

"Listen to me," Brennus roared. "The druid lies."

Lorne gave him a bow which was brief enough to be insulting.

"My lord, we have much to discuss," he said. "I beg our leave of you now."

"You will stay here," Brennus said. "All of you." He looked towards the guards. "Why are you still here? Take the druid away like I said."

As guards led me from the room, the four advisors left by another exit with Brennus screaming after them. They marched me along the hallways and down to the cells.

"One more for you," one said to the guard stationed at the door.

The guard gave me an inquiring look. It was Gwern, who had been on duty both times I came to visit Agata.

"So, druid, you've offended the kingling, have you?" he said, with something that might have been a grin. "Well, into the cells with you."

I answered his grin with one of my own and tried to look more confident than I felt. The advisors would be locked in private discussion until they decided how much weight to put on my "visions". If they decided to support Brennus, my execution was inevitable. But I had planted the seed of doubt and that was all I could do. The rest was up to them.

The other guards departed, leaving me alone with Gwern. I followed him to an empty cell, where he tossed me a blanket.

"Queen's order," he said. "Every prisoner receives a blanket now."

"Thank you," I said. "Would it be possible to send a message to the queen to tell her I am here?"

Gwern hesitated. "I could get into a lot of trouble for that."

"Don't worry about it then," I said. "I wouldn't want to cause trouble for you."

He considered me for another few moments, then nodded.

"If I have a chance to pass on your message quietly, I will," he said. "But I'm not promising anything. Brennus would have my head if he thought I was undermining him."

"Of course. I appreciate anything you can do."

Gwern closed the door and the bolt slid into place with a clunk. Only meagre lamplight made its way through the opening set high in the door, but I could smell well enough to know this wasn't one of the cells that were cleaned prior to the battle with Cullen. A mossy growth covered the floor and the air smelled of rot and mildew.

I wrapped the blanket around me and sat in the middle of the cell, where the stones seemed cleanest. The chill rose straight through the blanket. I pitied the prisoners who had been in here for days with no relief from the cold or the damp air. At least they had blankets now. I hoped Brennus's advisors would act quickly.

40

ARLEN

*I*f Brennus was allowed to be king, he would undoubtedly have me executed. And he would claim Agata. I couldn't even imagine what he would do to her. Rape, certainly, but I was sure he would also have a special humiliation in mind. Something to punish me, even if I never knew about it. I would be dead by then and likely Derwa too.

All I could do was wait. I could do nothing else to influence the advisors. I focussed on my breath, on letting go of my thoughts, and sank into a meditative state. It allowed me to block out the cold and the damp and the occasional sobbing from other prisoners. Every now and then, the realisation that I would likely die within the next few hours sprang back up. I pushed the thought away and told myself I wasn't afraid.

Eventually the door to my cell opened. Lamplight blinded me and I could see only a dark shadow as I raised my arm to shield my eyes.

"I'm so sorry, Arlen," Derwa said. "I've only just been told you were here."

My feet tangled in the blanket in my haste to get up. I tried to bow, but my limbs were stiff and didn't seem to work properly. My heart pounded. Surely the advisors would not have allowed Derwa to fetch me if I was to be executed.

"Come," she said. "Your questions must wait until we can talk in private, though."

As I climbed the stairs, my legs wobbled but at least my eyes were adjusting to the light. Gwern was gone and another guard stood in his place. He nodded at Derwa as we passed. So, something had changed, for it seemed Derwa now had some authority within the keep.

Two guards waited at the top of the stairs. I recognised both their faces, but didn't know them by name. They fell in behind me as Derwa led us at a sedate pace to her sitting room. The guards took up positions in the hallway on either side of the door as she closed it behind us. Coals burned in the hearth sending off a wonderful wave of heat and I stood as close as I dared.

"Oh, Arlen," she said, looking me up and down. "I'm sorry."

"It was not as bad as it could have been." I finally noticed the blanket still wrapped around my shoulders and let it drop to the floor. "At least I had a blanket."

"I will be able to do more for the prisoners very soon." Derwa nodded to a table set with a platter of cold meat and cheese, a loaf of grainy bread, and a jug of ale. "Sit and eat. You've been down there for a day and a half as best I can tell. I'll tell you what has happened while you eat."

"Am I to be executed?"

She gave me a small smile. "No. Your plan, such as it was, seems to have worked."

The relief that rushed over me was immense and my hands shook as I reached for a plate. My mouth already watered at the aroma of roasted meat and fresh bread.

"Was no food offered to you in that time?" Derwa asked.

I shook my head, already filling my mouth with wild boar. It was succulent and juicy. I swallowed too big a mouthful and almost choked.

Derwa frowned. "I gave instructions for the prisoners to be fed twice a day."

I washed down the mouthful with ale and wiped my mouth, worried I had embarrassed myself in my haste.

"I apologise for my rudeness," I said. "I have become far too used to regular meals since I arrived here. It wasn't all that long ago that a day without food would have been a fast rather than torture."

"Eat," she said. "As soon as we are finished talking, I will ensure food is taken down to the cells. Much has happened since you went to the audience hall with your tale of two futures."

She gave me an appraising look, but if she doubted my visions, she didn't say it.

"The senior advisors spent a whole day in discussion before they came to me. I was distracted with Hearn's funeral and didn't note their absence. When they weren't present for his burning, I assumed it was their way of expressing disapproval of him."

I paused between mouthfuls. "Hearn has already been farewelled?"

"We burned him on a pyre and the remains were buried. I did wonder why you weren't there."

"I'm afraid I was otherwise engaged, my lady."

She didn't seem to find my comment amusing. I kept eating as she continued.

"I finally received a request from Lorne for an urgent audience. Truthfully, I nearly ignored his message. I assumed he wanted to discuss Brennus's coronation and I wanted no involvement. When I met with the advisors, they told me of your visions and that they were unsure whether they could support Brennus. They have taken to heart your words about Girec making a sacrifice. If Brennus doesn't become king, he will be the sacrifice. It has been many years since such a thing has been done here, but they consider this the strongest way to demonstrate their censure of Brennus."

I swallowed hard. I knew my plan would mean death for either Brennus or myself, but it was still difficult to hear.

"And Girec?" I asked.

"They are undecided. He is too young and has not been groomed for this as Brennus was. They may allow him to take the throne in a temporary capacity with myself as regent. An opportunity for him to learn and to show them he is suited to the role. If he has proven himself by the time he comes of age, they will support him."

"And if not?"

She shrugged. "He must succeed. There is no other option at the moment. If I had borne Hearn a child, the situation might be different."

"Does Brennus know?"

"He won't be told anything until they make a final decision. They want to speak with you again first. But there is another problem that needs to be dealt with before either boy can take the throne."

I waited. What had I missed?

"The woman who calls herself Ida."

For a moment, I had no idea who she meant, but then my mind cleared. Ida. I had forgotten again.

"I keep noticing her briefly, but then I forget," I confessed. "How is it that you remember her?"

"Everyone keeps forgetting her. I assume she has laid some sort of charm on the people here. As to why it doesn't affect me, I have no idea. Perhaps she didn't think me important enough to bother charming."

"You are the queen. She should have thought you important."

"You know how the people here view me."

"Perhaps that will be different now Hearn is dead. You said his advisors requested audience with you, that they want you as regent. That already indicates change."

"I hope it lasts. I don't know much about Girec as Hearn always kept both boys well away from me. But from what little I have observed, he is not like Brennus. I assume that is why your vision showed him to be the most suitable candidate."

The slight emphasis she placed on *vision* told me she believed I had fabricated it. Did the advisors suspect, too? I couldn't ask without admitting what I had done.

"So, we need to deal with Ida and I hoped you might be able to suggest how," she said. "Surely your training has given you some experience with creatures like her? Is she fey?"

I told her of Fiachra's letter explaining about Uncle Diarmuid's muse and how she escaped on his death.

"I don't know how to stop her," I said. "My uncles have already tried and failed. Uncle Fiachra has been a druid for some ninety summers as best I can figure. If he was not able to stop her, then I don't know what I can do."

"He must be very old."

"When I last saw him, he looked like a man in his sixties, but he must have been at least eighty summers even then."

"Would he come here, do you think? His advice and experience in this matter would be very valuable."

"I don't know where he is. He was leaving Silver Downs at the time of his letter. The message I left with you, would it have reached home by now?"

"I sent the messenger on horseback with instructions to deliver the message with all urgency. He was to change horses as often as needed."

"Maybe Uncle Fiachra is on his way here now."

"We can only hope he arrives in time to advise us. What do we do about Ida in the meantime? She will likely act against us when she finds out about your visions. You were fortunate she wasn't present when you went to see Brennus."

"He might have told her since then."

"He has been kept under guard in his bedchamber. For his own security, of course." Derwa stood and stretched. "I must go to the kitchens and arrange for food to be taken down to the cells. We can only wait, I suppose. Until the advisors make their decision, we can do nothing else."

As I left Derwa, I fixed the image of Ida firmly in my mind. I couldn't afford to forget her again. In my bedchamber, I looked longingly at my bed. I couldn't remember when I last slept. Two days? Three? It might be as long again before I could.

I sat on the floor and sought a meditative state, still clinging to the memory of Ida. It was harder than usual, perhaps because of my fatigue. But finally I reached the place where my mind could drift freely and I was no longer aware of the physical world. I held Ida's image in my mind and let my thoughts flow around her as if she was a rock in the middle of a stream.

I knew little of how she had been created, only that Uncle Diarmuid had somehow brought his tale to life. He had managed to confine her in his mind and keep her there for his last sixty summers. What could I do as a druid? Ida was a problem that needed a bard and a strong one at that.

I considered asking the Old Ones for help. I could go back to the fey realm and try to find the rock that called itself Orm or one of his fellows. But how would I recognise them when they looked so like their natural surroundings? And would they expect me to immediately help them take their land back from the fey? I still had no idea how, or when, I was supposed to do that and I couldn't afford to be delayed in the fey realm. There was also the risk that Titania would know I was there. But perhaps I could convince her to help me? Would she act if she thought Agata was in danger from Ida? But I couldn't be sure Titania cared anything for Agata, and it might do nothing other than bring me to her attention.

Could the elementals help? Fire or Earth or Water might restrain a living being. Air could transport one. But I didn't know how strong Ida was or how long I could persuade the elements to hold her.

When I opened my eyes, the room was dark. I hadn't found any feasible solutions and I was so tired I could barely think anymore. I eased open the shutters to steal a glance at the sky. Dawn was only a couple of hours away. There was nothing else I could do tonight. I crawled into bed and fell asleep.

41

ARLEN

When I woke, the sunlight shining through the gaps around the window shutters was pale, so I knew the morning was still young. I kept hold of the memory of Ida while I slept, but I still had no plan other than to hope Fiachra's reply to my letter arrived today.

It was only as I sat up that I noticed the figure sitting in the corner. Despite his age, his back was straight. Although his hair was now mostly grey, he still wore it in the many braids I remembered from my youth. His face might have held a few more wrinkles, but he didn't look anything near the hundred-odd summers I calculated he must be.

"Uncle Fiachra."

I straightened my tunic, wishing I had thought to change into clean clothes before falling into bed. He rose a little stiffly and I suppressed the urge to help him. Something told me he would not appreciate being treated like an old man.

"We came as soon as your letter arrived." His voice was deep and melodious. "How fare things here?"

I told him about Brennus and Ida claiming the throne. My "visions" that would mean death for either myself or Brennus, and how I had been locked away while the advisors debated. About Agata's situation and Brennus's interest in her. I kept my summary as brief and emotionless as if I reported to Oistin. Fiachra's face was thoughtful and he stopped me only twice to ask questions. When I finished, he nodded.

"I have Seen some of this. Frustratingly brief glimpses. I have always believed that the only one who can destroy Ida is a bard of Silver Downs. One who is the seventh son of a seventh son. But I begin to doubt myself."

"You mentioned an apprentice bard in your letter. Is that who you mean?"

"There is one who is a seventh son of a seventh son. Only one. His name is Tristan, and he is in the kitchen. He was hungry after our journey and I wanted a chance to speak with you privately."

"About what?"

"When I received your letter, I went straight to Silver Downs to get Tristan because I thought he would be the one who must stand against Ida. He believes it still, because I haven't told him what I Saw last night."

A growing feeling of unease squeezed my stomach.

"It's you, Arlen," he said. "You and Agata. You are the ones who must face Ida."

"I'm not a bard," I stammered. "Nor the seventh son of a seventh son."

"The two of you have both the blood of Silver Downs and also that of the fey running through your veins. We know nothing of the power such a combination might create."

"I have no power. I'm barely even a competent druid. My visions are few and brief, and I can't communicate with the air elementals."

Fiachra raised his eyebrows. "Interesting. Your mother has such a strong affinity with Air that I assumed you would too. But no matter. Those things are irrelevant. You must have some other ability you haven't realised yet. Something unique to you and Agata. Unlock that and I suspect the rest will come."

"Agata," I said. "What have you Seen about her?"

"Little more than that this requires the two of you. I assume you have reasons for not sending word to your mother about finding your sister."

Although his tone was mild, I heard the rebuke in his words.

"Agata found me," I said. "I didn't send a message because she wants nothing to do with the mortal world. She has been raised to believe she's fey and the daughter of Titania. I couldn't tell Eithne I had found Agata, but that she didn't want to know her family."

"And she is still in the cells?"

"The guards won't release her without authorisation from the king."

He shook his head and his tiny braids swung from side to side.

"We will go now and release her. I can compel the guards. But before we do, there's one more thing you need to know. You will need my strength to deal with Ida. She very nearly defeated Diarmuid all those years ago, and he was strong in his ability. Once we have Agata, I will explain more. I will give you everything I have in order to defeat her."

"Do you mean…"

His gaze was steady.

"I will die. I intended to give my strength to Tristan, although he doesn't know. He wouldn't take from me as much as he needed if he did. Ida will be far more powerful this time, but three is an auspicious number. With you, Agata and myself, I believe we have a chance of defeating her."

No words came to my tongue. I wanted to argue with him, to tell him Eithne would never forgive me if I let him do this, but he was calm and steadfast. This was a carefully considered decision and he had already made his choice.

"I'd like my body returned to Silver Downs," he said. "You remember the ancient oak just to the south of the lodge? My parents are buried there and I would like to be returned to the earth in the same place. Don't let them burn me."

How does one respond to a request like that? My throat closed and I could only nod.

"Is she here because of me?" I asked when I thought I could speak again. "You said she might be attracted to a son of Silver Downs."

"She has probably followed you here. But if not you, she would have found another of our blood."

"Are you sure about this? There might be another way."

"I'm the last of my brothers left living," he said. "I thought she might escape when Diarmuid died. I prepared him as best I could, but I always knew I would be part of her end, even if I don't have the ability to stop her myself. I regret we didn't try harder to prepare Diarmuid as a child. We wanted so badly to believe the curse had passed over him that we didn't see the warning signs. I share the blame for her creation and I'll share the burden of destroying her."

"Why didn't Diarmuid destroy her instead of returning her to his head?"

He sighed heavily. "He couldn't. She was as much a part of him as he was of her. It would have killed him, too. So instead he took her back into himself. He paid many times over for what he did in creating her. And now it's my turn. I don't regret this, Arlen. It is necessary. I only regret that I didn't act when I could have, before he ever created her."

"Is there anything you want to do first?"

"I've said my goodbyes. I'm ready. Let's retrieve Tristan from the kitchen and then we'll release Agata."

As I followed him along the hallways, Fiachra walked with his back straight and his head held high. His braids swung slightly, and to look at him, one would not think he was a man about to face his own death.

The kitchen smelled of hot porridge and fresh bread, and my stomach growled in response. A boy of about fourteen or fifteen summers sat on a bench. Like all of our family, he was dark-haired and dark-eyed. With his broad shoulders and strong arms, he looked more farmer than bard. But he nodded gravely at me and I could see he knew the importance of what we were about to do. His eyes were shadowed. Perhaps he suspected that the impact of this event would be greater than he understood. He swallowed the last of his bread and stood.

"You found him," he said.

"This is Arlen." Fiachra nodded in my direction. "Your cousin. There is another cousin we must find now, before we pursue our task."

The boy was clearly bursting to ask questions, but he was wise enough to restrain himself in front of the kitchen staff and the two guards who sat in the corner finishing their meals. I led the way down to the cells. The rank odour was familiar now, although no less unpleasant. We paused at the guard's station and I was a little regretful it was Gwern on duty today. I hoped he wouldn't be punished for Agata's disappearance.

"We have come to retrieve Agata," Fiachra said.

Gwern looked puzzled for a moment, but he nodded.

"Of course." He took the lamp off its hook and led us to Agata's cell. "Hey, fey princess. Come on, you're going out."

"Where to?" Agata's voice was sulky as she emerged into the lamp light. When she saw me, she glowered. "So you came back."

"We have to go," I said, praying she wouldn't argue for once. I didn't know how long Fiachra's compulsion would last.

"Am I being released? Can I go home now?" She moved too slowly.

I grabbed her by the arm and pulled her out through the cell door.

"Just walk," I hissed in her ear.

She finally stopped talking and walked a little faster. Fiachra passed me a cloak which I was sure he hadn't been carrying earlier. I draped it over her shoulders and pulled up the hood to cover her hair. We hurried out of the cells, leaving behind Gwern and his lamp.

"Will he realise what happened?" I asked quietly as we walked swiftly through the keep.

"He shouldn't," Fiachra said. "He'll remember that someone came to take her away and that they had the proper authorisation, but he won't remember who."

I led them out of the keep and across the courtyard. Fiachra was barefooted, despite the midwinter cold, and he walked gently, as if savouring the earth beneath him. The air was crisp and clean, and the sky was a brilliant blue with just a few scattered clouds. A raven cawed nearby. I wondered whether it was the one I encountered while seeking signs for Hearn's battle with Fingen. There would be significance in that.

We didn't stop until we were hidden behind the stunted birches. Agata threw off the hood, although she left the cloak around her shoulders.

"Is somebody going to tell me what's happening?" she demanded.

"This is our uncle, Fiachra," I said. "And our cousin, Tristan."

She dismissed Tristan immediately, but her gaze lingered a little longer on Fiachra.

"Thank you," she said, and her mouth twisted as if they were words she didn't like to say.

"We need your aid," he said.

"I need to go home," she replied.

"Help us and I'll ensure you get home safely."

Her gaze turned scornful. "I don't need help from a mortal."

"Agata, please," I said. "Will you just listen to Uncle Fiachra?"

She gave me a long look, but eventually sniffed and looked away.

"Fine. I'll listen."

42

ARLEN

Fiachra explained to Agata about Uncle Diarmuid's death, Ida's escape and his plan to destroy her. As he spoke of his vision and his decision that Tristan would not be involved, the boy clenched his fists although he waited until Fiachra finished before he spoke.

"Uncle, this is not what we agreed."

"It is as it must be," Fiachra said.

"No, it should be me," Tristan said. "You said it yourself. It will take a bard who is a seventh son of a seventh son to do this."

"I don't understand it myself," Fiachra said. "But I Saw Arlen and Agata facing Ida. I fear…" His voice trailed away.

"You fear what?" Tristan asked. "I am strong enough. You know I am."

"Perhaps I didn't See you because you had already died trying to stop her."

"If it takes my death to stop her, it will be worth it," Tristan said.

"Eithne won't agree with that," Fiachra said. He shot me a glance I couldn't read. "You are like a son to her and I will not act against the vision. You will not be involved in this."

"The Sight can show possible futures," Tristan countered. "You've told me that yourself. How do you know this isn't just one possibility?"

"I have never been more certain of anything in my life," Fiachra said. "Trust me, Tristan. I know you came here expecting to do this yourself and I don't take this decision lightly. Now, I assume you have a tale prepared?"

Tristan nodded.

"Can you tell it to your cousins? Carefully. Don't draw on your ability and don't say her name. We don't want to attract her before we are ready. Arlen. Agata. You will tell the tale, so listen carefully to Tristan."

"And how do we access the bard magic?" Agata asked. For once her tone was interested rather than sulky.

"You won't," Fiachra said. "Or at least I don't think so. My guess is that your power is something to do with the two of you being together. Twin souls, or one soul divided between two bodies, depending on what you believe. There's something special about that. Something magic. It's different to the ability our bards have, but I think this duality of the Seen and the unSeen ones is what we need."

When I ventured into the fey realm to find Agata, something led me straight to her. Had she felt me, too, as I drew closer?

"Where should we do this?" I asked.

"Here will be suitable," Fiachra said. "My strength is greatest when I am connected with the natural world."

"Sadly there's little out here to connect to. As you can see, the trees are dying and everything else is already dead."

"It will be enough. I need only to have my feet in the earth and I can find the connections from there. Tristan, tell your cousins the tale while I prepare myself."

Fiachra took a stick from the ground and dug into the compacted earth, loosing it so he could dig in his toes. He placed his palms against a tree, seeking as I had to find the life within. There was much I could learn from my druid uncle and it would never happen now. My heart was heavy with regret for the knowledge that would be lost with his death. I listened carefully as Tristan told us his tale.

"Can you remember all of that?" Tristan asked when he finished. "The wording of the ending is particularly important."

I was well accustomed to memorising long passages, but Agata was flushed and looked unnerved.

"Can you say the last part again?" she asked.

What education had she received? I was taught lore and old tales and other arcane wisdoms. Oistin regularly tested our memory of such things. Agata had likely experienced none of that. While Tristan recited the end of his tale again, I went to stand next to Fiachra.

"What will happen if this works?" I asked.

"It should occur exactly as Tristan's tale says."

"And if it doesn't?"

He looked at me steadily. "She will be angry, we can be sure of that. She is strong. Probably far stronger than last time she was free. If we fail, she will likely kill us. From what you have said, she has already enticed Hearn into war twice over. Now that she has claimed the throne, who will she take her army against next?

"We thought the biggest danger to this country was at the battle front, where the southern armies still engage our forces. If they defeat us and sweep across the country, our whole world will change. They will force us to adopt their customs, their gods. Everything about our way of life will change.

"But I believe Diarmuid's muse is a bigger threat than the foreign armies. She sows discontent amongst folk in their own homes. For most folk the war against the invaders is happening a long way away. It has little effect on their lives except for the soldier sons who die in battle. But the muse sets neighbour against neighbour, brother against brother. The invaders might yet come and force us into submission. They want to rule us, but she would have us tear ourselves apart. There would be nothing left for anyone to rule over."

"That's why you are willing to die for this," I said.

His mouth twisted into a sad smile. "I've had a long life, Arlen. I'm the last of my brothers. My time is coming soon regardless of what happens today. If it takes my life to stop her, I'll be well satisfied with my choice."

Tristan and Agata were finally finished and came over to us. Fiachra pointed to a spot some distance away.

"Tristan, wait over there and don't do anything to draw her attention," he said.

"I can help," Tristan said.

Fiachra shook his head. "Stand back. I want to be sure you are returned safely home when this is over."

Tristan obeyed without further comment.

"Arlen. Agata," Fiachra said. "Come stand just in front of me."

We moved into position and he placed one hand on my shoulder and the other on Agata's.

"I'll send my strength into you as you tell your tale," he said. "You may or may not feel it, but trust it will be there. You must put everything you have into this tale. This is our one chance. She will take this as an attack and if we don't succeed, she will destroy us. With her on the throne, the entire country is in danger."

"Should we start now?" I asked.

He squeezed my shoulder gently.

"When you're ready, boy. When you're ready."

"There was once a bard," I said.

My voice didn't come out quite as strongly as I hoped and I wished I could start over. But Agata took my hand and the moment she touched me, I felt the connection between us renewed. Fiachra was right. There was power in the two of us being together. Strong power.

"He was not a very famous bard, nor a very good one," I continued. "But he was well loved by his family despite his flaws. In the pride of his youth he created a creature from nothing more than his words and the images in his mind. The creature came to life and when she left his mind, she committed terrible deeds. Eventually, and at great cost to himself, the bard secured her inside his mind again."

A tremble passed through the air. It was gone so fast I wasn't sure whether I imagined it. I hesitated and Agata took up the tale.

"Years passed and the bard kept the creature contained within his mind, right up to the moment he died." Her voice was clear and stronger than mine. "Then the creature broke free and emerged into the world again. Her name was Ida."

As if she had summoned the muse by speaking her name, Ida appeared in front of us. Her white dress whipped around her legs, although I myself felt no breeze.

"You fancy yourself as bards, do you, children?" she snarled.

I averted my gaze. Perhaps looking into her eyes would not affect me, but I wouldn't risk it.

"This time Ida was weaker than before, although she didn't know it at first," I said. "After the king to whom she had allied herself died, her power waned, for it was from him that she had drawn her strength."

"What is this?" Ida asked. "What are you doing?"

"Then came the arrival of a young man and woman," I said.

Tristan had obviously improvised here, changing the tale from what he had intended. Likely this section was originally about himself as a bard and the seventh son of a seventh son.

"Born of the same womb and in the same hour, they possessed but one soul between them," I continued. "And when the two halves of their soul were reunited, a mighty power was created. As they told the tale that would destroy Ida once and for all, they drew on the strength of a powerful druid, thus magnifying their ability many times over."

"Stop this at once," Ida shrieked.

She held out her hands towards us and I staggered as an invisible force hit me. It was only Fiachra's firm grip on my shoulder that kept me on my feet. Agata tightened her grasp of my hand as she took up the tale.

"Their words wrapped around Ida like chains." Her voice was still steady, although the hand that clutched mine trembled. "They contained her and confined her, and then they drained her power away, letting it siphon off into the earth, where it couldn't harm anyone."

Ida wailed, staring down at her own hands as if she had never seen them before.

"As her power drained, so too did her life force," I said. "Like her power, it drained into the earth, seeping slowly down into the dirt where it could never again come together to form a living creature."

As I finished, Ida's shape shifted. The edges of her form became undefined and instead of a woman, she was now a shining silvery blur. She sank down into the ground, screaming as the earth drank her up like a mug of spilled ale. In moments, she was gone. The three of us stood in silence.

"Is that it?" My voice was unsteady. "Is she gone?"

Fiachra swayed and collapsed. I wasn't fast enough to catch him. Tristan rushed over and stared down at him in horror.

"He knew this would happen," I said. "It was the price he was willing to pay for not preventing her creation."

"You took too much of his strength," Tristan said. Tears tracked down his cheeks. "He didn't tell me this might kill him."

"He did what he had to," I said and my voice was perhaps a little curter than he deserved. "And we should be grateful he was willing."

43

AGATA

My legs trembled as I stared down at the uncle I had never known. He lay with his limbs sprawled, his eyes unseeing. I had never seen death before. Was this how it would come for me, too, if I stayed in the mortal realm? Would I be alive one moment and fall down dead the next? My leg suddenly cramped and I fell. Arlen caught me before I could land on my dead uncle.

"You need a healer," he said.

"I'm just stiff from sitting in the cold for days on end," I said. "How long was I down there? Eight days? Nine?"

Arlen shook his head and didn't answer.

"Do you even know?" I asked. "I couldn't count the days in the dark, but you've been up here, free to come and go. Free to eat whenever you want and to bathe and to sleep in a bed. I'm sure you've been very busy while I was down there in the dark and cold, wondering if I would ever see the sun again."

"You have no idea what has been happening," Arlen said. "With the king dead and the succession in doubt, there were bigger issues that needed to be resolved."

I couldn't be bothered arguing with him any longer.

"Now that we've dealt with that creature, I'll be on my way," I said.

"You need a healer first and some decent food. You can sleep in my bedchamber tonight."

"I'd rather sleep in my own bed. I need nothing from you. I want to go home."

"I'm leaving for Silver Downs shortly. You could come with me. Meet our mother."

"No, thank you. I have no interest in meeting any other mortal relatives."

He gave me a dark look, then pointed.

"That path will lead you to the keep's gates," he said. "Keep following it to the town wall. I assume you know how to get back to the fey realm from there."

"I do."

"Agata, please, won't you at least stay long enough to eat?"

He gave me a look I couldn't interpret. It might have been sadness or maybe just weariness. I finally noticed the paleness of his face and the shadows under his eyes, and almost wanted to change my mind. This was my brother, after all. But he had left me in the dark for days.

"Farewell," I said. "Don't come looking for me again. I want nothing to do with the mortal realm. If our mother asks, I'm glad Titania took me."

The gate was open and nobody tried to stop me. Snow covered the road and masked the decrepit lodges as I ran through the town. Those folk who were out and about were bundled up in scarves and hats and patched cloaks. The breeze sent brisk fingers creeping in under my borrowed cloak.

My breath steamed in the cold air and as my muscles warmed, they loosened. Soon I ran smoothly. I didn't stop until I was back in the fey realm. I was badly winded, far more than I should have been. Perhaps the days spent in the damp cell damaged my lungs. Being back in the fey realm would cure that soon enough. I hoped it would also cure the horrible heavy feeling in my chest.

44

ARLEN

I left Tristan standing guard over Fiachra's body while I looked for Derwa. I found her in her sitting room, hunched over a table as she wrote on a piece of parchment. The room was warm and scented with a herbal concoction. Derwa was finally making this room her own.

I told her what happened and Derwa sent a pair of guards to retrieve Fiachra's body until we could take him home. They would look after Tristan also. I wanted him well away from me in case the next phase of my plan failed. Derwa promised to make sure he got home if I wasn't able to take him myself.

"Are you certain Ida won't return?" Derwa asked.

"Fiachra was confident she couldn't. We have killed her, in as much as a creature such as her can be."

"I'm sorry about your uncle. He sounds like a brave man."

"I doubt he would agree," I said. "But thank you."

A panting servant boy interrupted our conversation with a knock on the door. He sketched a quick bow to Derwa.

"My lady, the chief advisors request the druid attend them," he said, between puffs.

"Of course." Derwa stood and straightened her skirt. She looked unworried, although I knew her well enough to see through her facade. "Are they in the audience hall?"

The servant boy nodded and darted away.

"Are you ready, Arlen?" she asked.

I inhaled shakily. "I have to be."

She smiled and grasped my hand for just a moment.

"Good luck," she said.

My skin tingled where she touched me. When we reached the audience hall, the doors were already open, although guards stood on either side as usual. A brief *my lady* passed from the lips of one as we entered. Things were changing around Braen Keep.

I followed Derwa into the hall, walking a couple of steps behind her as was proper. Right now she was my queen, not my friend. And certainly not anything more. Brennus sat on his new throne. Beside him, Hearn's was empty. Was this where he expected Ida to sit?

Derwa stopped in front of the dais and looked coldly up at Brennus, then turned to the chief advisors, who were grouped to one side: Lorne, Cahan, Egan and Teris, along with Iver, who was absent the last time I spoke with them.

"Gentlemen." Derwa's voice was calm. "You wished to speak with the druid."

Her presence discomfited the advisors who shuffled a little closer together and hesitated before first one, then the others, bowed to her.

"My lady, we need to interrogate him about his visions," Lorne said.

"False visions," Brennus interrupted. His voice was overly loud and it echoed through the room.

"You will be silent," Lorne said to him. "If you wish to be present for this discussion."

"You can't talk to me like that," Brennus said. "I'm your king-in-waiting."

"That is yet to be confirmed," Lorne replied.

"Should this discussion not be held without Brennus?" Derwa asked.

"We have decided it would be appropriate for him to hear what the druid has to say," Iver said. "It is his future we discuss."

Derwa nodded and if she disagreed she held her tongue. I spotted Girec huddled against the wall behind the advisors looking as if he wanted to be anywhere but here. It was his future, too, being decided.

"Druid," Lorne said.

"My name is Arlen." I kept my voice pleasant. "And I much prefer to be addressed by name."

Lorne flushed faintly. "Well, then, Arlen, tell us again of your visions of the two futures."

I repeated what I told them previously, being careful not to embellish any details. I kept my words factual and unemotional so as not to seem as if I steered them in either direction.

"How certain is the future in which our country is laid to waste?" Iver asked.

"At this stage, I believe both futures are possible," I said. "We don't seem to have reached the incident that will force one or the other, although I feel we are close."

The men withdrew a little distance to talk amongst themselves. There seemed to be some disagreement amongst them, with the other four trying to persuade Egan. Heart pounding, I watched and tried not to look as if I strained to hear them. Girec was close enough to hear, but if anything they said gave him hope, he didn't show it.

Brennus sighed loudly and shifted on the throne.

"Will this take much longer?" he asked.

His voice held an unpleasant whine, and I stifled the urge to shake him by the shoulders. Maybe if that had happened to him from time to time, he wouldn't be quite as obnoxious. When the men ignored him, he repeated his question louder.

"Hush," Derwa said. "You are fortunate to be present, so try to act like a man instead of a boy."

Brennus glared at her.

"When I am king—" he started.

"Shut your mouth." Derwa held herself tall and glared back. "Right now you are a boy, and an insolent one at that. It is time I took some responsibility for your behaviour. Even *if*—" she put heavy emphasis on the word, "if you become king, there will be rules for you to obey and you will be required to respect your elders. Hearn allowed you to be ignorant, slovenly and rude, and that will change starting today."

Brennus opened and closed his mouth, but said nothing further. He continued to glower at her as the chief advisors finished their private discussion. Although I felt like cheering as she put Brennus in his place, now I wished she hadn't said anything. If he hadn't already been inclined to seek revenge on her, he certainly was now.

"Druid," Lorne said, then quickly corrected himself. "Arlen. Can you estimate how likely each of the two futures are?"

"They are equally likely," I said. "We are approaching the inciting incident from which the two futures will diverge."

"And do you know what that incident is?" he asked.

I hesitated as if choosing my words with caution, although this too was planned.

"It seems to me that the decision the chief advisors make regarding which boy will be king will determine all our futures."

"It's as simple as that?" Egan asked. His face was distinctly unhappy. It seemed he still disagreed with whatever decision the other four leaned towards.

I nodded. I was tempted to add more, but restrained myself. Too much now might push them in the wrong direction. The men retreated to speak quietly amongst themselves again. Brennus sighed, but wisely kept his mouth shut after Derwa fixed him with a glare. Eventually the advisors turned back to us.

"We will make our decision in the morning," Lorne said. "Both boys will be escorted to their bedchambers and kept under guard for their safety."

Brennus sat up straighter and opened his mouth to protest. At another look from Derwa, he changed his mind. Lorne nodded at me and I took that as my cue to leave.

I found Tristan in my bedchamber and a guard standing at the door. The boy lay on my bed and looked as if he had cried himself to sleep. I draped a blanket over him, then decided I should rest while I could. I lay on the floor and fell asleep almost instantly.

I woke to a soft knock on the door. My legs didn't seem to work properly as I stumbled the couple of steps to the door. I leaned against it to force it open and found Lorne waiting. The guard had retreated a few steps down the hallway to give us some privacy. Tristan was still sound asleep, so I stepped out into the hallway and eased the door shut.

"Have you made a decision?" I asked.

Lorne's face was grave.

"Girec will be king," he said.

My breath caught in my throat.

"And Brennus?" I asked.

"He is to be sacrificed. If your vision is true, then there is no other path open to us lest we destroy the country. We seek your guidance as to the most suitable method."

I swallowed hard. I was safe. So was Agata, and Derwa. And Girec.

"He should be drowned," I said. "Preferably in a body of water that is sacred to the gods."

"There is a pond a couple of hours' walk from here. Would that be suitable? Unfortunately there are no sacred sites in Braen Town. There were two some years ago, but Hearn had them destroyed."

"If there is nothing closer, that will have to do. Brennus should be given time to fast and meditate. Dawn is an auspicious time for a sacrifice. The chief advisors should come, and also Girec and the queen."

Lorne blanched.

"Is it really necessary for Girec to witness this?" he asked. "He is little more than a boy."

"And he's about to become your king. Let him see what his kingship is forged from."

He nodded. "As you say."

I left Tristan sleeping with the guard at my door, and followed Lorne to the audience hall. Both boys stood in front of the dais. A distance of several paces between them indicated they had no desire to stand next to each other. They were both pale with dark circles under their eyes. Derwa stood a little way from them, her face composed, although she clasped her hands tightly. I suspected she already knew.

"We have made our decision," Lorne announced without preamble. "Girec will be king."

Girec seemed to grow even paler. He nodded and continued to look straight at Lorne. Beside him, Brennus started and clenched his fists.

"This is ridiculous," he said, loudly. "Hearn named me as his heir. You should obey his wishes. He was your king."

"And now he is dead," Lorne said. "The king may select an heir, but if the heir is underage his choice must be confirmed by the chief advisors. Surely you learned this in your lessons?"

"So what is to become of me?" Brennus's tone became belligerent. "Am I supposed to watch Girec stumble his way through a role he has not been prepared for? We will be a laughing stock. Is that what you want?"

"You will not need to watch," Lorne said gently. "To ensure the future we are trying to avert never comes to pass, it has been determined that you will be sacrificed to appease the gods."

"The gods don't care who is king," Brennus said, but his voice trembled a little. "Hearn never paid any respects to them and we have done fine."

Derwa interjected softly.

"Hearn was responsible for much damage and grief, Brennus, as I am sure you are well aware. Braen Town was respectful of the gods many years ago. We can be again, but we feel it necessary to propitiate them. I'm sorry, but the decision has been made."

"You will be permitted to fast and meditate for the rest of the day," Lorne said. "Arlen can assist if you need guidance."

Brennus shot me a venomous look and spat on the floor.

"Hearn thought you a fool and a spy," he said. "I wish he could have seen that you are also a traitor to the crown."

I didn't respond.

"We leave tonight at midnight," Lorne said. He turned to the guards. "Take Brennus to his room. Keep him in sight at all times."

To Brennus he said, "From your response I assume you don't want Arlen to accompany you. If you change your mind, you need only ask the guards to send for him."

Brennus's response was to spit on the floor again. Lorne nodded to the guards and four stepped forward. One took Brennus by the arm, but the boy shook him off.

"Don't touch me," he snarled.

"Let him walk if he will do so willingly," Lorne said. "If he won't, carry him."

Brennus glared, but didn't respond. He walked to the door with his head held high, surrounded by guards. The audience hall was silent for a few moments until Girec spoke.

"Is it really necessary to kill him?" he asked in a very small voice.

The chief advisors glanced at each other as if deciding who would respond.

"He will forever be a threat to your kingship if he is not dealt with now," I said. "This disappointment is not something he will ever forget. One day, you will turn around and discover he has led an uprising to take the throne from you. Or you will find yourself poisoned in your own dining hall or your throat cut as you sleep in your bed. The people are uneasy because of Hearn's lack of respect for the gods. They need to know we have done what we can to appease them."

"Will it work?" he asked. "Will the gods favour us if you kill Brennus?"

"I See possibilities, not certainties. I only know we can't afford to let him live."

Girec inhaled shakily and nodded.

"I would have you stay in my court if you would, Arlen." His voice was stronger now. "I know Hearn had little respect for druids, but I would like to have you at my side."

I bowed, oddly touched.

"Thank you, my lord but I am not suited to be a king's advisor," I said. "I believe my master sent me here for his own benefit, not for Hearn's. I beg your leave to depart as soon as possible. My uncle came yesterday to visit me and died. I need to take his body home."

One day, perhaps, I would tell him why Fiachra was here. But not today.

"You may leave if you want," Girec said. "But I'd rather you stayed."

A guard entered and spoke quietly to Lorne.

"The druid master has arrived," Lorne said.

45

ARLEN

"Oistin is here?" My heart lightened. He must have Seen what had happened. I didn't dare hope he would carry out Brennus's sacrifice himself, but I would value his advice. I badly needed to speak with someone who understood my terror at what I must do tonight.

"Arlen, you stand over there." Lorne pointed to a spot beside the dais, then turned to Girec. "My lord, you should sit on the throne. Hearn's throne, not the new one. My lady, would you stand over there beside Arlen? The chief advisors will stand in front of the dais."

"Is something wrong?" I was confused about why Lorne set such a careful tableau for Oistin's arrival. "He has surely come to advise me."

"I am not so certain of that," Lorne said. "I knew Oistin as a boy. He was ambitious and ruthless. It was many years ago now, but there are those of us who have not forgotten."

"You must be confusing him with someone else," I said. "Oistin would have begun his training in his tenth year. A boy of that age can't display much ambition."

"He went to the druids late," Teris said, surprising me as he had never spoken directly to me before. "I too remember. I was about fifteen or sixteen summers at the time and he was two summers older.

His father was involved in a plot to overthrow Hearn's father, Braen, and take the throne. Hearn happened to overhear a suspicious comment, relayed it to his father, and the plot was uncovered."

"Was there any evidence of Oistin's involvement?" I couldn't reconcile the druid master I knew with the ambitious boy they remembered.

"No evidence that he was, but also no evidence he wasn't," Lorne answered. "He left to train as a druid shortly after. I remember being surprised, for he had always been touted as his father's heir. If their plan had been successful, he would have been king after his father's death."

"We are not making any accusation against him," Teris said. "But the circumstances were strange and it is odd that he would come here now. As far as I know, he has never returned since he left to study with the druids."

A guard announced Oistin's arrival and we moved into our assigned positions. Oistin strolled in, taking in his surroundings as he did. He must have noted my presence, but gave no indication he saw me. He paused a few paces from the chief advisors, who were arrayed in front of the dais as planned. Oistin bowed and looked up to Girec on the throne.

"My lord Brennus," he began.

Girec looked down at him, but said nothing. Lorne stepped forward.

"Greetings, Oistin, it has been many years since we last met." His voice was courteous.

Oistin barely glanced at him, but continued to direct his words to Girec.

"My lord, I have Seen what has been occurring here and it is clear to me you need a more senior advisor than the one I sent previously," he said. "I have come to offer my own services to you."

Girec held his head high and looked to Lorne for a response. He managed to convey an impression of not deigning to speak to Oistin himself, rather than not knowing what to say.

"Perhaps you have not Seen as much as you think," Lorne said.

Oistin finally looked directly at him.

"You dare question my ability?" he asked with a sneer.

Never had I heard the druid master speak so coldly and arrogantly. I hardly believed Lorne and Teris's words, but it was clear there was a side of Oistin I never suspected.

"My lord Girec is the king-in-waiting," Lorne said.

"It hardly matters which boy it is," Oistin said, hurriedly. "The point is that we have a child about to take the throne and he needs a senior advisor."

"He already has senior advisors," Lorne said. "People who know him and know the court here. People who are accustomed to advising the king."

"He needs a druid, not mere men."

"He has a druid. You sent him yourself."

Oistin's gaze flicked up to meet mine briefly.

"He is little more than a boy himself, with no experience of the world outside the community," he said.

"It seems to me that you are the one with little experience of the outside world," Lorne said. "Arlen has been here for some weeks now and has proven himself a valuable ally. The king-in-waiting desires that he stay. You have no qualifications that would recommend you to such a post compared to the one who already holds this position."

"Arlen will be recalled to the community," Oistin said. "He is clearly unsuitable for the role here."

"As I said, the king-in-waiting has asked him to stay."

"Arlen belongs to the community. He returns if I recall him."

"I don't believe that was negotiated when you sent him here, which was, as you know, in direct defiance of Hearn's wishes. Nevertheless, you surely cannot think the druid master outranks the king. Do you?"

Oistin's face turned a deep red.

"Of course not," he spluttered. "But I am the more experienced druid and it should be me here, not him."

"The king-in-waiting has made his choice."

"The king-in-waiting was supposed to be Brennus," Oistin countered.

"It seems that what you have Seen may not be accurate," Lorne said.

Oistin started to reply, but Girec cut him off.

"Druid master, thank you for offering your services. However, I intend to keep the druid you already sent. With his agreement, of course."

"And who will be your regent?" Oistin asked, with a hastily added *my lord*. "You need a senior advisor who can fully assist you in such a capacity."

I suddenly understood Oistin's aim. He wanted to be regent. Was this his plan all along? Had he Seen Hearn's death and the succession of a boy king? If he became regent, would Girec soon have an unfortunate accident? Did he choose me for this role because he thought I would be easy to remove when the time came? It wasn't my place to ask questions, but I would dearly like to know.

"Queen Derwa will be my regent," Girec said, with a nod towards her. Derwa stood to the side of the dais, her hands folded in front of her. She looked serene as she returned his nod. "This has already been determined in consultation with the queen and my chief advisors."

"She is unsuitable," Oistin began.

"Do you think to criticise me in my own keep?" Girec voice turned cold. "You may leave, druid master."

I noted the subtle gesture from Lorne to the guards, who promptly stepped forward, making it seem as if they acted on Girec's words.

"But—" Oistin got no further before Lorne cut him off.

"The guards will escort you out," he said. "I regret that we are unable to offer you a bedchamber for the night, but the guards will take you to the kitchen so you can eat before you leave."

Oistin drew himself up tall and bowed to Girec.

"That won't be necessary," he snapped at Lorne before he turned on his heel and strode out. The guards followed behind him.

The door closed and we stared at each other.

"That was unpleasant," Lorne said.

"I have never seen him act like that," I said. Any respect I still had for Oistin was shattered.

"He is little changed from the boy I remember." Lorne's voice was sad. "I hoped I was wrong about him, but I fear I wasn't. He thought to take the throne for himself."

46

ARLEN

I sent Tristan to the kitchen, telling him to amuse himself for the rest of the day and to take my bed tonight. I would see both him and Fiachra home within the next couple of days.

Home. It had been so long since I had been to Silver Downs. Would Eithne even recognise me? A fierce homesickness swept through me as I remembered wide pastures and singing streams. A big flat rock near a stand of beech trees. Another rock beside a river where one could lie and listen to the water flowing over pebbles. The woods, which I had been forbidden to enter as a child. The big lodge filled with children, some cousins and others the sons and daughters of those who worked on the estate. The workers' children had never been treated any differently to the children of Silver Downs. We played together and were schooled together. I barely remembered any of them now. Did they remember the son who went off to be a druid?

I pushed away the memories to focus on what I must do tonight. A boy would die. Mine would be the hands that held him under the water until he stopped breathing. I pictured the scene, walked myself through every detail. Sacrifices who were willing were usually not restrained, but Brennus would likely fight his fate. So his hands would need to be bound. He would struggle. I might need help to hold him under the water. It was not ideal, but I would work with what I had.

Brennus had to die, I firmly believed that. Sacrificing him to the gods would be seen by the people as a sign that change was coming to Braen Town. That a new king would mean a return to the old ways. A renewed devotion to the gods. People feared what they had heard about the invaders from the south and their new religion which forsook the old gods in preference for one new god. A sacrifice would show them Braen Town had not forgotten its past. I spent the day in silent meditation and made my peace with what I must do tonight.

Girec and Derwa already waited in the audience hall when I arrived. Girec was pale and looked unsteady on his feet. He and Brennus were never friends, but they had grown up together.

"My lord, are you well?" I asked.

He nodded in my direction but didn't speak. I looked to Derwa and she came close to whisper into my ear.

"He is distraught. He understands this is necessary but wishes there were another way."

"As do I."

"I am at war with myself," she confessed. "Is it still murder when the death is a sacrifice for the gods? Brennus is a bully and unsuitable to be king, but he's still just a boy. I know this was our people's way many years ago, but I thought those days were passed."

"It must be done," I said. "He will forever be a threat if he lives. This will show that Girec truly intends to bring change. I know some think sacrifice cruel and unnecessary, but many folk believe we should never have left the old ways behind."

"This will be much harder for you than for me," she murmured. "All I have to do is watch."

"That alone will be difficult."

I let myself touch her arm gently. The fleeting contact filled me with longing — longing for a different world and a time and place where we could be together. That would never happen now. After tonight, when she looked at me, she would always remember watching me sacrifice a boy who would have been king. The chief advisors arrived before I could say anything else.

"The guards are bringing Brennus now," Lorne said. He held up a canvas sack. "I have the items you requested."

Brennus entered, flanked by six guards armed with swords. He wore a white linen tunic and trousers with a thick cloak draped over his shoulders. A guard on each side grasped his arms, but he walked docilely between them. His gaze was vague and wandering.

"Has he been drugged?" I asked quietly.

"We had to," Lorne said. "For his own safety. He was trying to tear out his throat, saying it was better that he died by his own hand."

Even a willing sacrifice was often dosed to keep them calm. I was ashamed at my relief that this would make my task a little easier.

Night fell as we left Braen Town. The snow was hard and icy, slick in patches, and I walked carefully. Brennus slipped several times and would have fallen if not for the guards holding his arms. Another guard walked close to Derwa, offering his arm when she needed steadying. The air was frigid and still, creeping under cloaks and beneath collars. I wrapped my cloak tighter around me and tried not to think about how much colder the water would be. We walked in silence and without torches, for the moonlight was strong enough to light our way.

We headed in the opposite direction to the standing stones and I had not gone this way before. Trees were sparse at first, but became more common the further we went from the town. Eventually we came to a small woods. The guards lit torches, for the canopy was thick enough to obscure the moonlight. The trees were a mix of oak and beech, ash and birch. Frost sparkled on the moss that grew up the trunks and spread over fallen branches.

We moved between the trees, following some path only Lorne saw. He probably explored every inch of the surrounding countryside in his childhood. If he was anything like my cousins, he would have gone as far as a boy could walk and still return in time for dinner. I watched carefully for any sign we might have inadvertently passed through a fey portal, but the woods around us never changed.

At length we reached a clearing, in the middle of which was a pond, its surface veiled with patches of ice. The edges were scummy and it was not as inviting as the one in the fey realm where I met Agata and Orm, but it would do. The lamplight reflected off the water's surface, obscuring its depths.

We rested on oil skins and passed water flasks around. There was little conversation as we waited for dawn. I huddled into my cloak and tried to calm my pounding heart. Despite the midwinter cold, sweat trickled down my back. Derwa reached for my hand. Her hand was warm, although her fingers trembled, and I wondered at the sensation of skin on skin. I eased the corner of my cloak over our hands.

Brennus sat between two guards, his eyes vacant and his jaw slack. Girec sat alone and stared off into the trees. He was pale, but I hardened my heart. One day it would be he who gave the order for men to die. Let him know now what it was to hold that sort of power over someone, while he was still young enough to learn to respect it.

When the small patches of sky I glimpsed through the canopy lightened and the birds began their morning calls, I rose. Lorne handed me the sack he had carried and I removed its contents, one by one. A small clay pot of dirt scraped from the packed earth in the keep's grounds. This I handed to Teris. A bronze bowl, which I passed to Derwa. The tiny oil lamp and tinder I handed to Lorne. The last item was a raven's feather and that I kept for myself.

"Bring Brennus forward," I said.

The guards pulled him to his feet. He looked at me briefly, but apparently found me uninteresting and turned his gaze to the pond.

"On your knees," I said.

The guards tugged Brennus's arms until he knelt. I glanced around at those who had accompanied us. Derwa's face was sympathetic but resolute. Girec held his head high and tried not to cry. The senior advisors were grave and distant. The guards' faces were carefully blank, although more than one swallowed hard. Brennus had given nobody reason to intercede for him, but it didn't mean that what we did this morning sat lightly with anyone.

"Brennus," I said.

He didn't respond. I repeated his name more sharply and he finally looked up from the pond.

"Do you understand what is happening?" I asked.

He nodded, but his eyes were dazed and I wasn't sure he really comprehended my words. I hesitated, wondering whether I should wait until the soporific wore off. A raven croaked loudly and I made up my mind. I raised my arms to the sky and took a deep breath.

"I request the presence of the elementals. I ask that you bear witness to what we must do. Our country has been led astray by a king who was wilful and selfish, conceited and blind to all but his own satisfaction. Tonight we make atonement for his failings, and for our failings in following him. Tonight we sacrifice the one who would follow his path. We pray that by our actions the gods forgive us."

I indicated that Derwa, Lorne and Teris should move forward. I had explained earlier what they needed to do and each now carefully performed their part. Lorne cleared an area of snow and leaves and placed the little oil lamp on the dirt. He struck a flame and lit the wick. Derwa filled the tiny bronze bowl from the pond, then placed it beside the lamp. Teris set the clay pot of soil down with them and I added the raven's feather. Our offerings stood in a row on the bare earth. The fire from the lamp played across the surface of the bowl and the water darkened and flickered. I didn't let myself look at what it showed.

"We offer these gifts to the elementals. Fire and Earth, Water and Air. Bear witness to the terrible task we do tonight."

I held my hand out to Lorne and he passed me two final items. A rope and a linen hood. I knelt in front of Brennus and took his hands. He offered no resistance but stared at me almost curiously, as if he was a child encountering someone he had never met before. I tied his hands together in front of him.

"If you have any final words, speak them now," I said.

He looked at me dumbly. With a heavy heart, I slipped the hood over his head. He tossed his head back, startled, and the guards tightened their grip on his arms. But he offered no further resistance as I tied the string that would hold the hood securely.

I rose and stepped into the pond. The water was near freezing and already my skin burned. I had feared we might need to cut the ice, but it was patchy and thin enough that I could easily break through it. The bottom of the pond was slippery and I kept my balance with difficulty. My progress wasn't terribly dignified, but all too soon I stood chest-deep in the water. My teeth chattered and I already couldn't feel my legs.

I nodded to the guards, who lifted Brennus by his arms and carried him into the pond. He kicked when he felt the frigid water, but they held him firmly. By the time they reached me, their shirts were soaked through and water dripped from their faces. Neither looked at me and I wondered whether they volunteered for this task or were chosen. Once again, I held my arms up to the sky.

"Bear witness to our sacrifice," I called to the elementals.

The guards lifted Brennus by his bound arms and his legs and tipped him forward. I placed my hands on Brennus's head and pushed him under the surface. He thrashed and struggled, but the guards grasped him securely as I held his head under the water. Time passed too slowly and he fought for longer than I expected. But at last his body stilled. I counted to one hundred, then released his head.

"Bear witness to our sacrifice," I said. My throat choked with tears I couldn't afford to shed.

47

ARLEN

We took Brennus's body back to Braen Keep, where a pyre had been built in our absence. I watched with dry eyes as the flames took him, and tried not to inhale the scent of his burning flesh. It was only later in the privacy of my bedchamber that I let myself cry for what I had done.

Lorne sent a carefully-worded message to Brennus's family, explaining only that he had died but not the circumstances. We assumed Brennus would have boasted of being named as heir, but his family were in no position to demand any explanation other than what Lorne offered. They gave up all rights to the boy when they sent him to be fostered as a show of allegiance towards Hearn.

Girec said little, but he listened carefully to everything Derwa and the chief advisors said. He would make a fine king, I thought, given enough time to learn all that Hearn hadn't bothered to teach him. Although I regretted the necessity of Brennus's sacrifice, I did not regret the deed. The country would fare far better with Girec on the throne. And those women who were important to me — Agata and Derwa — were safe.

Girec's first act was to order the prisoners from Cullen's and Fingen's estates be released. They were fed, given medical treatment, and offered work if they wanted to stay. Some would likely depart to live with families elsewhere, but most probably had nowhere to go. Here they would have a roof over their heads and the promise of a job.

It was almost dusk by the time I escaped the discussions with Girec and the advisors. I was fiercely hungry, having eaten nothing yet today, so I went straight to the kitchen. I took my bread and cheese and braved the cold outside to find a quiet place to eat. I wandered with no real direction until I ended up at the three birch trees. There was nowhere to sit as a fresh layer of snow covered the ground, so I ate leaning against a tree. It was a simple meal, but the bread was fresh and the cheese sharp. I rested my head against the trunk and closed my eyes. The tree's life force was weak, but even that small connection revived me a little.

Tomorrow Tristan and I would take Fiachra's body back to Silver Downs. I intended to stay there for a while, but I already knew I would return to Braen Keep. I would have dearly liked to ask Derwa to come with me so I could show her my boyhood home, but she had responsibilities here now and a king-in-waiting who needed her. So I would return and eventually there would be time and space for Derwa and I to find out what we meant to each other.

I dreaded telling Eithne about Agata. What would she think of me when she discovered I found my sister but failed to bring her home? In almost every letter I sent home during my training, I promised to search for Agata as soon as I could. Would Eithne think I gave up too easily? Or maybe she would think I hadn't even tried. I needed to make one last attempt to convince Agata to come home with me.

My feet already ached as I left the keep and the moon was high in the sky by the time I reached the portal. The night was bitterly cold and frost crunched under my boots. Icicles rimed the branches of beech and birch, sparkling in the moonlight. The air was fresh and clean, scented with woodsmoke and snow. Yet as I passed through the portal, the winter night disappeared, replaced with woods on a warm summery afternoon. The trees were lush with new leaves and blossoms. I heard the chirp of squirrel and the song of woodlark.

I wasn't sure I would remember the path to the pond, for it had been a long, winding route. But the woods seemed to lead me straight there this time. I didn't know how often Agata came here, but it was the only place in this realm that I knew she visited. I hadn't decided how long I would wait.

My feet were throbbing and blistered and I eagerly anticipated soaking them in the pond's warm waters. But when I arrived, Agata was already there. She sat in the moss in front of the pond. Her long dark hair cascaded over her back and I thought she might be crying. I cleared my throat to let her know I was there and Agata spun around, already scrubbing the tears from her face.

"You shouldn't be here," she said. "This is not a place for mortals."

"The portal let me through. Surely it would have stopped me if mortals weren't permitted."

"Fool," she hissed. "Titania will know. She Sees you now. She hasn't decided what to do about you yet, but if she knows you are here, she will come."

"Come home with me, Agata," I said. "Meet our mother. See the place where you should have grown up. There's a portal to the fey realm on the edge of our lands, so you can come straight back from there."

"I have no desire to spend any more time in the mortal realm," she said.

Before she could say anything else, a woman entered the clearing. She wore a blood-red gown and her dark hair flowed unrestrained around her shoulders. I recognised her instantly even without having seen her before.

"So, the mortal woman bore two children." Titania inspected me as if I was a squashed bug. "How fortunate for her, but why were you unSeen?"

I kept my face blank, not wanting her to know how much I feared her. The queen of the fey. The woman who tried to destroy both my mother and my sister. The one who featured in so many of my boyhood nightmares.

"The children of Silver Downs have always had special abilities," I said. "I thought you knew that."

Her eyes narrowed. "Impudent. Just like your mother."

"If I had half my mother's courage, I would be proud."

"Your mother was a sickly runt whose only achievement was bewitching a half-blood fey."

"My mother escaped a fey prison to bring home the man she loved," I said.

"Impertinent wretch. I should have squashed your entire line generations ago."

"I think you would have if you could."

She narrowed her eyes and put her hands on her hips.

"Do you dare suggest a handful of mere mortals are more powerful than I?" she asked, her tone scornful.

"I think you're scared of us," I said. "I know you watch us. What I've never figured out is why."

Titania's face registered surprise as she looked down at something on the ground. Orm had arrived. I reached down to touch the rock's smooth surface and Orm spoke in a slow ponderous tone.

"I'll tell you why, young druid," Orm said. "It's because she knows your line will be the end of the fey."

"What is that?" Titania hissed. "And where did it come from?"

"This?" I kept my voice casual. "You mean to tell me you don't recognise an Old One when you see one?"

"There are no Old Ones here," she said with a snarl. Her gaze didn't leave Orm for a moment. "They died out long before we ever arrived."

"No, actually, they didn't. They went into hiding because they didn't think you were worth fighting. But now they'd like their lands back."

Titania laughed. "You think we'll just walk away? We've held this land for thousands of years. It's ours now."

"I think you'll find you're outnumbered." I had no idea whether that was true, but I hoped it was.

"There are hundreds—"

Titania stopped as the clearing filled with a variety of rocks and logs and bushes and trees. They stood silent and patient. Agata let out a shriek as something climbed out of the pond and stood beside her. It was vaguely human-shaped, but its limbs were too long and its hands and feet too big. Water sluiced from its body and puddled on the moss.

"What is this?" Titania asked. "How are you doing this?"

"I'm not doing anything," I said. "They're the Old Ones."

"No point us trying to talk to her," Orm said. "She can't hear our kind. Only mortals can."

That's why they needed me.

"Well, if the fey need to leave, they have to go somewhere," I said. "Is there an unoccupied place they can go to?"

"An island a few hours off the coast. North and to the west. Occupied by wildlife but no mortals. None of our kind there."

"The Old Ones know an island," I relayed to Titania. "It is uninhabited. I can arrange transport if you will leave willingly."

Titania screwed up her mouth as if she tasted something bitter.

"We aren't going anywhere," she said. "And I have no patience for dealing with mortals right now. Come along, Agata."

She walked away. Agata didn't follow her, too occupied with staring at Orm. Could she hear the Old Ones? After all, she had as much mortal blood as me. As Titania reached the edge of the clearing, the weeping willows moved, interlocking their branches to stop her from passing between them. Titania gave a squeal of fury.

"Let me pass this minute or I'll burn you all to the ground."

"You can try," Orm said.

"I think you'll find they don't burn," I said. "And it seems there are more Old Ones than you realised."

"We are all around," Orm said. "The woods, your homes, your furniture. Did you really think the trees grew into shapes so convenient for you?"

"They're everywhere," I said. "They made themselves useful so they could watch you. They're your homes and your furniture. The woods. They're everywhere."

"That's nonsense," Titania said, but her voice shook. "The homes we use were left by the previous inhabitants of this land. We merely moved into them."

"I thought they were made by fey magic," Agata said.

"That's just what we tell the mortals." Titania's voice was distant and she missed the look of fury Agata directed at her.

"Will you accept the offer of transport?" I asked.

Fatigue washed over me in waves and I could barely follow the conversation anymore. If Titania resisted for much longer, I would simply lie down on the moss and sleep while I waited for her to come to her senses.

"Lies. It's all preposterous lies," Titania said. "I demand you let me pass. Whatever mortal magic this is, it's not amusing."

"I promise you this is no mortal magic," I said. "It's the Old Ones."

"I think he's telling the truth," Agata said. "They showed themselves to me, too, but I can't hear them like Arlen does."

"Yes, well, you're more mortal than anything else, so I'm not surprised you're siding with him," Titania said.

Agata gave her a wounded look and tears shone in her eyes.

"I've tried to be the best fey I could," she said. "Even once I found out I had hardly any fey blood. But you've never given me a chance. It was all about revenge, wasn't it? You never cared about me at all."

Before Titania could reply, a tree root burst out of the earth and wrapped around her foot.

"What is this?" she shrieked. "Get it off me."

"We are all around," Orm said in the usual slow way.

The root crept up Titania's leg, wrapping around her limb. She screamed and tried to tear it away. It climbed over her torso and encased her arms. It slid over her neck and head. Soon only her eyes were visible.

"This is what we'll do if they don't leave," Orm said. "To each of them."

"If you don't agree, they'll keep you like this," I told Titania. "And they can do this to all the fey. You'll be stuck forever, trapped inside the tree roots."

Agata stared at Titania in horror.

"We have to leave," she said. "Think of it. Everyone we know encased in those roots. We can't live like that."

Titania blinked furiously.

"I don't think she can talk," I said to Orm.

"Oh," Orm said.

The roots uncovered Titania's face.

"Do you agree?" I asked. "Because I've been up all night and I'm really tired. I don't feel like talking for much longer, so now's your chance."

"I agree," Titania said. She somehow managed to make the words sound imperious as if she did me a favour. "Get this off me and the fey will leave. But you will provide us with transport."

Even as the words left her mouth, wind swirled through the clearing. It was strong, almost knocking me over, and brought with it the scent of honeysuckle. Agata's hair whipped around her face and she had to hold her skirts down with both hands. Orm, steady as ever, seemed unperturbed, although I sensed a faint humming from him. Perhaps he communicated with others of his species.

"I think the air elementals are offering to transport you," I said.

The elementals responded by circling me, faster and faster, almost lifting me off the ground in their eagerness. Meanwhile, the root leisurely released Titania, easing down over her body and back into the earth until the only sign of its presence was some disturbed soil. Titania glared at me.

"I assume you need time to prepare," I said. "There is a ring of stones a couple of hours walk from the portal. Go there and call for Air when you are ready to leave."

"This is all your fault," she hissed. "I knew the children of Silver Downs were trouble. I'll see the end of your line yet."

"Protected," Orm said.

"I think you'll find we're under the protection of the Old Ones," I said.

Titania let out a squeal of rage, then marched out of the clearing. The trees let her pass.

"Come, Agata," she called over her shoulder.

"Stay," I said to her. "Come back to Silver Downs with me. If you go with the fey, you'll have to leave forever. The Old Ones won't let them come back again."

She chewed her lip, and for a moment I thought she actually considered it. But she shook her head.

"I belong with the fey," she said and ran after Titania.

Then it was just Orm and me left in the clearing. The rest of the Old Ones had disappeared without me even noticing.

"Well, that's that," I said sadly.

"The girl will be back," he said. "Maybe not in your lifetime, but one day."

48

ARLEN

My heart was heavy as I trekked back to Braen Keep. My relief at convincing Titania to leave was outweighed by dismay that Agata had chosen to leave with her. At least the Old Ones would have their home back shortly. I, however, would have to tell Eithne that she would probably never meet her daughter.

Tristan and I departed for Silver Downs later that day. The healers preserved Fiachra's body to give us time to get him home. Girec provided a cart and a pair of oxen and there was plenty of room for Tristan and me, even with Fiachra and our supplies. I didn't see Derwa before we left and I didn't know whether to be relieved or disappointed. Maybe there was no possible future that a queen and a druid could share, but there would be time enough to find out.

Tristan and I spoke only as necessary while we travelled. Midwinter passed and the days slowly became longer, although no warmer yet. We camped beside the road at night, wrapped well in blankets. Tristan turned out to be proficient with a bow and provided fresh meat to supplement our supplies. I often saw him staring at the wrapped bundle that was Fiachra's body, but didn't ask what he was thinking. He clearly knew Fiachra better than I did, so he likely grieved our uncle.

I recognised nothing of what we trundled past. It had been too many years and I was too young when I left. But after a full sevennight of travel, we finally approached the Silver Downs lodge. It stood proud above its surroundings, all grey stone walls with creeping mosses and vines. It was not as big as I remembered, or maybe Braen Keep had skewed my perspective. The gardens out the front were different from my memory. Shutters had been recently painted and the barn extended. But when I inhaled, the smell of home rushed through me. It might look different, but it still smelled exactly the same.

As we arrived, a pair of young girls were out the front, playing a fighting game with wooden practice swords. They waved and scampered into the lodge to announce our arrival. My hands trembled a little as I climbed down from the cart.

Eithne was the first to come out of the lodge. Her mouth trembled when she saw me. She moved as if to hold her arms out to me, but checked herself. I went to her and embraced her. She was far too thin and fragile, with bones that seemed almost to poke out of her skin. She returned my embrace and her shoulders shook as she sobbed once or twice. She released me and turned to Tristan.

"It's done," he said before she could ask. "She is destroyed forever. But Uncle Fiachra…"

She held out her arms to him.

"He knew even before he left," she said. "He told me this would be his final journey."

Tristan cried into her shoulder and Eithne allowed her own tears to run freely down her cheeks.

"He should have told me," Tristan said. "I could have helped them."

Eithne met my eyes with a questioning gaze.

"It was Agata and me," I said. "Fiachra Saw it would be the two of us who destroyed her."

"You found Agata?" She covered her trembling mouth with her hand. "Where is she?"

"She chose to stay with the fey."

Eithne smiled sadly and shook her head a little.

"I should have known," she said. "I should have expected Titania would make sure she never came back to us, even if she was found."

"It's all she knows. Titania raised her to believe she was fey."

"Do you think she will come home one day?"

I didn't want to lie to her, but it felt wrong to tell her the truth.

"Maybe," I said.

"At least I know she is alive and well," she said. "I had thought…"

I knew what she had feared, for I myself had often wondered how Agata lived. Whether she passed her years in the darkness and solitude of a fey prison.

"She has been treated as a princess, as far as I can tell," I said. "She hasn't been mistreated."

"Except in that she was stolen from her family." Eithne's voice was bitter. "But she is alive while we mourn my brother. Fiachra thought Ida would find you."

"Why me?" I asked. "I had little to do with her until Uncle Fiachra arrived. She charmed me and I kept forgetting she was there."

"It was one of our sons who created her. Fiachra believed her power would be strongest near those of our line. She needed to be near you."

"Hearn is dead. The news may not have reached this far yet. One of his foster sons is to be king." I couldn't tell her of my part in the death of his other foster son. Maybe that would be a tale for another day. Or maybe it would be a secret I would hold close for the rest of my life. "And Titania knows about me."

Eithne reached for me even as she clutched Tristan tighter with the other arm. Her fingers barely grazed my cheek.

"Oh," she said. "Will she come here?"

"No. She won't bother us anymore. The Old Ones have returned and the fey are leaving. They have been banished."

Her smile was hopeful, like the sun peeking out past a grey cloud.

"We don't have to fear her any longer," I said. "Mother."

49

ARLEN

I spent the next sevennight at Silver Downs. Eithne and I didn't speak much for the first day or two. She would often walk past and hesitate, as if wanting to say something, then walk away. But gradually we both found our words and the years between us dissolved. She told me about what happened at Silver Downs in the years I was away. There were no other children for her and Kalen, out of fear that Titania would take them too.

I told her everything that happened with Agata and Titania. She understood why I hadn't brought Agata with me — perhaps better than I did — but it grieved her. I spoke sparingly of my studies, for there was much I wasn't permitted to tell, and of what happened at Braen Keep. If Eithne judged me harshly for the decisions I made, she didn't show it. The only detail I kept from her was my friendship with Derwa. It felt disrespectful to talk about her when things between us were still unspoken.

Once Eithne and I had said everything we needed to, my thoughts turned to Braen Keep and Derwa. Before I left, though, I wanted to explore the places I remembered from my boyhood. The hill where I could see out over the entire estate. The place where the twin rivers met. The woods on the edge of our land, not that I was ever permitted to enter them as a boy. I spent a morning walking across the estate, finding place after place that had some memory from my childhood attached to it.

I left the rock by the stand of beech trees for last. This place was special to Eithne, for it was here she fell in love with Kalen. I sat on the rock, listening to the wind whispering through the branches of the beeches, and imagining Eithne sitting in this very spot as a young woman. I could see why she liked this place. It was out of sight of the lodge and yet surrounded by Silver Downs land. The pastures were brown and mostly free of snow, for winter here had been mild this year. The rock was warm from the sun and weathered smooth. Woodlarks sang and somewhere nearby a raven cawed. Something rustled behind me. I ignored it, thinking it would be a vole or badger or squirrel.

"Arlen."

I jumped up when Agata spoke. She stood amongst the beeches, wearing a gown of forest green.

"Agata."

There were so many things I wanted to say and I had thought any chance of saying them was gone. But now she was here, my mind went blank.

"Just listen to me," she said. "I need to explain."

I nodded.

"I can't stay, so don't think that is why I am here," she said. "I need to remain with the fey. Titania has watched your family for a long time. Generations, I think. Your line — our line — has magic in its blood and she always feared we would become a threat to the fey. When Eithne was born, Titania thought she would be the one to rise up against them."

"Eithne would never harm anyone."

"She's strong and that makes Titania uneasy. She went into the fey realm and escaped with her mind intact. Very few mortals do that. And she was unSeen, which has always puzzled Titania."

"Eithne's birth was unSeen? Like mine?"

Agata's mouth twisted into a sad smile.

"Just like yours. She Saw me, but she only recently Saw you for the first time."

"That would have been after I finally accessed the Sight. I wondered whether it had broken something. Whether I would no longer be unSeen."

"I've never tried to See." Agata's voice was contemplative. "I wonder whether I have any ability."

"If you stay, I can help you find out."

"I can't. I've already told you."

"But this is where you belong." Having spent time with Eithne, I could see where Agata's stubbornness came from. "I've spent my whole life preparing to search for you. I promised Eithne I'd get you back. Everything I've ever done was about bringing you home."

Her eyes flashed and she scowled.

"It isn't your decision," she said. "It's mine."

"But you're mortal. I can understand you wanting to stay with the fey as long as you didn't know, but now that you do you should be here. With your family."

Agata put her hands on her hips.

"It's all about you, isn't it? It's about what *you* want for me, what *you* think I should do. What about what I want?"

"But how could you want anything else? You belong here."

"I belong with the fey."

I opened my mouth to argue, but she cut me off with a sharp swipe of her hand.

"Be quiet and listen. This is my life and it's my decision where I live. I know nothing about the mortal realm. Can't you understand that? The fey are all I know. They're all I understand. They're my family."

"Do they know you are mortal?"

"They do. It was difficult at first, but things are getting better since we went to the island. They're starting to accept me."

"Don't you want to meet our mother?"

"I don't want to give Titania any reason to go looking for her. Or for you. As long as I've chosen to stay, she's won. The fey might have lost their home, but she won against Eithne and I think that matters more to her than anything else."

I finally realised just how deep Titania's hatred of Eithne went.

"Will you come back one day?" I asked. "Spend some time with Eithne before it's too late. We will age much faster here than you will in the fey realm."

"I don't know. It's safer for all of you if I stay away."

Agata didn't stay long after that. She gave me a tentative hug before she left and I felt the connection between us renewed. As she melted away into the trees, I knew exactly which direction she went in. I would be able to find her again if I needed to.

It was only after she left that Sumerled revealed himself. We stared at each other and I supposed we each waited for the other to speak first.

"She hates me now," he said at last.

"Does she have reason to?"

Sumerled shrugged. "She thinks she does. That's all that matters."

"Were you following her?"

"I was looking for you."

I waited. He shifted his feet and looked out at the fields.

"So this is what he gave up the fey realm for."

"You mean Kalen? He gave it up for my mother."

"Can you give him a message for me?" His words came in a rush. "Tell him I'm watching over her for him. She's safe."

"Did you know she was his daughter?"

He finally looked me in the eyes.

"I suspected. She looks much like him."

"Why didn't you tell her sooner?"

"Because she would hate me. And I loved her."

"I'll tell him," I said.

He nodded and backed away into the trees. Just before he disappeared into the shadows, he spoke one last time.

"Tell him also that I understand. Tell them both."

"You understand what?" I asked.

But Sumerled was gone. His message might not mean much to me, but I suspected it would to Eithne and Kalen.

The story continues in
Book 4: *Swan* (A newsletter list exclusive)

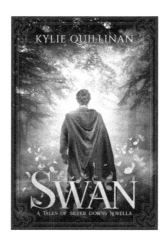

ACKNOWLEDGEMENTS

There were times when I thought this book would never be finished. I had written a first draft some time ago but threw it out and started again just a few months before publication. There's not much left of the original story, except for Derwa, who was there all along. Although she's not a point of view character, she was always integral to the story that I wanted to tell.

I didn't set out to write three books about courage but somehow that's what happened. Muse was a story about a boy who didn't want to be a hero. Fey was about strong women who readily step up to be heroes. Druid is about a young man who is courageous in so many ways, even though he thinks he is failure.

Thank you again to Deranged Doctor Design for a lovely cover.

Thank you to Eliza Dee for fitting me into your schedule so urgently and for editing this beast.

Thank you to my uncle, Peter Abraham, who doesn't report me to the police when every now and then he receives a message that starts with something like, "I'm decapitating somebody and I need to know whether the blood will gush or ooze."

Thank you to Donald Maass for his comments on the story you're not telling that finally helped me to understand what Arlen's true problem was.

Thank you to Juliet Marillier for her comments on writer's block that finally loosened my words.

Thank you to Cathy Yardley for her help with tying things together at the end and brainstorming the final scene. There are so many elements that I finally managed to weave together thanks to those thirty minutes we spent talking.

And last, but not least, to Neal, Muffin, Lulu and Frehley: Thank you for being there waiting for me when I finished this book.

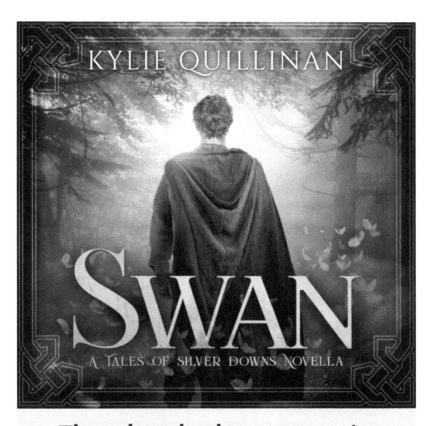

Three hundred years ago, six brothers were cursed to live as swans. This is their return.

Subscribe to receive your free copy of Swan, the epilogue novella for the Tales of Silver Downs series.

ALSO BY KYLIE QUILLINAN

The Amarna Age Series

Book One: *Queen of Egypt*
Book Two: *Son of the Hittites*
Book Three: *Eye of Horus*
Book Four: *Gates of Anubis*
Book Five: *Lady of the Two Lands*
Book Six: *Guardian of the Underworld*

Daughter of the Sun: An Amarna Age Novella

Tales of Silver Downs series

Prequel: *Bard*
Book One: *Muse*
Book Two: *Fey*
Book Three: *Druid*
Epilogue: *Swan* (A newsletter list exclusive)

Standalone

Speak To Me

See kyliequillinan.com for more books and newsletter sign up.

ABOUT THE AUTHOR

Kylie writes about women who defy society's expectations. Her novels are for readers who like fantasy with a basis in history or mythology. Her interests include Dr Who, jellyfish and cocktails. She needs to get fit before the zombies come.

Her other interests include canine nutrition, jellyfish and zombies. She blames the disheveled state of her house on her dogs, but she really just hates to clean.

Swan – the epilogue to the Tales of Silver Downs series – is available exclusively to her newsletter subscribers. Sign up at kyliequillinan.com.

Lightning Source UK Ltd.
Milton Keynes UK
UKHW010250090223
416650UK00002B/486